PARIS POLO MATCH

Paris Polo Match

Ami Hendrickson

MUSEINKS PRESS

PARIS POLO MATCH
Copyright © 2025 Ami Hendrickson
All rights reserved.
Published by Soul Sparks Press

ISBN: 978-1-968944-06-3 *(paperback)*
ISBN: 978-1-968944-07-0 *(ebook)*

Book design by Rae Ganci Hammers

1

Colt Starting

THE BAY COLT FLUNG HIS HEAD up in the air. From a vantage point seven feet above the ground, wide eyes stared down at the weedy man who held the rope attached to the horse's halter in one hand and a long wooden stick in the other. Nostrils flared. The colt snorted. Muscles tensed. He was a volcano on the cusp of eruption.

"*Aidez-moi, Madame Alvarez!*"

"Easy, Cédric." Mayla kept her voice low, hoping it sounded more confident than she felt, enunciating her words so the twenty-odd people gathered around watching could better understand her American-accented French. "Don't lose your temper. You are balancing on a knife's edge right now. If you push him, he will blow up. But—" she continued as the man began to relax, "if you quit now, you teach him that freaking out is the answer."

"*Pardon?*"

"Keep doing what you were doing. You have a polo mallet in your hand, that's all. It's not a whip. It's not a snake or a stick of dynamite. It won't hurt him. You were swinging it. Keep swinging it. Quiet. Calm. Steady. That's it."

The colt's handler had terrible timing. The warm June morning had drenched him with sweat within five minutes of his participation in the training clinic. Slick and sticky, stiff and awkward, he failed to read many of his horse's cues.

Mayla stood outside le Polo Parisien's smallest turnout paddock, watching the drama inside. The whole thing could go south in an instant. The horse could explode, injuring himself, or Cédric, or her students, or her...

She had a hundred things she could be doing—should be doing—since traveling all day yesterday. She had tack to clean. Clothes to wash. Horses to exercise. Her stomach rumbled, reminding her that the kitchen cupboards needed stocking. It also reminded her that those who wished to eat had to work. She rested one foot on the lowest rail of the fence. "I could jump in there and take over."

Hope brightened Cédric's red face.

"But if I did, you wouldn't learn how to help him deal with things that scare him in the future."

Hope died, drowned in despair and perspiration.

"Stand your ground. Breathe. Easy. Don't chase him; he'll run away from you every time. But don't back off either. That's it!"

The horse's high head dropped slightly.

The handler lowered his mallet and started to relax.

"No," Mayla said. "Don't stop. Don't give up. He is starting to come around, to trust you, but if you quit too soon, everything you've worked for is lost."

Cédric shook his head. "*Non.* He is too big for me."

Mayla climbed into the paddock. She stood five-foot five—considerably shorter than her student, though she refrained from pointing that out. "You are tired. And you can't train when you're exhausted." Taking the lead rope, she ushered the man out of the ring. "Take a short break. I'll try to show you what I mean."

By the time the change of handler took place, the bay held its head like a giraffe again. Its tension and nervous energy electrified the lead rope.

Mayla picked up the mallet, hefting it in her hand. At fifty-four inches, it was longer than she generally used when playing, but—as with the trainer—the size of the stick didn't matter.

Putting no pressure on the lead rope, she began gently swinging the mallet. As soon as the mallet began to move, the horse went back to Volcano Mode, snorting and dancing in place.

The mallet swung, rhythmic as a metronome.

The colt backed to the end of the rope, making little jerking motions with his head, spoiling for a reason to explode and drag her with him as he headed for the ends of the earth. Each jerk tested the rope for resistance.

Mayla stood her ground, her momentum never changing.

"How many of you signed up for the 'Polo Women 101' series that starts later today?" she asked.

Seven hands went up, prompting the bay to pop his head even higher and snort with alarm.

"I don't often do colt starting clinics. Usually I work with horses that are already broken to ride, but I owed Cédric a favor—" *And I'm short on cash.*

"Thank God and all that's holy." Cédric held a cool bottle of water to his forehead.

"In any case, the approach is the same every step of the way. If you're riding with me later, I'm glad you're here now," Mayla told the students. "This is a good introduction to how I train."

"And a better introduction to why you want her to owe you," said Cédric.

The bay snorted like a steam engine.

"I want to emphasize that this horse is doing nothing wrong."

"He is also doing nothing right," Cédric groused, massaging a sore shoulder.

With the bay balanced on the edge of flight, Mayla explained:

"He is young. You got him up early, threw him in a box on wheels, and brought him here. Now, you're asking him to trust you. He's not so sure he wants to do that."

She moved the mallet slightly closer to the horse. "The way he sees it, I've got this scary thing in my hand threatening to attack him. I'm going to keep making this movement over and over until— There! He's standing still.

"That's good. But it's just the first step. It's too soon for me to stop yet. I keep swinging...back and forth...back and forth. Soon he'll realize there is nothing to be afraid of. No reason to be afraid. You see?"

The horse stopped popping his head against the line. He stretched his neck out toward her, the same move he had made with Cédric moments earlier.

"His feet have stopped, but his brain hasn't kicked in yet. If I stop what I'm doing, or if I suddenly do something different, I have changed the rules on him, and we're back to square one," said Mayla. "Remember, what's the key?"

"No surprises," her students chorused.

"*Bien.* Horses hate surprises. So do I, for that matter."

The colt dropped his head still further. Soon, ignoring Mayla completely, he began to chew as if he had a cud.

The swinging stopped.

"And now he's showing us his Inner Cow." Mayla reached out with the mallet and rubbed the horse's flat face with the wooden end. The animal stood calmly, chewing on nothing.

"When a horse starts acting like a cow, eating nonexistent food, he is processing all the new material you have given him," Mayla said.

"That is when you stop. Relax. Reward him for using his brain. Give him a chance to assimilate the information."

A rather fluffy woman, wearing a floppy straw hat that had seen better days, stood on the periphery of those auditing the clinic. Her boots, breeches, and blouse were all of top quality craftsmanship, exuding the kind of relentless shabbiness only the truly wealthy can achieve. Though she watched with avid interest, paying close attention to the lesson, an underlying agitation plagued her.

Mayla tried, but couldn't get a read on her. "Are there any questions?"

With an apologetic air as if she and an entourage of teacup poodles were asking to move in rent-free, the woman raised a hand.

"Yes?" Mayla nodded at the woman while making a mental note to insist all participants in future clinics wear name tags. She doubted barking out "You there! What's the matter?" would encourage anyone to share.

"My Ombré, he is usually calm and docile. But he is terrified of silly things, like clippers."

A murmur of understanding rustled through the onlookers. Several nodded their heads in solidarity.

The woman continued with a bit more confidence, her voice figgy and warm. "He often acts like this horse did when something frightens him. He tries to run away. If he can't run, he—as you say—'freaks out.' I tried to trim him this morning…"

Setting her jaw, she overcame her embarrassment, pulled out her phone, and showed Mayla a short video on which played out an all-too-familiar scene:

A buckskin gelding stood quietly in crossties, an extra lead rope attached to his halter. His owner approached holding a small battery-operated trimmer. With an air of trepidation, as if diving naked into a piranha pool, she held the lead rope with one hand and turned the trimmer on with the other.

The horse did, indeed, freak out. No other words could do justice to the spectacular display of rearing, eye rolling, striking out with his front legs, leaping forward, breaking free of the crossties, and dragging the poor woman off her feet.

"That was this morning?" Mayla said.

A nod.

"Are you OK?"

A shrug.

"I believe I will be."

Now Cédric's horse paid no more attention to the swinging mallet than to the croaking frogs in the nearby woods. His neck drooped as if his head were too weighty to hold up. His ears flopped like telephone poles after an earthquake. An attitude of Zen acceptance enveloped him.

"One of the worst mistakes either of you can make is to run away," Mayla said. "If the horse runs away, he learns he can avoid things he fears. If you run away, he learns you are not trustworthy."

"You forget one thing," Cédric said. "If I run away, I get to live for another day. I get to live as a coward, *c'est vrai*, but I get to live."

Ombré's owner leaned close to a tiny, birdlike woman standing near her and whispered something her ear. Though her voice was low and her words were not for the general assembly, years of playing polo had tuned Mayla's hearing:

"The days lived in fear are the longest of one's life."

"Fear has no place in training," Mayla said. "Every time we interact with the horse, we are training it. Done properly, the training process replaces fear with confidence."

"And done improperly?" asked the woman in the floppy hat.

"It teaches the horse that those who should be his advocates, his partners, his protectors, are liars and frauds at best. Or sadists at worst."

Mayla nodded toward Cédric. "Your goal, always, is to remind your horse that when he is with you, he is home. The two of you are stronger together than you are apart. Ultimately, you are going to put your life in his hands. And you both need to have a partner you can trust."

She continued working with the horse while she spoke. Soon, she could rub the mallet all over his body, his legs, his head, his ears. The bay stood, cow calm.

Mayla handed the mallet and rope back to Cédric. "Now it's your turn."

With renewed confidence, the man continued his colt's training.

"He needs to know that no matter what you do, you will never hurt him," Mayla said.

The unclippable Ombré's owner tentatively cleared her throat. "But that's not entirely true, is it? I mean…There is always an element of danger. In everything. And polo looks like quite a hard-hitting sport."

"What is your name?"

"Laudine." The hat flapped as the woman bobbed her head.

"It's true, Laudine," Mayla admitted. "Eventually, when you are on your horse, swinging the mallet, playing the game, he might get hurt. Even though we take every precaution, from extensive conditioning to wrapping the horse's legs, it's possible. Anything can happen in polo. But a polo pony trusts his rider. He understands the two of you are partners chasing the ball across the field, in it to win it together."

The little woman standing next to Laudine twisted her straw-colored hair, weaving it around her fingers. "I'm just so afraid of making a mistake," she said. "Of ruining my horse. He knows much more about the game than I do."

Several onlookers voiced similar worries.

"Mistakes are inevitable," Mayla said. "I have made so many.

"Ten years ago, when I was looking to buy my first polo pony instead of leasing other people's horses, I found a quick little half-Thoroughbred mare I loved."

"Cantata," said Cédric, gently bumping the mallet against his horse's sides while the colt stood, patient as a monument.

"That's right. Cantata was the first pony I owned by myself. There have been many since, but I knew she was special as soon as we met. When I rode her—every rideoff, every sprint for the ball, every play—I felt like Supergirl. Invincible.

"She knew more about polo than I did. I could tell where the ball was by watching her ears. Cantata never missed a trick. So, when she started slowing down a few months after I bought her, I lost sleep with worry. Even with the best feed and the best training regimen, she grew slower and slower. I had to call the veterinarian."

"What was wrong with her?" Laudine wondered.

"Nothing. The vet informed me that Cantata was in peak physical condition for a mare who was six months pregnant."

The thin woman had stopped twisting her hair, but she jumped like a startled fawn when the rest of the assembled students laughed at the story's punchline. The laughter fazed her more than it did the bay, who stood with his neck horizontal to the ground, nearly asleep.

"That spring, when Bogo was born, all legs and attitude, no one was happier than I," Mayla said.

"What happened to your mare?" someone asked.

"She's seventeen now and still loves to play. We're a team. Come see the exhibition games later this week; you'll see her in action."

Mayla clapped Cédric on the shoulder. "You did well today."

As the onlookers applauded, Cédric made no effort to hide his smile of pride.

"I've made every mistake you can make, including asking a pregnant mare to perform like a top-notch athlete," Mayla said. "No one is perfect; mistakes are inevitable. You will make many of your own. But if I can help it, you won't make mine."

2

The Assassin

IT WAS A MISTAKE to think he could fly anonymously.

As Thiago boarded the big Boeing 777, the first class flight attendant greeted him with a pre-programmed smile and a flute of champagne balanced atop a silver tray.

Thiago saw no reason to start guzzling champagne merely because he stepped on the plane. "It's one o'clock in the afternoon," he said. "What are we celebrating?"

"Your arrival, of course! Welcome... "

In mid-greeting, recognition dawned.

"*Señor Calvo.*"

Awe wiped the smile from the attendant's face. A nameplate dangled from a pin emblazoned with *Sécurité et Sûreté* on his uniform lapel. Self-consciously, he rubbed his arm across the "ALBERT" engraved in the brass. For a few lax seconds, he stared, speechless, until his training kicked in. The smile returned, hiding his awareness of who his passenger was behind a veil of professionalism. A very thin veil.

Thiago removed his sunglasses. So much for anonymity.

"Welcome!" the star-struck Albert repeated. "This plane has been recently renovated. Refurbished from stem to stern. Entirely safe and functional, so no worries there."

"I had no worries," Thiago told him. "Until now."

The attendant leaned forward as if sharing a thorny secret. "I heard rumors that you were going to Europe as a hired assassin. Now I know they are true!"

Thiago mimicked the man's conspiratorial air and whispered. "Best not to use the word 'assassin' on an international flight, *si?*"

"Ha!" Albert sobered, unsure whether or not Thiago was making a joke. "Oh. Yes. Indeed. Only too happy to comply. This way, please."

He escorted Thiago to his seat, a comfortable recliner of generous proportions upholstered in putty-colored leather, with a matching footrest that was larger than any of the seats back in steerage. Four windows lined the wall. Beneath the windows ran a long table on which sat a lamp, a set of gray pajamas, a pair of slippers, a Vevier-branded amenities kit, and a bucket chilling more champagne.

Heavy curtains, gathered into an artful, discreet bundle, hung between the recliner and the wide aisle separating Thiago's enclave from the one next to him, which was empty. While the passengers in economy sat packed like pickles, ten to a row, here at the front of the plane there was room to spare.

Thiago's phone buzzed with a text.

Albert hovered with ingratiating courtesy. "Would you like to see the cockpit? Meet the pilots? Have a drink? I should be only too happy to give you the Grand Tour."

"Thank you. No."

The attendant melted into the periphery, hissing to another crew member, "Do you know who that *is?* Thiago *Calvo!* Move a little left, I want to take a picture. Ssshh! I know we're not supposed to. Now, shut up and move."

Thiago stowed his carry-on and checked his phone. The text had come from Sergio:

Call me.

While the plane boarded, Albert tried, and failed, to find something near Thiago that required his attention. He wiped down every flat surface with a disinfecting cloth. He rolled a lint brush over the curtains. He cleaned the windows until they squeaked in protest.

"First class welcomes you, *señorita*. *Señor*. Champagne?"

As Albert tweezed imaginary fuzz off the carpet nearest Thiago's seat, a different flight attendant ushered in a woman, thin as a swizzle stick, and a man with a thug-like swagger who shadowed her every move. The woman walked with practiced boredom on stilettos so high, she was practically *en pointe*. Her makeup was both flawless and excessive, what Abu would call a "five-hour face." She looked as if she were headed for a runway instead of an intercontinental flight.

The couple found their seats. Tough Guy was either a bodyguard or the boyfriend, Thiago decided. Possibly both. Though he treated Swizzle Stick with solicitous attention, offering her first choice of seat, pouring additional champagne, and stowing her bags for her, she treated him with all the deference of a used toothbrush. She sat and took out her phone, scrolling on it with the same detachment as she approached everything else.

While business class, premium, and economy passengers boarded, Tough Guy prowled the cabin, peering out windows at the runways of Ezeiza Ministrio Pistarini and opening storage doors. When he was finished, he drank his champagne with the enthusiasm of a toddler taking his medicine. He refilled his glass and emptied it twice more in quick succession, then sat down, instantly falling asleep.

Thiago placed his call.

"What have you done?" Sergio demanded when he answered the phone.

"What are you talking about?"

"A chef! You sent me a Cordon Bleu chef! *La verdad de la milanesa!* I know she came from you. Don't deny it."

Thiago laughed. "Why would I deny giving you a gift?"

"It is too much. I cannot possibly accept, but of course I will. Am I dying? I'm dying, aren't I?"

"You are sick, my friend, but you will survive. You can't ride. Can't go outside. That alone is torture. But when we last spoke, you complained about the soup. Soup is sacred. No one should ever have to complain about soup."

"The last time we spoke, I complained about having strep."

"And about the soup."

"Maybe. But mostly about the strep. And about having to practically beg you to fill in for me on the team. You couldn't leave Buenos Aires, you said. You were swamped with work and your father is only recently recovered from his illness. What changed your mind? Was it my promise to make your visit enjoyable, my Zoelie, my irrefutable logic, or my blistering intellect?"

"All of the above," Thiago laughed. He had no intention of discussing his change of heart with Sergio or anyone. "Is she a good cook?"

"She arrived this morning in time for breakfast. I proposed to her before lunch."

"Isn't that a bit fast?"

"Clearly, you have not tasted Madeline's vichyssoise."

3

Few Fly

WHACK!

The little white ball whizzed through the air, causing two people in its path to quickly leap aside, then utter prayers of praise for fast reflexes to any deity who might be listening.

"*Pardonnez-moi!*" The diminutive woman who had spent the morning's clinic twisting her hair cringed. Her name tag read "Yvonne."

"Be careful!" Mayla said. "Remember: look before you swing."

"I did," Yvonne replied. "But it did not go where I looked." She held her foot mallet in both hands and flexed it tentatively. "This is a formidable weapon."

The quiet, introspective way she said the words raised little hairs of warning on Mayla's arms.

"Nothing in polo is a weapon," Mayla said, projecting her voice to make certain everyone heard her. "Not your mallet; not you; not your horse. Safety is the number one priority. The only thing you hit with your mallet is the ball, though you can hook an opposing player's mallet and keep them from making a play."

"Of course." Flustered and a little embarrassed, Yvonne ducked her head as if trying to hide between her shoulders.

Yvonne, Laudine, and five other female would-be polo players stood in a ragged semi-circle. Each held a foot mallet, a shorter version of a polo mallet. Each wore identical expressions of frustration.

"Let's go through it again," said Mayla. "We'll apply what we learned about keeping the swing on the same plane. Hold your mallet in your right hand. Rotate your shoulders and your torso to the right. Good. Now... "

Mayla found herself suddenly at a loss for words. Instead of following instructions and going through the training motions, Laudine put the head of her mallet on the ground and pushed her considerable weight on it, bending the flexible cane shaft.

"Is there a problem?" Mayla inquired. Foot mallets were strong, but nothing is indestructible.

"*Oui*. It is crooked." More pressing and jamming ensued.

With a smile that felt as if it had been etched in glass, Mayla reached out a hand in a mute request for the abused mallet.

"I am trying to straighten it."

"Yes, of course. But that would ruin it." Mayla held up the foot mallet for all to see. "The shaft is not perpendicular to the head. It attaches at an angle so the sweet spot—along the flat side; never at the tip—more readily connects with the ball."

She demonstrated, sending one of the practice balls sailing straight and true into the beautiful blue Parisian sky.

Laudine bowed her head, embarrassed. "*Désolé*."

"No problem," Mayla assured her. "Thank you for identifying something I should have taught, but didn't because I take it for granted."

Handing the foot mallet back, she said, "Polo is like life. It's not all right angles and straight lines. The equipment is literally built to take your twists and turns into consideration. Let's practice the off-side forehand and you'll see what I mean."

She walked among her students, talking them through the motions of a basic shot. "As you start your swing, move your mallet first. Then let your hand follow it back and down. As you complete your swing and follow through, keep your arm straight; don't bend at your elbow."

With satisfying *whacks*, seven balls lobbed into the air.

"Good," Mayla said. She adjusted a few students' grips and helped Yvonne to better understand how to use her shoulders to initiate the swing.

Soon, white orbs dotted the sky like snowballs, each flying farther and truer than before. The strikes grew stronger as confidence increased.

When the students had whacked all of the balls away from them, Mayla said, "We'll work on your follow-through before we go where the balls are and send them back here. First, let's review proper mallet grip."

She walked around, double-checking techniques. "Don't grab it like a baseball bat or a cricket bat. Spread your fingers out, pointing your first finger toward the mallet's head. Imagine you are pointing to where you want the ball to go."

Yvonne swung, stiff as a robot, her lips pressed together in a white line. Telling her to "loosen up" would probably do no good. Mayla suspected the woman had no more idea how to relax than she did to turn lead into gold.

"Breathe in," she instructed everyone, though she kept her attention focused on Yvonne. "Breathe out. Good. Do it again: as you breathe in, turn your body and prepare your swing. Now, as you breathe out, follow through with your whole arm. When you get to the end of your swing, open your hand and let go of whatever is holding you back. Literally throw the mallet away. Its trajectory will mimic the trajectory of the ball."

The foot mallets arced away from the students' outstretched hands like blunt-nosed javelins. Yvonne smiled, watching her mallet soar.

The students retrieved their equipment and practiced hitting balls again. All made progress, but Yvonne's was the most dramatic improvement.

"Your technique is quite good," Mayla said. "The practice you do here on the ground will really pay off when you get on a horse."

"Laudine talked me into signing up for this clinic," the tiny woman confessed. "I almost didn't come. I never thought I'd be good enough or strong enough to play well."

"Me neither," several others nodded.

"Here's a little-known secret: the vast majority of players are low-goal amateurs. Everyone starts at the same place: the beginning, learning the game from the ground up. All crawl. Most walk. Some run. A few fly. And that's OK.

"Polo is the great equalizer. While the younger, taller, stronger players may achieve a higher goal rating faster, that doesn't keep the others from enjoying the game. It's fun for everyone."

Laudine wrinkled her brow, as if fun were something other people enjoyed. "Isn't it difficult to be a woman and hold your own on the field with the men?"

The words were so quiet, Mayla wouldn't have understood the question if she hadn't heard it a hundred times.

"I won't say I've never had a problem with it. But the worst pushback I had was ten years ago."

"And—?"

And I was twenty-one: young and naïve and it gutted me. Mayla smiled, though she knew it stopped short of her eyes. "As you can see, I refused to let it stop me."

Mayla smacked a ball in the air, then dribbled it, bouncing it on the end of her mallet. "You're not playing *against* the men; you are partnering *with* your horse. Horsemanship has nothing to do with gender. There are many great women players. I'm not alone—and neither are you."

Hoping she conveyed both support and encouragement, she said, "Now, let's get on our horses and we'll start the mounted part of the lesson. I have a good feeling about you!"

Though the good feeling lasted all through the riding lesson, it vanished when Mayla put away the equipment after her students had left for the day. In its place was a tiny trickle of concern. She checked and double-checked, counted and recounted, but there was no getting around the fact.

One of the foot mallets was missing.

4

Takeoff

ALBERT APPROACHED WITH THE DEFERENCE of a Victorian butler. "Dinner will be ready soon, Señor."

He pulled out the travel table and spread a white linen cloth over it. In short order, a glass of wine and a *mise en bouche* of an artfully assembled leek tart appeared.

Thiago stood and stretched until he heard his back crack. "Albert," he said as the attendant walked toward the food prep area.

"Sir!"

"You promised me the plane was entirely safe and functional. Told me not to worry. Yet we spent the past five hours sitting on the tarmac."

"And now we are flying. Safely. You see? I told the truth."

Albert hesitated. He looked around the cabin, furtive enough to draw attention to himself. No other attendants were in sight. After an indecisive moment, he wheeled around and returned to Thiago's seat.

As if by magic, he produced a fashion magazine, a trendy publication filled with more advertisements than articles. He flipped to a dog-eared page: an advertisement for Vevier clothing and jewelry. Thiago saw himself staring from the page, brooding and introspective—what Abuelita called his "pirate face"—in high-contrast, glossy glory.

"I could get fired for asking," Albert said, breathless at his audacity. "And you probably get asked this all the time, but, may I have your autograph?"

Thiago obliged. Truth be told, he got requests for selfies more often than for autographs. In general, he didn't mind granting either one. Fans kept the game alive and thriving, though the adoration of Argentinian devotees burned with such a white-hot fervor that he sometimes felt guilty for wanting his privacy. The only good thing about going to Paris was that there, he would not be recognized.

Albert blushed and bowed his thanks. "I'll be right out with your food, sir. Just push this button to let me know if you need anything."

Behind him, two signal lights lit up. He ignored them and left the cabin.

Thiago stretched again, limbering up his muscles. He ambled over to the restroom, more to move his legs and wash up before eating than from any real call of nature. He was keyed up. On edge. Cagey. After spending the afternoon in travel limbo, on board but going nowhere, an unsettling combination of tension and boredom plagued him.

Across the cabin, Swizzle Stick rummaged through her amenity bag. She set out the Vevier-branded lip balm, hand cream, sleep mask, earplugs, compact mirror, and more in an array beside the complimentary slippers and pajamas. She moved languidly, detached, her face a beautiful mask of jaded disgust as if she had expected the sort of swag she would get at Cannes. Finding nothing to interest her, she pulled out a magazine and began paging through it.

Though she never looked his way, Thiago couldn't shake the feeling that she was sizing him up.

A thirteen-hour flight coupled with the additional five-hour time difference between Buenos Aires and Paris should have brought him into Charles de Gaulle bright and early tomorrow morning, allowing plenty of time to get to know the horses and get a little sleep before tomorrow night's event. But the lengthy delay on the runway had trampled his plans. He hated to admit it, but Pa had been right: he should have just taken the jet.

Ducking into the restroom, Thiago washed his face and hands. He couldn't say he was surprised at the scheduling snafu. It was to be expected. Paris never agreed with him. That's one of the many reasons why, when Sergio's invitation came on Monday, he had been inclined to reject it. He probably should have, instead of asking Pa what he thought.

"My son! A force of nature! Of course you will go. Such an honor!" Pa had said, gesturing so broadly his cigar smoke formed arcane symbols that hung like spectres in the humid air. "You must live while you are still young. Do the dangerous, the exotic thing, before you are a husk of yourself, like I am."

Pa, who had always dreamed of playing internationally, considered the matter settled and abandoned himself to the joys of vicariously living his dream. But Thiago had refrained from calling Sergio and accepting the invitation. Playing polo at home was ideal. He had a string of exceptional ponies, his teammates were as close as his own brothers, and he could still keep an eye on Pa and the details of the family business. His reservations over the irresponsibility of leaving town to run around Europe for two months had continued. Furthermore, there was no escaping the fact that the last time he had played in Paris had been disastrous.

It was Abuelita, not Pa, who ultimately changed his mind. His grandmother had come to visit him late Monday evening on the tiled patio where he was balancing bank statements.

"Always the responsible one," she said, after sitting quietly for some time.

The quiet reprimand in her tone was so unlike her, Thiago had looked up in surprise.

"I've been thinking of Tía Nina a lot lately," she said, reverently speaking the name of her dear, departed sister.

"Oh?" Thiago said. "Has she come to you in a dream?"

"Don't be so quick to scorn dreams. They are the best part of us."

"Did she give you a message?"

Abu wagged a cautionary finger at him. "*¡Che boludo!* I didn't say I spoke to her. I said I've been thinking of her."

"And?"

"When I wonder whether I should do something, I remember that Nina will never have the opportunity to ask such questions."

"You think I should go play in Europe?"

"I don't know. You said yourself these Monde du Polo people encourage their players to be grooms and exercise boys as well."

Thiago knew she was goading him, but he responded anyway. "And you think *I* think I'm above all that?"

"I do not dream of suggesting I know what you think." Abu smiled, enigmatic and wise as the Mona Lisa. "But it could be fun."

Fun.

The word bothered him. It rankled, festered, like a splinter. It's not that he couldn't remember the last time he had fun. He remembered it vividly. But he had been a boy then. A very long time had passed since. Fun was no longer something on which he focused.

With the shade of Tía Nina hanging over him, he had accepted Sergio's offer.

As a result, he was running late, flying halfway around the world to a city that held nothing but bad memories.

May as well go eat dinner.

He returned to his seat to discover that it was taken; the leek tart gone. Swizzle Stick had made herself at home in his absence. She thumbed through her magazine as Thiago sat opposite the recliner in the footstool that served as a companion seat.

She looked up at him from beneath long, dark lashes and folded a page back to display the Vevier advertisement.

"This is you?"

Thiago shook his head.

The girl studied the picture. Looked at him. Then back at the ad. "No. This is you." She leaned forward, compressing the space between them. Her hand slid up his thigh, purposeful as an anaconda, though not as warm. "You are famous?"

"No."

Fingers squeezed; the boa constricted.

"I am," she said.

"Really?"

She grabbed the champagne from the table and took a drink straight from the bottle. "Yes. I am going to Paris."

"With him?" Thiago tipped his head toward Tough Guy, who was glaring in their direction.

The girl shrugged a shoulder. She tossed her head. Drank some more. "You are going to Paris too?"

"That is where the plane is headed."

She tipped the bottle again, growing boozier by the moment.

The plane hit a pocket of turbulence and dropped suddenly. Swizzle Stick missed her mouth, spraying champagne everywhere.

Thiago sighed. Not his idea of "fun" at all.

With a squeak of alarm, Albert came over, wringing his fingers, flustered as a Chihuahua in a room full of Dogos. "I'm sorry, madam.

The captain has turned on the seatbelt signs. I must ask you to go back to your seat."

Swizzle Stick destroyed him with a look that could melt tires. "My friend here, the mister model, he does not mind."

Poker-faced, she waited for Thiago to cave. To fall under her spell. To say it was fine, she could remain, maybe have a little more champagne...

"It's OK," Thiago said. "You stay."

Swizzle smiled.

Thiago got to his feet as the plane bucked like an unbroken colt. Without another word, ignoring the girl's outraged gasp at being left behind, he retrieved his bag and walked across the aisle to an empty seat.

Albert followed close behind, drew the privacy curtains, and laid a fresh tablecloth on the new table. He bowed, formal and proper, but with a devilish glint in his eye. "Well played, sir. As I said: dinner will be ready soon."

5

Conditioned Responses

THE EARLY MORNING SKY glowed salmon and green as Mayla opened the shed row doors. Horses whickered happy hellos, no doubt wondering what had taken her so long to get here.

According to her phone, the time was 5:45 a.m.

She checked outside: no students in sight.

"Adequate conditioning is a critical part of training your polo pony," she had told them at the end of yesterday's clinic. "Be here bright and early at six o'clock."

Predictably, this encountered some resistance.

"*À quelle heure?*"

"Six."

"Tonight? Oh no! I have plans—"

"I think she means in the morning."

Seven pairs of suspicious eyes had fixed upon her. "That can't be right."

"It is," Mayla said. "And before you mutiny on me, I'd like to point out that a six a.m. call time is a full two hours later than I generally start exercising my horses."

"*Merde*," murmured someone standing in the back of the group. "And a full two hours earlier than civilized people get out of bed."

Though Mayla had laughed along with everyone else at the little joke, she had neglected to mention that the early morning sessions were what separated the serious students from the time wasters.

Wondering if anyone would show up, she groomed and saddled Bogo. Before the girth was tightened, she was happily surprised to discover five of the seven students from yesterday had arrived.

Four of the ladies gathered in a friendly knot, discreetly keeping their distance from a woman whose name embroidered in pink on her custom-made polo shirt proclaimed her "Proue."

"I don't know why we have to get up so early to train," Proue complained, leaving no doubt in Mayla's mind as to the identity of yesterday's back-of-the-group griper.

"Conditioning is separate from training," Mayla said as the women tacked up. "Both are important. Training teaches the horse what you want her to do. But conditioning gives her the ability to do it.

"As for the time: early morning is ideal. It's usually cool. The horses have the opportunity to limber up before breakfast, but can still relax and recharge before they have to work hard either playing or training later in the day."

"So. Early." Proue sighed audibly and *tsk*-ed.

"Wait! Wait! We're here!" Laudine's large frame moved with surprising agility as she hurried toward them. She carried a giant stainless steel carafe in one hand and balanced a box full of croissants and *pain au chocolat* in the other. A canvas bag slung over her shoulder held cups, sugar, and cream.

Yvonne hurried behind her, leading two horses tacked and ready to ride.

"Coffee, for afterward." Laudine placed her things in the tack stall where the team stored its saddles, bridles, and other equipment. "We are late. It is my fault. *Désolé.* I turned one road too soon and then it was just one-way after one-way."

"All the wrong way," Yvonne agreed.

When everyone was mounted, Mayla led the way to the exercise track, a half-mile oval of graded, stone-free dirt wide enough for ten horses to stand abreast.

"When I condition my horses, I generally ride one and lead four or five others," she said. "Today, each rider will be responsible for just one horse. Focus on maintaining a steady gait while staying with our 'herd.' Keep together. Ride relaxed. We're going to walk and trot in both directions, beginning with the walk."

She moved Bogo forward onto the track. Her students followed.

"Let your horse stretch forward and warm up. Some of you may be used to riding with constant contact on the horse's mouth. Make an effort not to do so. Loosen your reins, as long as you don't lose control."

A few of the ladies who Mayla had privately dubbed "dressage queens," gave little mews of apprehension.

"Try it," she encouraged them. "I promise you won't ruin your horse. No need for you to carry him every step he makes. Let him carry himself for a change."

They moved out at a brisk, ground-covering walk.

"The key to conditioning is LSD: long, slow, distance work. Though polo is a game that moves fast and pivots on a pin, no magic pill will instantly make your horse fit. Going from full speed to a stop, to changing direction, to running again all takes a toll on ligaments and joints. That's why we condition. Before a horse can spend a chukker starting and stopping and turning quickly, he must first have strength and endurance. Heart and lung capacity, bones, and muscles don't develop overnight. You've got to do things slowly, building your pony up over time."

"A slow burn rather than a one-night stand," said Yvonne.

Mayla nodded. "You could say that. Proper conditioning involves a lot of walking. And trotting. It's about consistency rather than constant speed."

Proue slouched atop her stunning Andalusian gelding like a cloud raining on a parade. "This is boring."

Said the spoiled little rich bitch.

Mayla bit her tongue and refused to dignify Proue's remark.

One woman was less circumspect. (Dauphne? Darlene? Mayla couldn't remember. Nor could she see the lady's name tag, though the riot of curly hair spiraling out beneath her helmet made her more than memorable.) "A morning on my horse is better than a morning spent anywhere else," she said. "And this is a nice change from riding in endless patterns in the ring. I signed up for this clinic series because I wanted to learn new things and spend more time riding. So far: success! I've done both."

"Yay for you," said Proue. "What I have learned is that no matter how much I like my horse, I'd rather be in bed at five a.m. My Frederic, he complained so loudly this morning when I left his side. I had to pet him until he went back to sleep."

"Your dog?" said Yvonne.

Proue leveled a *you-want-to-go-there?* stare. "My husband."

"Ah," Yvonne said, backpedaling. "My boyfriend doesn't care what I do, as long as it doesn't get in the way of his cello practice."

"My husband is away on business. But if he were here, he would take Frederic's side." Laudine's soft words poured oil on the frothing conversational waters. "Of course, Herb complains about everything I do. Especially if it involves my horse."

Yvonne quietly confided in Mayla. "*C'est vrai.* If she likes it, he hates it. Ombré he despises. Her art, which is superb, he ridicules. You should see what she does with wood and stone. He does not care.

Neither she nor I can figure out what old Herb wants, but it sure as hell isn't her."

She looked across the track at her friend and sighed. Raising her voice so everyone could hear, she said, "Never trust a man who doesn't like horses."

That was something on which they all concurred.

When they had completed one full lap around the track, Mayla said, "While we finish up the walking portion—Stay together, ladies. Don't let your horses drag their feet.—let's review what we covered yesterday. What is a chukker and how long does it last?"

"It's a seven-minute period of play," Proue yawned.

"But it seems like forever," Yvonne said as the others nodded in agreement. "Yesterday's practice chukker nearly killed me."

"Seven minutes of heaven," Mayla said in English. But the joke was lost on her listeners. Either they didn't understand the reference or they were too tired to find it funny. "How many chukkers to a game?"

"Four."

"No, six."

"I thought it was eight."

Mayla waited till everyone had weighed in. "You are all right," she said. "It depends on the league. Here, for the Monde du Polo games, we play six."

"But beginners, like us, play only four, yes?" said Proue.

"Thank God," said Yvonne.

The missing foot mallet crossed Mayla's mind. Perhaps if she formed her next question correctly, the culprit who took it would confess. "Does anyone have any unexpected takeaways from yesterday? What did you leave with that you didn't have when you came here?"

The question landed with all the finesse of a cannonball. No one looked the least bit guilty.

So much for subtlety. She would make a terrible detective. Mayla prayed her students would attribute her awkward phrasing to the natural shortcomings of an American speaking French.

As they walked their horses, the silence stretched, awkward and empty.

Finally, the curly-haired Darlene—or was it Darla?—spoke. "I liked that thing you told us about the natural progression of players. I don't know why, but it really resonated with me."

"All crawl," chorused several ladies with all the reverence of repeating a religious mantra. "Few fly."

The woman's horse jig-jogged sideways enough for Mayla to read the small square affixed to her shirt: DOREEN. "I also appreciated how you didn't make us feel like failures when we did something wrong," she said.

"The biggest revelation, to me, was how you can desensitize an animal to anything if you keep picking away at it," Laudine said.

"It's true," Mayla said, glad that yesterday's demonstration had made an impression. "Time and patience are all you need to get a pony to accept things it would normally run from. For instance, if a horse is afraid of the mallet, then hang mallets everywhere around the paddocks and barn so she gets used to seeing them all the time. Eventually, it becomes part of her life."

They rode on, the horses snorting in time to the rhythmic footfalls.

After several yards, tiny Yvonne cracked a mischievous grin. "I don't know about anyone else, but I discovered that I really, *really* liked hitting the ball."

A few ladies applauded: a charter meeting of Ball Hitters Anonymous.

Suddenly, as if they were all part of a single organism, the horses raised their heads and pricked their ears. As one, they looked in the direction of a man who hurried toward them from the barns.

His long hair and stubbly beard hid his features the way moss hides granite, which only accentuated the menace boiling out from him. Stomping on bowed legs, his jaw set like he planned to pick a fight with an aristocrat, he was edgy as a guillotine, and less welcoming. Little clouds of dust scuffed up from his well-worn boots. He gestured toward the club entrance. "Stupid womens! Get out!"

"Here comes a winner." Laudine's fingers tightened on the reins. Ombré shook his head at the tension on his mouth.

"Keep riding. Stay together and follow me," Mayla said. "I'll take care of this."

Anger propelled the man. As he neared their group, he stopped, standing on the edge of the track with feet apart, hands on his hips like a surly wannabe superhero.

Mayla never slowed. "Bruno Carrizo. Is there a problem?"

She gave him her sweetest, most angelic smile while leading her students past, forcing him to walk alongside them if he wanted to be heard.

"Get out," he repeated, his French stilted and heavily accented. "This is no a bridle path for pony rides. Out! Or I call security."

"Please do. Tell them a hateful troll is harassing the guests."

Bruno squinted his hard, dark eyes, taking in every detail of Mayla, her horse, and her students. He spat on the ground, then reached up, grabbing for Bogo's reins.

Doreen's gasp of alarm spurred Mayla to action. Spinning the excess rein in her right hand, she whipped it forward. The bight, heavy with buckles connecting the left and right reins, cracked down on the back of Bruno's bare hand.

Cursing, he jerked his hand away.

Laudine's quiet "*Bravo*" made Mayla smile.

Bruno scowled. "You womens. Prancing around and—"

He jumped aside, cursing louder than before, but with less invention, as Mayla moved Bogo sideways. True to her instructions, her students followed. Soon, a wall of horses crowded the man off the track, onto the grass.

"Okay, Sparky, run along and play," said Mayla. "The grownups are busy. Ladies: let's pick up a trot."

6

Sleight of Hand

SOMETHING WAS WRONG.

Someone moved beside him. Someone was in his bed, with their hands around his neck! He was trapped. Pinned down. Held against his will...

Thiago awoke with a start, hyperalert. Though remnants of his dream vanished, the claustrophobia that woke him put down roots and set up housekeeping.

The cabin shuddered, throbbing from the drone of the big jet engines. They were still aloft, which was reassuring, but now that he was awake, the feeling of wrongness remained.

So did the body beside him.

What the hell?

Awareness slowly dawned. Swizzle Stick lay spooning him, lying close, sharing the same seat, rubbing his shoulders, kneading his neck. As Thiago regained his bearings, her hands crept under his shirt and slid onto his chest. Though her fingers were warm and her movements adept, everything in him recoiled.

Thiago remained still. With forced detachment, he said, "We don't know each other this well."

"You will know me soon enough," she purred. Her left hand dipped into his pants and started redecorating like it owned the place.

"*Pará che.*" Taking her hands off him, he sat up.

"You like it. You like me. I know you do."

"This is not a service I requested."

She huffed, pouting pertly. "How can you say that? We could be beautiful together."

Her gaze lingered on his shoulders, then slipped down to his abs and traveled down his body in frank admiration. When she finished her appraisal and raised her eyes to meet his, he read her mind. She wasn't a deep thinker.

"I'm sure we could," he said. "You are already beautiful."

She accepted this as a basic truth, as if he had said "the sun is hot" or "icebergs are bad for cruise liners."

"But no." Thiago kept his voice low, impassive, empty of emotion. He opened the privacy curtains and turned on the vent, letting in the silver light of early morning and blasting the confined space with fresh air.

Confusion creased her perfect forehead. "Don't you want to play?" She sucked on a finger that had recently been south of his equator.

Thiago doubted anyone had ever refused her before. "I'm not in the mood for games."

Sighing as if unsurprised to discover that he, too, bored her, she moved to stand.

With reflexes honed from years of lightning-fast decisions, Thiago reached out and grabbed her wrist. He closed his fingers enough to make certain she couldn't slip through them, but he put no pressure on her.

She tried to pull away from him. She might as well have tried to fly alongside the aircraft.

"Don't...Don't hurt me!" she said, her voice high and frightened, like a child's, though no fear flared in her eyes. "Let me go!"

"You are no model," Thiago said, pushing the call button. "But you are a remarkable actress. I'll say it just once: leave it."

Albert appeared at the end of the aisle. One look at the altercation sent him hurrying toward them.

The girl's empty eyes held neither regret nor remorse. A flick of her free hand produced Thiago's passport from wherever she had hidden it.

Thiago checked to make sure he still wore his watch. His relief at still having it must have shown on his face, for Swizzle Stick sneered. She had evidently judged the watch and deemed it worthless. She had no idea it was the most valuable thing he owned; his only true treasure.

"How may I be of assistance?" Albert asked.

Thiago held out his hand, waiting. "Everything."

Swizzle Stick's left nostril twitched, telegraphing her irritation. She produced his wallet and phone.

"Coffee, please," Thiago said.

"Of course. Only too happy."

As Albert scurried away, Thiago released his captive.

She took her time standing. With sultry indifference, she sauntered to her seat. Pretending to ignore everyone else in the cabin, she pulled the compact from the amenities kit and repainted her lips a shade of red found only in the blood of innocents and the most expensive, exclusive makeup lines.

Thiago checked the contents of his wallet and the SIM card on his phone: all present and accounted for, though the disconcerting undercurrent of wrongness continued.

Tough Guy lay motionless on the other side of the cabin. Though stretched out in his recliner bed, he was too still, too stealthy to be asleep.

While Thiago watched, the man's eyes cracked open and swept the room, taking everything in. When they rested on Thiago, they stopped and stared, challenging and malevolent.

Albert returned with coffee so hot, dark, and strong, it dissolved any residual ties to dreamland.

They would land in a few hours. Might as well stay awake, Thiago decided. Besides, his skin was still crawling where his uninvited guest had touched him while he slept.

7

Best Laid Plans

MAYLA CROUCHED OVER CANTATA'S WITHERS as the gray mare hurtled down the field. Past the white-topped gazebos. Past the long white barn shed rows with their red roofs and the Eiffel Tower punching up into the skyline behind them. The peaked roofs of the dormers on the Polo Parisien Clubhouse streaked by.

No matter where in the world she played, the game was the same: she and three other players mounted on elite equine athletes rode into battle against a similarly skilled team, chasing a little white ball, doing everything in their power to knock it between goal posts at one end of the field without allowing their opponents to send it between the goal posts at the other end. The fields all had the same measurements, the same manicured turf, the same markings.

But not all fields were created equal. No. The Parisien was something truly magical. Perhaps it was the cultured sense of history and tradition that permeated its grand, century-old grounds. Or maybe it was because ten years ago, this place had been her home when she had none and had helped mend her very young, freshly broken heart.

She had been back for less than a week, but every time she returned, it was like greeting an old friend. Though separated for months, they resumed their comfortable relationship as soon as they reunited. The smell of leather and sweat, wood shavings and French soil intoxicated her, adding further joy to the exhilaration of guiding a fast horse down this field of perfect green in the world's most lovely city, feeling the power of sitting astride a thousand pounds of pure muscle that responded to her every cue. Though she thrilled whenever she played the game, playing polo in Paris was as close as Mayla came to feeling at home.

She shadowed a young man who rode well, but who was new enough to the game that he overthought every move. He stood a little too far out of his stirrups. Prepped for his swing a little too soon. Swung a little too late.

Still, he was keen, engaged, and a fast learner. Like the team he captained, his reflexes and response time had sharpened notably since the first play of the chukker. If he kept this up, he would soon be one to watch.

As he prepared to swing, Mayla snicked the ball away from him and sent it flying back toward her goal. No point in letting things come too easily for the boy.

Her opponent sat back, checking his horse's momentum, compressing and focusing all the animal's power in its haunches before unleashing it in a new direction—a textbook rollback.

Good job! Mayla knew firsthand that there was nothing like playing against pros to make hungry amateurs up their game.

Today's exhibition match with players from Université de Flambeaux was the perfect way to blow off a little steam before tonight's party. The collegiate team all played well enough, but they presented no real challenge. Tomorrow, the three-day Monde du Polo exhibition series began, pitting Mayla's Team North America against the South American team. She couldn't wait to play them: they were the best of the best.

No sense in getting complacent, however. She closed her legs around Cantata's sides. Together, they rocketed after the ball.

Between chukkers, Mayla switched ponies, transferring from one saddle to the other without touching the ground. She patted Bogo and collected his reins from Rochelle, her groom.

"Looking good out there," Rochelle said.

"Thanks, but it's easy to look good against low-goal players."

"Some of them are OK."

"Talking about anyone in particular?" Mayla asked.

A bright blush colored Rochelle's pretty face. Rather than reply, she loosened Cantata's girth, giving the mundane task her full attention.

"Their Number Three isn't bad," Mayla prodded.

"That would be Philippe."

Mayla tried to keep her game face on, but Rochelle's smile so disarmed her that she found herself smiling too.

Though Philippe rode well enough, from the little she had seen of him on the ground—front and center in all the promotional events but missing in action when it came time to do any real work—he had struck her as a *parvenu*, embodying the worst traits of narcissistic social climbers. Still: Rochelle had not asked Mayla's opinion, so she kept it to herself. She remembered being young and in love.

"Your Philippe knows a thing or two about the game," Mayla said. "If I'm not careful, he's going to go pro and steal my groom away from me. Then who would help me run LaMay Farm when it becomes a reality?"

"Have they accepted your offer?"

"Not yet. Fingers crossed."

Mayla double-checked the mallet strap around her wrist. "Here's a thought," she said. "Why not ask Monsieur Philippe to be your plus-one tonight at the Palais Brongniart magpie? *Très romantique*! And who knows? He might find a patron."

Still blushing, Rochelle ducked her head, her hair falling over the patch covering her right eye. Her smile faded. "*Merci*. But I am just a groom. I have no extra ticket."

"Ask him anyway. I'll give you mine."

"I couldn't accept!"

"*Pffht*."

Rochelle squinted her good eye; a mute question.

"It's an American thing," Mayla said. "It means 'don't talk nonsense.'"

"Mm-hm. You are already lending me a dress. It is too much that you should have to go alone."

"I'll find some old thing to wear." Mayla knew the girl caught her sarcasm as she spoke of her gorgeous vintage gown. She turned Bogo toward the field. "And you know me: I fly solo."

Moments before the next chukker began, she and Bogo jumped the low railing separating the sidelines from the field.

As the game resumed, Mayla savored the memory of Rochelle's happiness. Young love. So radiant. So joyous. She smiled ruefully. So quickly jaded.

An inelegant knot of players converged on the ball. Mayla guided Bogo into the scrum and hooked Philippe's mallet, hampering him from making a bold shot. She might be responsible for his good fortune with Rochelle this evening, but for the moment, she dedicated herself to being his greatest foe.

8

Unhappy Landings

THIAGO ROLLED HIS NECK, stretching out the knots accumulated during the nightmare of a flight. So much for planning ahead.

He avoided the crowded baggage claim free-for-all. Most of his luggage, his mallets, boots, and helmet, had been sent ahead on Monday, shortly after he accepted Sergio's invitation.

Instead of arriving at a reasonable hour, ready to take on the day, he was stuck at the airport in the frenzy of the midday rush. For the hundredth time, he remembered why, even with first-class surroundings, all the champagne one cared to drink, decadent meals from famous chefs, practically prescient attendants, and interesting in-flight felonies, he hated flying commercial airlines.

At least he had a driver waiting for him once he got to Paris, he had told himself while airborne. Well, here he was, but the representative for Car Noir was dead set on withholding any information of use. Thiago knew his French was adequate, but the man behind the counter raised eyebrows high, pinched nostrils in disdain, and pretended not to understand. When the rep showed no inclination to acknowledge Thiago's native Spanish, he switched to English and tried again.

"I have a reservation. Here is my confirmation."

With extreme condescension, the man considered the number displayed on Thiago's phone. "That was hours ago. You're late."

"Yes. My flight was delayed."

"The driver, he is out."

"No problem. Just give me another one."

A ghost of a smirk haunted the man's mouth as he frankly appraised Thiago's inexpensive watch and worn jeans and deemed him unworthy. "All are out. Perhaps tomorrow."

Thiago forced a smile. "Monsieur—?"

"Laurent," the man admitted.

"Monsieur Laurent. I am tired. Work with me here. I don't want to go over your head, but I will if I have to."

Laurent shrugged, pious, brittle, and smug. "My head needs no going over. *Je le regrette*, but what can be done?"

Thiago refrained from itemizing all the things a capable company representative might find possible. Instead, he spoke to his phone. "Siri. Call Étienne Travert."

Laurent's face went frog-belly white. "Sir, I hardly think that's necessary."

Oh, but it was.

"Étienne! Thiago Calvo. *Ça va bien? Oui.*" Though Thiago spoke calmly, each word added to the rep's rising unease. "Just got in. I told you one day I'd get around to visiting your city. I'm a hired assassin for the next few weeks."

Laurent uttered a strangled *eerp*—the phonetic equivalent to the last sound a rodent makes upon tripping the wire of a mousetrap. His long pale fingers scrabbled on the countertop.

"I've got a series that starts tomorrow. Runs through Sunday. You're coming? Great. Listen, I hate to bother you, but I was wondering if I could count on you to honor a car confirmation."

With broad strokes, Thiago sketched his situation while Laurent listened white-lipped with anxiety.

"Thanks, Étienne. See you tonight." Thiago handed the phone to Laurent. "I believe the owner of your company would like a word."

⚜

"Good afternoon, Important Someone. Welcome to my beautiful city. I am Mourad, your joyful and attentive driver. It is my honor, my privilege, to take you where you wish to go."

A trim, dark man in his early fifties, wearing a tailored white shirt and black suit, stood at attention beside an elegant charcoal sedan. With a white-gloved hand, he opened the back door.

"I've never seen a B7 treated as if it were a limo," Thiago confessed.

"In the hands of Mourad, the Alpina, she is treated like royalty." The driver bowed slightly. "As are all who ride inside."

Thiago allowed himself to be ushered into the vehicle. He sank into the hand-stitched Merino leather seats. Entering the sedan was like entering a magical bubble. As soon as the door closed, the chaos of the airport vanished.

Mourad took his place behind the wheel. "Where to, Monsieur?"

"Le Polo Parisien."

"Very good. While we drive, do you wish for silent Mourad or chatty Mourad?"

Unsure how to answer, Thiago said, "Is there a 'quiet conversationalist Mourad' option?"

"But of course." The rearview mirror reflected the good humor sparkling in the driver's eyes. "Shall I pretend I do not know you, sir?"

Thiago tensed. This was why he never took taxis. Or Uber. The last time he tried public transportation, the scruffy guy behind the wheel recognized his name. He never heard the end of it. During the drive, he endured two movie pitches and hyperbolic praise over Calvo Land Development's business park project. Explaining that those were all his father's doing and not his hadn't deterred the driver. After the boy snarled traffic and nearly caused an accident when he tried to take a selfie with him, Thiago had sworn he would do his own driving while at home in Argentina. There, he was used to being recognized. He hadn't thought he would have the same problems here, but he couldn't help asking, out of morbid curiosity, "*Do* you know me?"

Mourad could not hide his grin. "Who does not know the great eight-goaler Thiago Calvo?"

"Many people," Thiago told him. "Outside of my home country, most people."

But Mourad was not one of them. An avid polo fan, he raved about Team Argentina's performance under Thiago's leadership at last year's Polo Internacional.

"You faced off against the fierce and ferocious dragon of Dubai. It roars. It flames. It plunders. Then, in the eleventh hour of the eighth chukker, in you dart, the fearless *chevaliers*, snatching bits of meat from the dragon's teeth! Remember that? Of course you do! You must! How could anyone forget?"

As the trees lining the A1 on the outskirts of the city gave way to graffiti on the uninspired concrete walls funneling traffic on the Boulevard Périphérique, Thiago learned he rode with "polo fan Mourad." It was the first thing about this trip he didn't mind—it helped take his mind off the well-creased paper in his wallet taunting him, weighted down with broken promises and missed opportunities. Paris: the most romantic city in the world for everyone but him. The last time he visited had been the worst defining moment of his life.

He reminded himself that Sergio hadn't contracted strep just to torment him.

Part of him remained unconvinced.

As Mourad reiterated highlights from his last few seasons ("When you played against the Saudis last September, and your stirrup broke? That long drive down the middle, then you juggled the ball on your mallet—what, four times!—before windmilling it through the goal. Pure poetry! Remember that?"), Thiago tried to reconnect with the honor he had felt when Team South America asked him to come join them in Sergio's place. The other players were good. He knew with his eight-goal handicap, he had something solid to offer. But why did it have to be Paris? London, or Dublin, or even Dubai would have been preferable.

The ride was so smooth and Mourad's chatter so effortless, time passed quickly. A few tunnels later, the green expanse of the Bois de Boulogne swallowed them up, engulfing them in its shadowy coolness.

"*Pardonnez-moi,*" Mourad said. "I talk more than enough, yes? What good fortune brings you to my beautiful city?"

"Paris belongs to you?"

"But of course, Monsieur. She belongs to all who love her, which is all who visit her."

Thiago didn't have the heart to explain how he had lost his love for Paris long ago. Instead, he said, "I have a Vevier photo shoot on Saturday."

"Watch? Or clothing?"

"Both."

"You are wearing a ChronoMétreur now?" Hope tinged Mourad's voice. "I have never seen one..."

"Sorry to disappoint." Thiago leaned forward to show the man the old watch he rarely removed except for games. Wouldn't do to damage it. It's not like it could be replaced.

Mourad nodded as if he understood. "I get it," he said, trying—and failing—to sound like a cool American. "You don't want to get mugged. Watch ain't worth your life."

"But the real reason I'm here is because I'm playing for Team South America, filling in for Sergio Chavez."

Mourad's hands gripped the steering wheel more tightly. "You are playing in my city, after riding in my car. Today I am both favored and blessed."

Thiago wished he could say the same as they pulled up to the tall, green gates of the club.

As he got out of the car, he noticed a scrimmage underway with a local team—wearing garish orange—taking on one of the pros. He saw the red, white, and blue colored polo shirts and assumed the pro team was French. Even from a distance, he could see the pro players were good. Very good. They knew their stuff.

He shook off his jet lag and began to look forward to testing his mettle against the best France had to offer. Maybe Paris would be good to him this time around.

Suddenly, a bright chestnut gelding broke away from the tangle of horses and bolted down the field, streaking after the ball like a comet. Its rider moved as if part of the horse, fluid and graceful, mallet high, with no wasted motion.

The sound of the ocean roared in Thiago's ears. His heart pounded as if he were in danger of being trampled.

"Mourad," he said in a voice he barely recognized. "I'll need a driver for the next few days. Know of anyone who would like the job?"

"Do not taunt me, Monsieur. To be sure, it would be my honor."

"Good. I'll call Travert and personally request you. Meet me here tonight at eight," Thiago said as the gelding flew out of view.

His mind whirred, putting all the pieces in place.

Red, white, and blue shirts.

Not French. *American.*
He hadn't known she would be here.
He should have known she would be here.
What had he gotten himself into?

9

Surprise

MAYLA AND BOGO LEFT the rest of the players far behind. As they raced across the grass, she looked around to make sure she knew where the others were. She hated surprises.

Out of the corner of her eye, she saw a dark sedan saturated with money and privilege glide through the side gate. A tall man stepped out of the car, dark as a shadow, self-assured as a panther.

Thiago.

Surprise.

Mayla tried to breathe, but her lungs refused to respond, as if all the air had been sucked off the club grounds.

Intimate images floated like bits of fluff and flotsam in the vacuum that remained. Mayla had a vision of long golden fields of Argentinian wheat, of vineyards laid out in neat rows with crenellated mountains rising in the distance, of olive orchards and green evening skies, of fragrant leather and silver bits and sunbaked days full of hard work and possibilities. Memories flooded her of loving every moment of being awake and alive, of feeling for the first time that she belonged. That was when she had believed she was a princess in a fairy tale. Before she learned the fairy tale was a lie.

Her heart flopped like a newborn foal. When she tried to swallow, her mouth was dry as sawdust.

Distracted by visions of her past, Mayla didn't notice Victor, easily the worst player on the Flambeaux team, until he was at her elbow. He smacked the ball, stealing it away from her, and rode off whooping with delight.

Mayla watched him go, nonplussed.

Thiago was here.

She wanted to hate him; had tried hating him for years. For a while, she had even convinced herself that she *did* hate him.

But she didn't.

Seeing him again had put her off her game, which underscored that she had been lying to herself all this time. The thought filled her, not with hatred, but with fury.

⚜

Bogo played in the spray from the hose as Mayla washed him down. He gleamed like burnished copper in the light of the afternoon sun.

The match had ended moments ago, but by the time Mayla dismounted, Rochelle had already untacked the other horses and removed their leg wraps. Now, she ran electric clippers over stubbled manes, roaching the coarse hair off completely, but leaving the forelocks.

"Why don't you go see if the Flambeaux players could use some help," Mayla suggested. "I've got this covered."

Rochelle's smile of gratitude was infectious. She put clippers and horses away in record time before scurrying over to the big orange horse vans that sported the Université de Flambeaux logo. Straight and true as an arrow, she aimed for the golden-haired Philippe, who was strutting around, proud as a stud colt.

As Mayla finished up in the wash area, she spied Yvonne hurrying in her direction. A showy fascinator of lime tulle, fabric begonias, and extravagantly long feathers perched like an exotic alien bird on the side of her head, dwarfing her tiny frame. Laudine, in a more understated hat, followed at a more leisurely pace.

"You were electrifying! So inspiring! We were completely enthralled!" The bird hat bobbled with excitement as Yvonne jigged in place, still energized from the game.

Mayla searched in vain for pins or ties, hoping to determine how the hat remained on Yvonne's head. She also tried to come up with the right thing to say that would make the tiny woman confess to taking the foot mallet. She found solutions to neither problem.

Bogo's coat glowed like a flame as Mayla scraped sheets of water from his body. "It's good to see you ladies here. I didn't know you were coming to our little exhibition."

"Neither did we, to be honest." Laudine huffed a bit from the exertion of keeping up with her friend.

Yvonne agreed, sending the bird into seizures. "When we signed up for your clinics, we bought tickets for the whole series. Then we realized we had never actually seen a polo match."

"Watching them online isn't at all the same," said Laudine.

"We wanted to know what to expect before we saw the real thing tomorrow."

"And what did you think of your inaugural game?" Mayla asked.

"It's so fast. So competitive. So precise," Yvonne said.

"Herb is right: I have no business playing," Laudine sighed.

"But look how far you have already come," Yvonne told her, backing away from Bogo, who wanted to taste her hat. "You hit the ball in practice today! Twice."

"*Et alors?*" Laudine wasn't convinced. "Those Flambeaux students are low-goal players, yet they ride like kings. Herb says I ride like a sack of potatoes."

Yvonne's face wrinkled as if she smelled a week-dead skunk in a sewer. "You ride just fine. Herb is an ass."

Laudine didn't argue.

"Every. Player. Starts. Somewhere." Mayla picked up a rough-napped terry towel and began to scrub Bogo, rubbing him dry. When she reached his withers, he stretched his head and neck straight out in front of him, rolling his eyes back in ecstasy and wiggling the tip of his nose as if he were an elephant.

"I guarantee you every one of those players, at some point, was right where you are. All crawl.

"But you? You are way past crawling. You're learning to walk. Running isn't too far away."

"Some run. Few fly," Laudine said, more to herself than to Mayla.

"That's right. Now, I can't speak regarding Herb, but there is nothing wrong with the way you handle a horse or the way you ride."

Bright tears of appreciation welled in the woman's eyes. "We owe you a huge debt of gratitude, Madame Alvarez. These clinics for beginning players..."

"Like us," Yvonne said.

"Like us. These are enlightening. I have learned so much already. I look forward to tomorrow's lesson."

"You inspire me, not only to learn to play, but to play well," Yvonne said.

As the women gushed about their newfound polo appreciation, Mayla thanked them. Her words and smile were genuine, and normally she loved few things more than comparing notes with new converts after a game, but thoughts of Thiago crowded her mind, distancing her from the conversation.

"You are busy," Laudine finally said. "And, no doubt, tired. We'll be here for tomorrow's clinic, but won't take up any more of your time today. Besides, I am inspired. I need to go home to my studio and get to work."

They said their *à bientôt*s and walked away. Mayla watched the bobbing bird hat till it disappeared into the crowd of people, speculating on the probability of Laudine's artistry having anything to do with its creation.

She dropped Bogo's lead rope on the ground, allowing him to nibble some grass while she untaped his tail. Keeping her hands busy, surrounded by horses, brought out the best in her. Today, more than any day in a long time, she needed to do some thinking.

10

The Asado

THE TEAM SOUTH AMERICA ASADO was ostensibly to welcome Thiago into their ranks, but he knew the boys well enough—some he had played with; others he had played against—to know they leapt at any opportunity to party.

He met the whole team, trainers, coaches, and grooms, and immediately felt at home…with one exception. Bruno Carrizo, a peacocking four-goaler, greeted him warmly enough, but watched him with eyes like a feral dog, hard and calculating. Even as Thiago returned Bruno's handshake, the hairs on the back of his neck itched with distrust as if he were back on the plane, hanging out with Tough Guy and Swizzle.

As the friendly match between the North Americans and the local collegiate team ended, many of the North American players followed their noses and came by.

"They say it is to introduce themselves," Remigio, the South American team captain, said. "But we all know they only want our food."

"Guilty as charged," the North American players agreed.

Thiago doled out a few little gifts of goodwill and rather enjoyed the good-natured roasting the North American players gave Remigio for bringing him in as an eight-goal assassin. He sized up his opponents, several of whom he had played against at one time or another. The two teams were fairly evenly matched. Tomorrow's game should be interesting.

As he scanned the faces milling around the fire, however, the game was not the foremost thing in his thoughts. Rather, he searched the crowd for a slight, dark-haired spitfire who rode like an angel and bedeviled his dreams.

Mayla would come, he rationalized. She may not have forgiven him. God knew he never had. But she would come. His hopes rose and fell with each new arrival.

It didn't take long before everyone from North American team arrived. Everyone except Mayla.

Your eyes deceived you.

You only thought you saw her.

Keep this up and you'll lose your edge. Might as well go back home without bothering to unpack if you can't focus on what's important.

That's what you get for projecting. For indulging in a pointless daydream.

Why did the cold, dispassionate part of his conscience always berate him in his father's voice?

As if Mayla would happen to be in Paris at the same time he was. As if he would reel her to him like a fish on a line after all these years. He had her once; he lost her, plain and simple. She wasn't his. And she wasn't here.

"It appears your whole team is present," he remarked to Moe, the paunchy, raunchy North American coach, who had eaten an impressive amount of sweetbreads.

Moe nodded, then reconsidered. "All except Alvarez. She's probably still taking care of the horses."

Thiago's heart tripped over itself, then raced to make up for lost time.

"She doesn't have a groom?" He kept his tone light, pretending he didn't care.

"Sure. Sure." Moe gestured with a greasy fork toward the fleet of Flambeaux horse vans. "But Rochelle's over there making nice with some pretty French boy. Alvarez doesn't mind. She likes to do things herself anyway."

As Moe wandered away in search of more food, Thiago finished his wine, preoccupied. He drifted away from the party.

"Had enough of us already?" Remigio asked.

"I'm going to go introduce myself to Sergio's horses," Thiago said.

"You know them well enough," his captain said, offering to refill his glass. "You used to own four of them."

Thiago waved off the refill. "True. But that still leaves a few I need to meet."

"Chevaliers de la table ronde / Goûtons voir se le vin et bon!"

As an impromptu French drinking song broke out that made up in volume what it lacked in musicality (*"Goûtons voir! Oui! Oui! Oui! / Goûtons voir. Non! Non! Non!"*), Thiago left the laughter behind and headed toward the shed rows.

11

Idol Chatter

MAYLA WAS IN THE PROCESS of untying Bogo's tail and combing it out when Carson LeVallier, Team North America's dashing captain, approached, sipping from a sterling bombilla stuck in a silver rimmed, grapefruit-sized gourd.

"You and your maté," Mayla said.

"It's iced, so it's tereré. *Avec citron*," he said, offering her the business end of the bombilla. "I'll share."

Mayla took a taste from the silver straw. Unlike Carson, she was not a raving fan of the earthy South American iced tea, but she had to admit that few things better quenched her thirst after a game.

"That's delicious."

Carson nodded. "It's the good stuff. The South Americans are having a party. A full-fledged asado. Guess who they brought in to pinch-hit for Sergio?"

Noncommittal, Mayla said, "Thiago Calvo."

"Can you believe it? Someone must have told him of my addiction, because he brought a whole kilo of maté from his family's estate. You know how they say you should never meet your idols? Well, they're wrong. He's amazing!"

Carson stopped abruptly, suspicion clouding his eyes. "Wait, now. How did you know he was coming? Who told you? And more importantly, why didn't you tell me? As Captain, it would have been nice to have a little warning."

"Believe me, if I had known, I'd have told you," Mayla said. "I saw him arrive during the match. I don't know what the big deal is. You're both eight-goalers. You're just as good as he is."

Carson flashed a cheeky grin. "Oh, Honey. Have you *seen* the man? Unlike you, I can think of more than just polo."

Mayla finished brushing Bogo's tail and put the gelding in his stall, where he promptly rolled in the fresh bedding. When he finished, he stood and shook, but tiny specks of wood shavings clung to him like packing peanuts.

"Ugh! Look at you; you're a pig," she said.

"I need a refill," Carson said, making empty slurping sounds through his straw. "Want to come meet Thiago?"

Meeting Thiago ranked near the top of Mayla's list of Last Things I Want To Do, falling somewhere below "swim the English Channel," but above "lick a metal pole on a cold winter day."

She was sweaty and grubby after playing in the hot sun for the past hour. Though she knew she had done well up until the time Thiago saw her, that didn't change the reality of her last, botched play. However, she restrained herself from heaving a sigh and pasted a smile on her face instead.

"Sure."

Might as well get it over with.

"Oh, curb your enthusiasm," Carson said. "You don't fool me. I know there's nothing wrong with your eyesight. Calvo practically reboots the 'tall, dark, and handsome' franchise. Besides, even if he were a toad—which he isn't—he's as charming as a twelfth-century knight. Did you know—"

As Carson gushed about Thiago's prowess on the field and fanboyed about his Vevier sponsorship, Mayla steeled herself. She would shake hands as if she were happy to see him again. She would be grown up. Gracious. She would pretend that seeing him didn't fill her with sadness about what they had and what she'd lost.

But she knew she was cracking open the door for disaster. She was no actress. So, when she and Carson arrived at the South American party, where the team *asador* grilled chicken and blood sausage, lamb and flank steak to mouthwatering perfection over a wood fire, Mayla's smile was genuine when she learned Thiago had left moments earlier.

12

Who's to Blame?

AT THE BARN, Thiago looked in on Sergio's ponies. He renewed his acquaintance with those he already knew and spent some time in the stalls grooming each of the horses he didn't. One bay mare in particular drew his attention. Lithe and limber, she moved with a quiet confidence.

"So you are the celebrated Zoelie," he whispered, watching the delicate ear closest to him swivel back to listen. "Sergio thinks I came because of national pride. But really, it was because this was the only way he would ever let me ride you."

He brushed the glossy body and ran his hands over the mare's perfect legs, looking for blemishes, but finding none.

"Because of you, I am here, *reina*. I blame you."

He held out a horse biscuit filched from the feed room. Zoelie, regal and aloof, took it from his palm, ate it, but did not deign to ask for more.

After leaving Zoelie's stall, Thiago wandered the shed rows. He told himself that he was simply interested in seeing the competition. He knew he was lying.

He recognized Mayla's mounts instantly: though all the North

Americans' ponies were in top shape, hers were the only ones who sported forelocks. Most players roached them off, but Mayla had always argued they helped keep gnats and flies out of the horses' eyes and refused to cut them. Some things never changed.

Mayla, however, was not around. The pang of Thiago's disappointment surprised him.

What was he expecting? That she would be waiting demurely for his arrival? That after ten years of refusing to respond to, or even acknowledge, his attempts at reconciliation, she would melt into a warm puddle of forgiveness? No. Not the Mayla he knew.

Thiago brought the last horse biscuit out of his pocket and flipped it back and forth across his knuckles as if it were a coin. The repetitive motion helped him think. Usually, it helped him to focus his thoughts on strategies for play. Now, though it brought back memories, it offered no answers.

◈

As Carson polished off yet another gourd of tereré, a stocky Team South America player staggered around the table that had been turned into a makeshift bar. He scowled when he saw Carson. At the sight of Mayla, however, he leered with naked contempt.

"Lemme guess. Here to see Thiago?" he said.

"Hello, Bruno. We just wanted to say 'hi.'" Mayla tried not to let her dislike of the man color her words.

Bruno, however, didn't care who knew his opinion of her. "Of course." He waggled nonexistent breasts and struck a truly offensive pin-up pose. "Ohhh, Thiaaaaago," he breathed. "Hiiiiii."

Carson growled, a pit bull on the defensive.

Tension crackled in the air. The remaining members of both teams noticed the exchange and veered in their direction.

Mayla smiled, sweet as nectar. "I'm worried about you. Especially since a bunch of beginners ran you over this morning. How's your hand? Are you OK? Looks like something left a nasty welt."

Bruno hid his hand behind his back. His face darkened with anger.

Before he could speak, Mayla chattered on. "As for Thiago: I wanted to talk with him about Faustino. See how he's doing."

"Pah, *gorda*!" Bruno spat. "What do you know of the great Faustino? He is a stallion unlike any of your insipid American ponies."

"Insipid?" Mayla turned to Carson. "Isn't that sweet? Someone's been building their vocabulary."

But Bruno was on a roll. "Faustino is a true warrior with nerves of iron. A little woman like you is unfit even to clean his hooves."

"I'm honored that you hold him in such high esteem," Mayla said. "Because I trained him."

"Oh ho!" Remigio hooted. "*¡Genial!*"

Everyone within earshot laughed at Bruno's expense.

Bruno's cold eyes narrowed. The cords on his neck stood out in anger. "You lie," he snarled.

Carson bristled and stepped forward, hands clenched in dangerous fists. Mayla put a hand on his arm to stop him.

Leaning slightly toward Bruno, she lowered her voice. "You're a swine: all ham and no bacon," she said in Spanish.

Switching to English, she said, "Trots like a jackhammer, flawless lead changes, and a stop so true it makes an atheist believe in God. That's my boy." She smiled sweetly. "If you see Mr. Calvo, tell him Mayla was here asking about 'Tino, OK, *chou chou*?"

She blew the enraged Argentinian a kiss. Turning on her heel, she took Carson's arm and walked away.

As they followed the footpath that skirted the exercise track, Mayla felt Carson staring at her. Without looking at him, she knew his mouth was quirked to the right, mutely questioning what had just happened.

"What?" she finally said.

"You never told me you worked for the Calvos."

"It never came up."

Carson waited for Mayla to tell him more. He waited in vain.

"Well," he sighed as they neared the little dormitory-like flats that housed the team members, "though I enjoy a good smackdown as much as the next guy, I'm glad we left when we did. I need to get a tie for tonight. Want to come with?"

"Didn't you get one—a nice one—two weeks ago?"

"I did. That was London. This is Paris. It's not like I can wear a tie from London in Paris. Listen!" He cupped an ear. "Rue du Faubourg Saint-Honoré is calling."

"I hear nothing," Mayla said.

"Of course not, because you claim to hate shopping."

"I do, for anything other than horses."

"I worry about you, Alvarez. For a woman who can recognize over four hundred bloodlines, not to mention clone stock, across multiple breeds, I despair of you ever having an eye for quality."

A vision of the beautiful farm she coveted flashed into Mayla's mind. She imagined the rolling hillsides dotted with broodmares and foals, the house and barns updated, new fencing, a green gem of a polo field, and a wide, smooth exercise track. As soon as her offer was accepted, she could start making the vision a reality. "I can spot quality a mile away when it's got four hooves," she said. "That's the only time it really counts."

Mayla tried to suppress a yawn, but failed. She surveyed her dingy clothes. "Sorry, Carson. You're on your own. I'm covered in sweat and horse hair. My whites are no longer white. I'm going to go to my tiny flat, shower in my shot-glass-sized bathroom, and rest up before the magpie tonight."

The enormous oak door of the Parisien's "Maison Bleu" guest cottage creaked open to reveal a suite of rooms decorated in classic, mid-nineteenth-century understated good taste. This apartment was not for players, Thiago knew. This was usually reserved for the patrons. Sergio had certainly made good on his promise that he would make Thiago's stay enjoyable.

The luggage he had sent earlier in the week awaited him in the slate-tiled anteroom. Per his request, nothing had been unpacked; he hated opening doors and drawers in a new place as if he were on a treasure hunt for his things.

Thiago stretched in a doomed attempt to combat the effects of too little sleep and too much traveling. The four-poster bed, situated to make the most of the breeze that frisked through the cottage, beckoned to him. A nap—a short siesta—was what he needed. As soon as he lay on the bed, however, his thoughts raced too fast for any relaxation.

Mayla.

In Paris.

They were together again, after all this time.

He almost laughed. Maybe he was in a science-fiction story, stuck in a loop, doomed to relive his greatest shortcoming once every ten years for eternity.

No. He knew better than that. He was no pawn at someone else's command. He made his own decisions. And he lived with the consequences.

Thiago rose from the bed less rested than when he lay down. He didn't need sleep. He needed a ride. Nothing else cleared his head or sharpened his thoughts as well.

He stripped off the shirt he had traveled in, ambled into the bathroom, and splashed bracing cold water on his face until all thoughts of sleep fled.

Creak.

Thiago froze.

In the mirror, he watched the cottage door ease further open.

Mayla! Though his heart swelled with misplaced hope and optimism, not for a second did he think she was actually crossing his threshold. The headstrong Mayla he knew would never compromise like that.

A hawkish nose poked into view.

All hope and optimism vanished.

"Bruno." Thiago cracked his neck, regretting his failure to shut and lock the door. "What do you want?"

Uninvited and unwelcome, Bruno skulked in. A wine-scented draft followed him.

"Expecting someone else?" He sneered at Thiago's state of undress.

"Certainly not expecting a *borracho* like you."

Ignoring the insult, or perhaps embracing it, Bruno swept the cottage with an appraising eye. "Doing all right for yourself, ain't ya?"

"It's time for you to go now."

"I just got here." Swaying, Bruno blinked several times, trying to bring Thiago into focus. "*You* just got here. Thiago Calvo! The great nine goaler—"

"Eight," Thiago said.

Bruno swatted at the correction as if it were a gnat. "Nine soon enough. Everyone knows it. Everyone. All the sponsors. All the patrons. All the women."

Thiago placed a hand on the man's shoulders to steer him toward the door, but Bruno ducked aside and flung himself into a Louis XV armchair. The lovely antique squeaked in protest as he swiveled sideways, flinging his legs over the padded arms.

"Women ruin everything," Bruno groaned. "They're everywhere.

Think they can do anything." He hiccupped, waiting for Thiago to join him in solidarity.

"Go back to your flat and sleep this off," Thiago said. He had no intention of encouraging this nonsense.

Bruno, however, would not be deterred. "They want to play, it should be against each other."

"You afraid to play against them?"

Bruno sulked, silent.

"Where did this come from?" Thiago asked. "Did you ask someone out and get turned down?"

Bruno belched in disgust. "It's not a sport for them! Do you know the North Americans have a woman on their team? Do you?"

"I do. I know that you and she are both four-goalers. And she's likely to move up soon. Sooner than you."

"They cheat. They're weak—" A fermented burp filled the air.

They have a woman, but we have a pig, Thiago mused. The North Americans clearly had the better deal.

Bruno continued cataloging his list of grievances. "They have thoughts."

"God forbid."

"He should. They ruin everything they touch. And they lie."

"Dishonesty is hardly gender specific. Let's go."

Thiago grabbed Bruno by the back of his shirt with one hand. The other hand went under Bruno's arm, with the thumb pointing up into his armpit. With a decisive movement, he hoisted Bruno out of the beleaguered chair and guided him toward the doorway.

"The American girl claims she trained your Faustino! Pah!" A stream of curses littered the air.

"She's right," Thiago said, enjoying the look of idiotic horror that twisted Bruno's face. "She worked for my father the year he shattered his shoulder. She was a groom then; wanted to play more than anything…"

With a pang that pricked his conscience, he heard the truth of his words. A truth he had refused to recognize when it mattered.

"She should have stayed a groom. Known her place and stayed in it."

"Speaking of knowing one's place. It's time to leave mine and go back to yours."

As Bruno realized he was being shown out, he became even crankier, which Thiago hadn't thought possible. He deliberately wiped his feet on the slate floor rather than the mat, grinding dried clods of horse manure into the cracks between tiles. "Nice house."

He walked away, grumbling just loud enough for Thiago to hear him. "Rich boys have it all without even asking. No one ever tells them 'no.'"

Thiago had no interest in telling him how very wrong he was.

13

Vintage Dreams

FRESHLY SHOWERED, Mayla toweled her short hair dry as she considered the two gowns. They hung side by side on the wooden wall molding originally intended for holding picture frames. For the first time, she wished she hadn't promised Rochelle she could borrow an evening dress. She owned two. Only one of them—a chic little black number she had picked up this spring at an estate sale in Milan—fit Rochelle. As for the other one…

The gorgeous vintage gown, the color of twilight, adorned with shimmering shooting stars, draped her body and flowed as if it were made for her. Too long for Rochelle, it fit Mayla as perfectly today as it did ten years ago. She never wore it without thinking of Thiago. She could only imagine what he would think when he saw her in it tonight.

Would he remember getting it for her?

She did. Vividly.

Two days before they had planned to visit Paris together, they had gone to an auction, a dispersal of a private collector's entire estate, including polo ponies and breeding stock. While on one of her innumerable errands for Thiago's father, she had seen the dress and fallen in love with it. She had never been much interested in clothes, or fashion, or labels. Jeans or whites and polo shirts were the only things she cared to wear. But that dress…

She had been covered in horse hair and dust, as usual. Not daring to touch the gown, she had stepped behind where it hung on display, lining herself up in a full-length mirror nearby.

Something very close to magic moved. A feeling of belonging seeped into her. It wasn't the promise of wealth or luxury that the dress held. Rather, it was a sense of security. "You are here." The words were almost audible. "Here is home."

For a brief moment, she had allowed herself to indulge in a fantasy in which she made a home with the man she loved. This home was a far cry from the poorly maintained, densely populated projects of her childhood. It wasn't a hotel room, or a player's flat, or a groom's apartment. No. In her mind's eye, she saw it all: a house big enough for children, small enough for companionship, that overlooked a farm of green pastures filled with fast horses. Her home. Her farm. Her Thiago. But even as the dream took shape, her phone had dinged with a text from Señor Calvo. The magic vanished as she ran out to do her boss's bidding.

She had not known Thiago had seen her looking at herself in that mirror, but something of the magic that hit her must have affected him as well. After dinner that evening, very late, he had arrived at her apartment over the broodmare barn. Without a word, he had handed her a soft parcel. "For Paris," he had said, boyish charm shining in eyes that looked at her with a man's desires.

How young he had been then. How young they had both been. And how foolish.

A lump of emotion caught in Mayla's throat. Hot tears threatened. *Pull yourself together*, she demanded. She never cried. Certainly not over a breakup that happened when she was hardly more than a kid.

Leaving the little black dress where it was, she took her gown down from the wall. Carefully, she put it back into its garment bag, zipped it closed, and hung it in the back of the armoire that served as her little closet. Whatever magic may have been present in the dress—or between Thiago and her—all those years ago, was long gone.

⚜

Thiago stood in the shower as the water pounded over him, rinsing away the last few hours of work. He had just finished riding the five horses of Sergio's that were new to him, testing their gears, seeing how they turned, noting what cues they preferred for leads, for speeding up, and for slowing down.

Sergio knew horses; no doubt about it. When he had asked Thiago to fill in on the team, he had known exactly how to play his cards. Though the prestige of playing for Argentina as part of Team South America held significant weight, he had to have known that access to Zoelie was the *pièce de resistance*: the winning argument that made Thiago agree to come.

Now, after a thorough workout, he knew beyond any doubt that the little bay mare was a spectacular ride. Light, fleet, nimble, willing—she was everything he had hoped she would be.

And yet, instead of glorying in working with this magnificent creature, he had been distracted the whole time he was in the saddle. It didn't matter what he did, how fast he rode, or how far he pushed himself or his horse; thoughts of Mayla fluttered in his head like flags in a hurricane.

For ten years, he had tried to speak to her, hoping she would listen to him, praying she would let him apologize. Every attempt had been in vain. Over the next three days, they would be on the same polo field, in the same city. Tomorrow, they would be adversaries. Tonight, however, their teams were the guests of honor at the Monde du Polo soirée. Tonight, they were on the same side.

Thiago turned off the hot tap and braced against the icy water blasting against his body. The temperature change was so quick it took his breath away. In the shock, all extraneous thoughts vanished.

Five minutes later, when he turned off the water and stepped out of the shower, he had a plan of action.

Perhaps it was fate. Perhaps providence. All he knew was that something mystical had aligned planets and stars to bring him here. Tonight, he had the rare opportunity to see Mayla again. He intended to make the most of it.

Rochelle swept out of the bathroom and twirled around the apartment. The black evening dress hugged her in all the right places, accentuating her curves and showing off arms toned from hours of grooming, sweeping, and shoveling. Her long, light hair was piled atop her head in a messy, trendy updo. A tiny orange crystal flame bedazzled the bottom corner of her black eyepatch. "How do I look?"

"You are a vision." Mayla put down her phone. "A little flirty; a little dirty. Philippe is lucky beyond belief."

Rochelle waggled a cautionary finger. "We'll see how lucky the boy is," she chirped.

Mayla laughed. "He got a free ticket to the hottest event in Europe tonight and he has a date with a dancing queen who is the best groom on four continents. Lucky already."

Rochelle indicated the phone. "Any news?"

"A bit. Some of it's even encouraging. The title is clear. No one else has been sniffing around. No showings to anyone since we were there."

"And no one had looked at it for months before we went," Rochelle said, reminding Mayla of what they both already knew in an effort to stay positive.

"Still no word on whether the owner will accept my offer, though," Mayla said. "He has until the end of next week. Guess I'll know one way or the other by then. I keep wishing I could just give him his asking price, do a wire transfer and make the place mine, but—"

"If you did that, you would be made of money. And you and I would never have met because this would be an alternate universe," Rochelle said. "Don't forget—the place is hardly a turnkey operation. The house and barns need a lot of work."

"Tell me something I don't know." Mayla grabbed a corner of the blanket, fell back on her bed, and rolled herself up like a burrito. "If I raise my offer, I'll have nothing left for all the repairs that need to be done."

Rochelle's phone dinged with a text alert. "That's Philippe," she said. "He's on his way to the magpie. I've gotta go."

"He's not picking you up?"

"It's out of his way to come get me, so we'll just meet there. I don't mind."

Mayla frowned. "Can I just go on record saying that it's a rookie move?"

"Noted."

Rochelle started rummaging around the cramped flat, moving pillows and books. "Where is my purse?" She tossed aside both clean clothes and dirty laundry. "Was Carson here lately? Maybe he stole it. You know how much he hates it."

Mayla unrolled herself and joined in the search. "Carson is a snob, but he's no thief," she said.

"Voilà!" Rochelle upended a polo helmet and shook out a shimmery, silver pouch—a clever little thing with a sterling gag bit top and a drawstring closure. "Philippe will love this. So chic. He has such good taste...I wonder if he also tastes good."

She giggled like a high school girl, a sound Mayla had never heard her make before.

As Rochelle critically inspected her makeup while chattering about Philippe's many good qualities, both real and imagined, Mayla padded into the corner of their apartment that held a sink, a hot plate, a mini-fridge, and an electric kettle. Calling it a "kitchenette" was an exercise in hyperbole. She raided their fridge, considering the Mason jar holding the remains of the wine she and Rochelle had uncorked on Monday to toast their first night in Paris, but settling for an opened bottle of almost-still-sparkling water instead. Tucking it under one arm, she tore off the end of a baguette and scored the last of some cabécou cheese.

As she nibbled, she made sure to say "mm-hm," and "you're kidding," and "I had no idea" in appropriate places.

"That's better!" Rochelle turned away from the mirror.

For the first time all evening, she took in Mayla's yoga pants, t-shirt, and fuzzy socks. Now it was her turn to frown. "Why aren't you ready?"

"I think I'll sit this one out."

"You have to go," Rochelle said. "It's expected."

"If I always did what was expected, I wouldn't be playing polo," Mayla said. "It's no big deal."

But it was. And she knew it.

"The patrons won't be pleased. They're there to meet you, you know."

"They're there to meet everyone. I'm a lowly four-goaler. There will be lots of better players there."

Rochelle sank into their only chair, concerned, at a loss. "Is it Bruno

Carrizo? Did he say something to keep you away?" Wide-eyed, she asked, "Did he threaten you?"

"Hardly," Mayla snorted. "He's just an ass."

"*Marie Jésus Joseph*!" Rochelle said. "You gave me your only ticket, didn't you? That's why you're staying home! I feel terrible. I'd have never accepted it if—"

"My name is on the guest list," Mayla said. "No ticket required. I just...don't feel like going."

"Hmmph." Rochelle wasn't falling for Mayla's line. "You love these patron parties. You're the one who named them: 'Meet and Greet Persons of Influence and Enterprise.' Something had to happen to make you stay home." She nibbled a fingernail. "Is it a man?"

Mayla thought she kept her expression neutral, but something must have betrayed her.

"It IS!" Rochelle gasped. "I can't believe it."

She kicked off her heels and started scurrying through the apartment, flash cleaning. "Who is he? Do I know him? Do you have a date? You never date. Is he coming here?"

"Stop!" Mayla laughed, moving to stand in the girl's way. "Go to the party. Drink lots of wine. Dance with your Philippe. I will be fine."

"You're also rhyming. You never do that either. Should I be worried?"

"Go on. Get out of here."

"You'll tell me all about it later," Rochelle said, throwing her shoes back on as she ran out the door.

"Promise," Mayla said.

Quiet descended on the apartment as soon as her flatmate left. Mayla reveled in it...for about five minutes.

She sat on the edge of her bed, chewing on baguette crumbs. Thoughts of the gown packed away in the armoire nagged at her. Her stomach rumbled, reminding her that great food was certain at the magpie.

"So it's come to this," she said aloud. "The Parisien's biggest event of the season, and you're hiding here because of the mean boy who hurt you years ago. Well, suck it up, Cupcake! Grow a pair and get out there."

She stood and dumped the fizz-free water into the bidet, still muttering to herself. "You'll see him. You'll be polite. You'll smile and make small talk like adults and then you'll move on."

Taking a deep breath as if diving into a bottomless pool, she opened the armoire, took the plunge, and retrieved her dress.

14

The Magpie

A grand piano played Debussy, filling the cavernous *Nef* of the Palais Brongniart with a lyrical waterfall of sound that underscored the quiet murmuring of conversation. In one of the many alcoves leading into the room, a wind ensemble discreetly tuned their instruments. Golden lights positioned at the base of the thirty marble columns marking the perimeter lent a rich, warm glow. Arching overhead two stories above, if any of the guests had deigned to look, two-hundred-year-old paintings in rich blues and gold framed the vaulted glass ceiling.

Wine flowed. Dressed all in black, demure servers circulated bearing platters. Crudités with vinaigrette and bagna cauda for dipping. Canapés of different geometrical shapes bearing a delectable assortment of caviar and patés. Assorted *amuse-bouches* too tedious to identify, but so satisfying to devour.

Thiago strode across the parquet floor of the massive Nave with the words of Mourad still echoing in his ears ("Enjoy yourself, Monsieur, as you party with your Important Someones. When you have had enough enjoyment, I shall be your awake and alert driver taking you safely home.") He accepted a glass of wine from a passing server as he considered the "important someones" filling the place.

Though many in attendance looked vaguely familiar, with faces one often saw peering from society news, overseeing foundations and funds, or swirling in the same social circles, none of them appeared particularly awake or alert, drifting about in a self-induced stupor of inflated ego and affected ennui.

As if to prove his point, he saw a tall blond man shake his head in contempt at a young woman who happily hurried toward him, stopping her in her tracks. Thiago was too far away to hear what the man said, but from the woman's stricken face and brittle smile, he knew.

He turned away from the sad little scene to see a dapper Frenchman about his father's age moving in his direction with a large, red-faced man in tow.

"Étienne!" Thiago shook hands and leaned forward, kissing the air for *la bise*, the cheek-to-cheek greeting.

"Thiago Calvo," Étienne Travert said. "You've had quite a year, son! Quite incomparable!" He turned to include his florid friend in the conversation. "May I present Monsieur Vernon de la Foret. I insisted he come with me tonight to meet you. He suffers, you see, from too much money and too little polo."

Monsieur de la Foret laughed. "I don't understand the damned game. To me it's just people on horses whacking a ball."

"I fear he is a hopeless case," Étienne said. "This is why I bring him to you."

"I would be honored to explain the game to you, Monsieur," Thiago said. "But you would still be an outsider. Do you ride?"

"I hunt a bit."

Étienne stared, dumbfounded.

A mental image of the overweight Mr. de la Foret jumping any sort of obstacle on a horse in pursuit of hounds presented itself to Thiago. He forced himself not to laugh.

"That should serve you well, then. Come to le Parisien tomorrow. We have an exhibition game in the afternoon—I am sure Étienne will be there. Come early, if you like, and I will show you what you are missing."

A stick-thin woman with a model's pout appeared at Thiago's side. "You're a player, aren't you?" Her sultry undertone promised that she played games too. Another woman cut from the same mold joined them, running a manicured finger around the rim of her wineglass.

"Yes," Monsieur de la Foret said, speaking to Thiago, though unable to take his eyes from the newcomers. "Perhaps it is time I learned more about this game. Tomorrow, then."

The saxophonist began to play. A lively pop tune masquerading as classical music filled the Nave. Hips swayed. Shoulders shimmied.

Thiago endured grasping hands while making polite, noncommittal conversation with the people who crowded around him. Knowing they cared no more about polo than he did about them, he searched the enormous hall, looking for Mayla. He saw only a sea of smiling teeth and blinking eyes.

The gold and marble room full of exquisite food and expensive tastes dimmed a little; the party became somehow tarnished, incomplete, when he realized she wasn't there.

❧

As Mayla entered the *Nef* via *l'Espace Réaumur*, she noticed Thiago immediately. A throng of people, mostly women, gathered around him, practically hiding him from view but making him impossible to miss. Young women giggled. Older women vamped. Very old women simpered. Nothing about him had changed—and really, why would it? He was definitely "to the manor born."

Looking away from Thiago's melee, she spied Carson headed in her direction holding two glasses full of champagne.

"Didn't go shopping after all?" she asked when they met.

Carson mimed clutching at pearls. "Have you no eyes? Do you not see?"

"It's a nice tie," Mayla said. "But it doesn't look a whole lot different—"

"Stop right there," Carson told her. "Don't say it."

"—than the one you got in London."

Carson heaved a theatrical sigh. "It breaks my heart that you can't tell Hermès from Savile Row."

A lively swing number began. Mayla saw Philippe dancing with two girls—one a vaguely recognizable minor celebrity. She searched for Rochelle and finally found her, standing alone. Placing her hand in the crook of Carson's arm, she steered them both toward Rochelle's dim alcove.

"He-he-he doesn't care for me at all," Rochelle said, breathing in sobs. "All he wanted was to get in the door and come to the party so he could meet women with money. Or, in his words, 'people who count.'"

Carson flexed a fist. "I'd like to teach him how to count. To five."

Mayla wanted to laugh at the lame joke, but Rochelle's heartbreak sobered her. Poor kid.

"He's a snake," she said. "You're too good for him. He doesn't deserve you." Though true, her words were too banal to help.

She wanted to say, "You'll meet someone. Someone who sees how amazing you are. Someone who treats you like a queen. Who respects you. Who has your back no matter what." But who was she to talk? She'd never been that good of a liar. And she knew as well as anyone that such men did not exist.

A handsome server approached, bearing a tray of sinfully delicious food.

"I'm not hungry," Rochelle mumbled, wandering away. She chose a dark corner where she could watch Philippe while cocooned in her sadness.

Carson selected a handful of flaky *vol-au-vents* piled high with rich fillings, "Don't look now," he murmured through pastry, "but you've caught someone's eye."

Thiago? Mayla's stomach pretzeled. "Who?"

"The divine Madame Delacroix, *mécène magnifique.*"

An old woman, bedecked in emeralds, made her way in their direction. She must have been radiantly beautiful half a century ago; her posture would have put a ballerina to shame, and her smile still stunned.

Mayla was grateful for Carson's whispered heads-up, for Madame Delacroix evidently felt she needed no introduction.

"Such a lovely gown," she said in a voice like whiskey mixed with honey. With a hand so pale it appeared light blue, she caressed the fabric, tender as a lover. "From another time. Another time...A private collection, I believe." She stared at Mayla with sharp, bright eyes. "Would you like to sell it, my dear?"

Something moved to Mayla's right, subtle as sunlight. Distracted, she glanced toward it—

Directly into Thiago's eyes.

It was as if no time, no distance, separated them. He held her gaze from across the room, more intimate than a touch.

Heat scorched Mayla's cheeks. She became acutely aware of her heartbeat pulsing in her ears.

With an effort, she closed her eyes, tearing herself away from the connection, reinstating Madame Delacroix as the center of her attention.

The old woman's expression softened. "Ah. No. For you it holds meaning more than money."

"A gift from an old friend," Mayla said. "He died."

It was the lie she always told when asked about her dress. It was a good lie. People heard it and murmured vague condolences.

No one ever questioned it. Until now.

Madame Delacroix's glance flicked toward Thiago and back so quickly Mayla wondered if she had imagined it.

The patron sipped her wine, deliberate as a surgeon. "I see," she nodded. "Such a tragedy, when someone is lost forever."

She patted Mayla's arm, smoothed the skirt of the dress one last time, and drifted away into the crowd.

"What just happened?" Carson said.

"I have no idea," Mayla said, draining her champagne, trying to regain the composure that had abandoned her.

✺

He saw her the moment she entered the room.

At the sight of Mayla wearing the first—and last—gift he had ever given her, Thiago breathed in, quickly, involuntarily, as if he had dived from an Arctic cliff and was rushing headlong toward the sea. The party, so dim half a second earlier, experienced an instant infusion of light. Jewels glittered more brightly. Music moved more passionately. The crowd around him blurred into insignificance. Though Mayla stayed in the shadows, to him she shone as if in a spotlight. Even if he wanted to, he couldn't have taken his eyes from her. And he didn't want to.

His lungs began to complain, begging him to exhale. She did that to him. She'd always done that to him: made him forget to do critically important things, like breathing.

She was a vision. A visitor from his past. For years, dreams of her had haunted him. But the reality blew the fantasy to dust.

She exuded more confidence than the last time he had seen her. He watched as she took Carson's arm and walked across the Nave, moving with an athlete's economy of motion, assured and graceful.

He thought he had grown used to living without her. Now he recognized how wrong he had been. Ever since she left, his heart had flat-lined; nothing had moved him. That wasn't living. Seeing Mayla again revived him like nothing else he had ever encountered. Every cell in his body felt restored and renewed.

Every cell also felt something else…

Inspected.

Thiago blinked, unable to shake the feeling of being pinned to a board on the wrong side of a magnifying glass. Unsettled, he looked away from Mayla to discover old Madame Delacroix standing near his elbow, gazing at him with the intensity of a lioness hunting a gazelle.

She followed his original line of sight and spied Mayla. "Lovely girl. Exquisite gown," she said. "Scandalously short hair, though."

There was nothing remotely wrong with Mayla's hair. Thiago almost opened his mouth to say so, when he saw the knowing twinkle in the lioness's eyes.

"I knew her," he said instead. "In another time."

Madame Delacroix patted his arm. "Perhaps the time has come to know her now."

She moved away faster than he had thought she could. As soon as she left his side, the space she vacated was immediately taken over by people crushing around him.

She made a beeline to Mayla. Thiago saw her touch the dress… touch the woman.

He couldn't help but think of how she once was *his* woman. His in the same sense that his arm and leg and head were his. He didn't own them; they made him who he was. Losing any part of himself would be a hardship. Would handicap him. But it wouldn't compare to the pain of losing Mayla.

As he watched, Mayla looked his way—

Time stopped.

Energy surged through his body, quickening his pulse, intense as a lightning strike. Thiago heard the roar of the surf. He felt the southern country sun warm his face. He felt carefully crafted layers of his character stripped bare as she saw into his soul.

He wanted to explore her forever, starting now. But long before he was ready, she closed her eyes and looked away. He tried, but he couldn't do the same.

Without thinking about it, he took a step forward. The people pressing in on him twittered in surprise. Another few steps and the tightly packed bodies relaxed enough to let him escape. He walked toward Mayla, hoping to stop time again.

15

Dancing Queen

MAYLA'S HEAD SPUN in reining-horse circles. She tried to blame the champagne, but she knew she hadn't had enough to cause her thoughts to tumble like this.

"Thiago Calvo, incoming." Carson finished off the last of his pastry. He looked at Mayla quizzically. "Time for Carson LeVallier to be outgoing... "

Mayla stood rooted in place, her heart hammering as it always did whenever she saw Thiago coming in her direction.

Stand your ground, she told herself. *Be a rod of iron.*

But iron rods draw lightning. As Thiago closed the gap between them, Mayla could almost taste the electricity in the air.

"Mayla."

How long had it been since she heard him say her name? No other man had ever said it like that, breathing it as if he were naming a star.

"Hello, Thiago."

She spoke with confident detachment, amazed at the strength and steadiness of her voice. Inwardly, her head was still spinning, a portion of her mind shouting like a kid on a rollercoaster.

Oh.

My.

God.

He looks even better than I remember. And I remember a hell of a lot. Plus, he smells amazing. Cloves and anise and wood smoke and hay. Good enough to eat. And I am soooo hungry...

She set her empty wine glass on a passing platter, relieved and a little surprised to note that her hands weren't obviously shaking.

What now? She couldn't make small talk with him. The whole charade of "How are you?" "Fine." "How's your father?" "Fine." would drive her mad within moments. If he mentioned the weather, or said something about how she looked in the dress, she felt certain she would scream.

"Would you like to dance?"

She looked into his fierce, dark eyes and saw a hunger there that mirrored her own. She blinked, wondering if her thoughts were as readily read.

Yes! YesYesYesYes! She would love nothing more than to have him put his hands on her, pull her close, and move with her.

"I would love to," she said, keeping her voice low because there was no other way she could control it. "But first, I have a request."

⚜

Thiago wanted to make sure he had heard correctly. "You won't dance with me until I've danced with someone else?"

"That's right."

Mayla flashed a smile he knew well: her combat grin. She wore it like armor before every game, gearing up for battle. Though it had been years since he had seen it, he recognized it immediately.

With some surprise, he noted that it was not directed at him. She was inviting him to be a conspirator, rather than declaring him a foe. He nodded: a knight accepting his quest.

"Make it good," she said. A challenge, rather than a command.

Thiago felt Mayla's eyes on him as he walked away from her. She was so self-possessed. So measured. So controlled. Of course, those were a few of the things he had always loved about her. His stride lengthened as optimism surged through him. She hadn't changed.

The girl to whom Mayla had directed him hid in the shadow of an archway. As he came up beside her, she tried to make herself smaller, take up less space. He recognized her as the key player in the drama he had witnessed earlier; the girl whose heart he had seen kicked to the ground.

"Rochelle?"

She jumped, startled as a doe.

"I'm Thiago Calvo." He bowed as if the place belonged to him. "May I have the honor of a dance?"

Though her shyness remained, her hesitation vanished. She placed her small hand, calloused from hard work, in his. So she was a horse person too, Thiago thought. He noted the patch over her eye. Not a polo player, though. At least...not anymore.

He led her to the dance floor as if she were royalty. The distinctive notes of a tango began. For a moment, Thiago worried that Mayla's plan—whatever it was—would backfire. The tango was a difficult dance. He loved it, but if his partner wasn't both confident and competent, it could be disastrous.

Rochelle squeezed his hand lightly. She stood a little straighter, a slight smile playing on her face.

Thiago banished his worries. Whatever Mayla had planned, it wasn't to humiliate this poor girl.

He placed his right hand across the small of her back, pulled her close to him, and began to move.

In less than two beats, he knew he was dancing with a master. Rochelle understood every cue he gave her. She balanced on air, it seemed, twisting back and forth with meticulous grace as they wove a complicated pattern across the floor.

They locked eyes, selling the sensuality of the dance. He could read her well. The sadness and vulnerability of a few moments ago had vanished. In their place reigned confidence, gratitude, resilience.

The dance progressed, their moves growing bolder, more fluid. When people applauded after one sequence, Thiago realized they were causing quite a sensation. He had no idea why Mayla made this request, but he knew she was watching.

Everyone was watching.

A barrage of flashes strobed over them as photographers snapped pictures. As they spun around, Rochelle ethereally light in his hands, Thiago noted a mild disturbance in their audience. The arrogant French boy he saw earlier pushed rudely past Étienne and Monsieur de la Foret, leaving in a huff.

After another spin, Mayla caught his eye. Nodding in the direction the spoiled brat had taken, she smiled. *Dios mío,* how he loved her smile. How he had missed it. It warmed him as completely as a June afternoon.

Funny, he mused as the song finale began, thinking about Mayla being happy made him happy.

Distracted by thoughts of Mayla *here, tonight,* he tightened his grip. Rochelle kept smiling, but her eye flashed with pain. Murmuring an apology, Thiago relaxed and readjusted his hand.

As their dance ended, applause filled the hall.

"*Merci, Monsieur,*" Rochelle said as she hugged him. "My evening was a misery. You have saved it. I am in your debt."

"Not so, *princesa.* Thanks to you, I have danced with an angel," he said.

They kissed politely and went their separate ways. Rochelle hurried out of the hall and into the night. Thiago shrugged out of his tuxedo coat as he spoke briefly to the musicians. Then he headed for Mayla.

⚜

After asking the musicians to play a tango, Mayla stationed herself in the arcade between the Nave and *l'Espace Réaumur*. She leaned against a cool marble pillar, observing the little intrigue she had un-leashed on the glitterati.

How many events such as this had she attended at the Calvo estate? There, she had served as one of the staff, working all evening in stiff, unyielding shoes, saying *"si, señor"* and *"con permiso."* She remembered commiserating with Thiago afterward, each trying to convince the other that they had endured the greater burden during the course of the event.

Once, when Thiago complained, "I must smile and nod and pre-tend to be interested in the very vacuous talk that streams from the mouths of so many of my father's friends," she had responded without thinking, "I must smile and nod and pretend not to be offended at the very scandalous propositions from the hands of so many of your father's friends."

The prospect of people he knew propositioning her, touching her, had filled him with a righteous anger so protective, it had brought tears to her eyes. Good Lord, how she had loved him.

"Stop it," Mayla hiss-whispered to herself as she watched the tango progress. "You are no longer a giddy, practically homeless kid working for his dad. You have grown up. Start acting like it."

Orchestrating this little drama, she had to admit rather guiltily, wasn't the most grown-up thing she had ever done. Still...

"Good riddance to bad news," she murmured when Philippe stormed out.

She would act like a grown-up tomorrow.

Rochelle was positively radiant by the time the dance ended. About time that girl had something good happen to her.

Thiago graciously directed all applause toward Rochelle. Though people tried to hem him in as they complemented him, he moved forward with purpose, his eyes fixed on Mayla. He traversed the space between the two of them in an instant, not stopping until he stood so near she could feel the heat radiating from his body. He offered his hand.

"Have I fulfilled my quest, Milady?"

"Admirably. You made an ungrateful ass very jealous. Thank you."

She took his hand. As soon as they touched, her pulse raced as if she had sprinted a mile. Her heart hadn't behaved this way in years. Sometimes, she had questioned if it was still capable of such nonsense. She wondered if Thiago knew how he affected her, then silently berated herself for caring.

There was a time when she would have melted into him, allowing him to enfold her like a human comforter, wrapping herself in him. Well, she wasn't a lovestruck kid anymore. But neither was he.

The musicians played a haunting opening chord that lingered... strengthened...and launched into a spirited salsa. Mayla's heart constricted as if squeezed in God's own hand. *Mi Lupita.*

She looked at Thiago and found herself stranded in his eyes.

She knew what he was doing, playing their song, reminding her of what used to be, when nothing stood between them and the future was bright with promise.

Nothing could change their past. Nothing could undo his betrayal. But tonight she wanted nothing more than to forget about it for a little while.

He did not lead her to the dance floor. Rather, they stayed on the rose and gray tile of the more intimate area *l'Espace Réaumur* offered.

As Thiago took her in his arms, Mayla released a breath she hadn't known she had been holding. His hands, steady and strong, guided her with assurance. Together, they spun and swayed, circling each other, coming together, then moving apart, partners in a provocative pattern.

Her senses sharpened. Every nerve sang when he touched her. She studied him, looking for flaws, trying to find something to dislike.

She looked in vain.

He was the same Thiago she had always known, but with notable differences. He was calmer. More contained than when they last met. Then, he was a gangly colt: unproven, full of himself, high strung. But now, he had matured with more charm, more charisma…more gravity.

It would be so easy, Mayla conceded with some alarm, to let him pull her out of her world and back into his.

No.

Remember what happened last time.

She remembered.

She could not allow history to repeat itself.

There was a reason she had refused his repeated attempts to get in touch with her. She had always feared she would put her dreams on hold for him if they met again, and she knew doing so would make her come to resent him.

They could dance tonight. Spend some time catching up, perhaps. But their time was in the past. They had no future together.

16

Ain't Misbehavin'

THIAGO DRANK MAYLA IN WITH HIS EYES, memorizing every motion, saturating himself with the vision of her. The way she lifted her chin. The way her neck moved and her eyes gleamed. How her hips swayed. How her body beckoned. How she held her slim shoulders, lifting her hands toward him, inviting him to touch her.

He never felt stronger than when she was in his arms. The fabric of her gown, light as a summer breeze, caressed his fingers as he crushed her to him.

She smelled like rain and jasmine. Her voice, low and full of laughter held in reserve, made his soul sing in harmony.

Thoughts of her had warmed his heart since he was eighteen. He had been a boy then, following in his father's footsteps. But the thoughts that had brought him happiness all these years were thin shadows when compared to the real thing.

He lightly balanced Mayla's hand in his, spinning her in dizzying circles, soaking up her smile. Once, he had held her heart in his hands and in an unguarded moment he had let it slip through his fingers.

Thiago breathed in. As he filled himself with the air that danced around her, he vowed he would not lose her again.

⚜

Mayla could not feel the ground beneath her feet. She almost looked down to see if she was flying. She didn't; choosing instead to enjoy the illusion as long as it lasted.

All too soon, however, the song ended.

Reality returned.

She felt the wide plane of Thiago's back, the muscles tight and solid, sliding smoothly under his shirt. She considered the short stubble on his chin; it took every shred of restraint she possessed not to run her thumb along his jaw, pull him close to her, and kiss him like she used to. At the base of his throat, his pulse beat steadily.

If only hers would behave so well.

"There you are!" A heavy-set man wiped his flushed face with one hand while he clapped Thiago on the back with the other.

Startled, the moment they had shared fled.

"*Oui,* Monsieur de la Foret?" Thiago said, polite to a fault.

"I have decided to take you up on your offer to teach me this confounded game," the man boomed. He wobbled his head from side to side, inordinately pleased with himself.

Thiago put his arm around Mayla's waist as naturally as if she were part of him. "Excellent. Shall we say noon tomorrow?"

He drew her closer. She melted toward him, reminded, again, of gravity.

"Mademoiselle Alvarez here plays for Team North America. I'm sure she would be happy to join us and show you—"

De la Foret looked through Mayla as if she were no more substantial than a spiderweb. "Oh ho," he leered, wobbling his head again. "No need to bring in the ladies' league to a man's game."

At Mayla's side, Thiago tensed. His hand tightened on her hip. She sensed him brace to deliver a rebuke.

Though there had once been a time when she would have given anything to hear him rally to her cause, she quietly placed her hand on his. No need to make a scene. Wealthy sponsors were critical to a club's existence. She knew that. So did he. The whole reason for to-night's soirée was to introduce the sport to more people who could afford to become patrons. Even if they were cretins.

"I understand," Thiago said, taking her cue. "Would you prefer if I asked my groom, Valentin, to assist instead?"

Mayla's heart stopped. She nearly choked in surprise.

"Valentin?" she squeaked, her thoughts a jumbled scrum.

"Yes," Thiago said without looking at her. "That would probably be best. Noon tomorrow, then?"

As the two men solidified their plans for the private lesson, Mayla excused herself. She went to the ladies' room to freshen up and make some attempt at self-control.

Thiago had not brought a personal groom with him. She knew that as well as he did. She understood what he wanted her to do. What she didn't understand was *why*.

Was he mocking her? She had always known he was a prankster, but had never known him to be deliberately cruel. Many things could change about a person in the course of a decade, but surely the funda-mental character remained the same.

Was this an attempt on his part to acknowledge the role he had played in their breakup? Was he trying to make amends? The possi-bility concerned her, but not nearly as much as the realization of how much she appreciated his gesture.

What was wrong with her? Less than twelve hours ago, she had been fit, fine, and focused on her game. Whole days could go by without her brooding over him. Any thoughts of Thiago that happened to hijack her mind had been filed under "Love Stinks" and "Disappointment." Since seeing him this afternoon, however, memories of the bond they once shared tantalized her while simultaneously reminding her of why they were no longer together.

Mayla squinted at the stranger who peered at her from the mirror. She methodically catalogued everything Thiago had ever done wrong. The list was short but significant. It included only three items: not standing up to his father, dismissing her dreams, and betraying her trust. An impressive trifecta.

Remember, you trusted him once, built what you thought was a relationship carved in stone, to discover it was nothing more than a sandcastle.

But she needed no reminding.

She was a grown-up; so was he. They could dance together, ride together, spend some time together. She would even play along with this little game of his. He had trusted her when she asked him to dance with Rochelle. She would return the favor. It might be fun. Perhaps doing it would give her a sense of closure.

"We are *not* getting back together," she ground out between clenched teeth. No matter how charming, how gallant, how supportive he was now, he had shown his true colors years ago.

Mayla left the ladies' room and went outside, avoiding the gala. Avoiding Thiago. He held her in his arms moments ago, yet she yearned for more. That was why she had to leave. Tempting though it was to go back to the party, she headed for home. She needed to gather her thoughts, get hold of her emotions before she met him on the field tomorrow.

She escaped through the massive columns illuminated for the evening with teal and orange lights: Polo Parisien's club colors. Taking off her shoes, she tripped lightly down steps still warm from the summer sun.

She could do this, she told herself with forced conviction. She could have some fun without planning a future. Thiago had broken her heart once, but she had collected the shards and patched them up as best she could. All she had to do for the next few days was guard the shards, keep them safe, and not fall in love again.

17

The Chapel

THE MOON LIT THE WAY as Mayla slipped into her apartment, padding quietly on bare feet.

"You don't have to tiptoe. I'm awake," Rochelle said from her pocket-sized bedroom.

Mayla gave up trying to be quiet. "I'm sorry it didn't work out with your Philippe."

"He wasn't *my* Philippe. I think he is only his *own* Philippe."

Mayla removed her makeup and changed into an oversized t-shirt. "You danced like a dream, you know."

"*Merci.*" Excusable pride floated on Rochelle's voice. "It was fun. Monsieur Calvo, he dances well. But you know this, yes?"

"We danced too," Mayla admitted.

Rochelle came into the kitchenette, rubbing sleep from her eye. "And yet you came home?"

"We have a game tomorrow. I've got to get some sleep."

"Mm-hm." Unconvinced, Rochelle took a carrot from the wee refrigerator.

"However, I think we have a date."

This grabbed the girl's attention. "Yes? You and Calvo?"

Mayla hedged. "Well, sort of a working date. And I have to wear a mustache."

Rochelle groaned. "Ugh. I will never understand you Americans' sense of humor."

Crunching on her snack, she padded back into her room.

Mayla lay down on her narrow bed. She doubted she would be able to sleep, but she was wrong, for she was soon dancing in her dreams.

⚜

Jet lag, Thiago mused, is the true bane of the twenty-first century.

He hadn't slept in nearly forty-eight hours. Exhausted, he lay down on the enormous bed in his cottage, his mind spinning faster than the ceiling fan above him, hurling questions at him, refusing to let him rest.

Why did he bring up Valentin? Did Mayla think he was taunting her? She had run off as soon as he mentioned the name, leaving him stuck with the extremely self-important de la Foret.

Listening to the man talk about tariffs and shipping practices was even less interesting than hearing his father discuss real estate development. Furthermore, as the night wore on, his sleep-deprived brain played tricks on him; he kept thinking he saw Tough Guy from the plane lurking in the midst of the partygoers, which cast an uncomfortable pall over the event. As soon as he could politely do so, Thiago had extricated himself from the narcissistic billionaire's clutches. He left the soirée shortly afterward.

To cap things off, even the ride back to le Parisien had been oddly unsettled. Mourad—though both awake and alert, as promised—was so subdued, so preoccupied, that he said little. His driving was faultless, but Thiago missed his earlier verve. Midnight had come and gone, replacing the magic and mystery of the evening with the cares of a new day.

Thiago inhaled deeply. He held the air in his lungs until silver sparks flared like tiny fireworks behind his closed eyelids. Then he blew his lungs empty, refilled them, and repeated the process. This usually helped him relax, paving the way to sleep. Tonight, however, drifting off was as difficult as holding onto a lungful of air.

It was so quiet, he could hear the rhythmic *tick-tick-tick* of the ceiling fan gently gyrating on its swivel base. Nothing else moved. Vague rustling outside the open windows made soothing sounds that should have lulled him to dreamland.

Two hours passed. He was still as awake as ever.

Moonlight streamed in the window, casting otherworldly shadows on the walls. Tomorrow, the moon would be full. Even tonight, it was bright as a searchlight. Try as he might, however, he couldn't blame it for his sleeplessness.

Resigned, Thiago rolled out of bed. Pointless to stay there.

He dressed and strolled to the barn, moving through pockets of air that were alternately warm, then cool, then warm again, separate and distinct as if belonging to different worlds, each with its own atmosphere.

Once at the shed row that housed Sergio's horses, he approached Milagro's stall. The gray stallion had come to the Calvo estate when Mayla worked there as his father's groom. Though Thiago hadn't seen the horse since he was sold as a four-year-old, he had followed his distinguished career with pride.

Milagro was awake, trying unsuccessfully to attract the attention of the mare stabled next to him. He turned his head and whickered a friendly greeting as Thiago drew near.

"I know how you feel," Thiago commiserated.

He bridled Milagro in the stall, led him outside, and vaulted onto his bare back.

The horse's body bunched up beneath him, offering to take flight if given the correct cue. Thiago encouraged him to relax and walk in a long, low frame instead.

Rather than turning toward the polo field, they made their way to the bridle paths that spiderwebbed the woods around the club. Choosing a path at random, Thiago asked the horse for an easy trot.

As the trees closed in around them, it occurred to Thiago that Mayla was the first rider Milagro ever carried. Her hands were the first to guide the bit in his mouth. Her quiet touch was the first he'd ever felt on the reins. Mayla was the one who taught him to start, to turn, to stop. There, on the path to the unknown, thinking more of his past than his future, Thiago put the stallion through his paces.

How far they rode, he didn't know, but the moon had moved across much of the sky and dawn tinted the horizon before the lights from the polo grounds were visible far ahead through the trees. It was nearly time to get up, and he had not yet slept. Thiago didn't mind. No longer tired, he rode easily, his muscles limber, his spirit at peace.

⚜

Mayla awoke at six, cursing herself for sleeping in. She jumped out of bed and scrambled to get dressed, but relaxed when she saw Rochelle's neat note propped against her coffee cup: *Everybody's walked and fed. Good luck today!*

A good groom was worth her weight in gold. Rochelle was both peerless and priceless.

As she paced the tiny flat, Mayla replayed the events of last night, examining the nuances of each word and action under the spotlight of hindsight. By seven, she was still jittery, on edge. Hardly ideal for her game against Thiago and Team South America later today.

The horses may have had their morning exercise, but she hadn't. Though thoughts of Thiago refused to be banished, Mayla pushed them off to the side. They went unwillingly into the shadows where they prowled the perimeter of her brain, looking for weaknesses in her defenses so they could return and take center stage.

Mayla focused on deep breathing as she moved through several yoga poses that required her concentration. Warrior Two...Warrior Three... Half Moon...Camel Pose. The edginess began to fade, but she knew better than to try for the King Pigeon, which required her undivided attention. She could achieve it only on the best of days. The clamor of her thoughts underscored that today was not one of those days.

After yoga, Mayla threw on running shoes, grabbed a bottle of water, and trotted out the door. Her destination was less than ten kilometers away. Six miles. Perfect for a morning jog.

A paved footpath meandered through the *parc du bois*. Within a few kilometers, she emerged out of the cool greenness of the woods, on the western border of Paris.

She followed Rue de Longchamp, plunging into a maze of grand old Lutetian limestone buildings. Bright, jaunty awnings and narrow balconies fenced with ornate black iron jutted overhead. Tables and chairs crowded the sidewalk outside cafés, inviting patrons to sit a while. Incongruously large wooden doors, some intricately carved, others painted purple, or red, or blue, occasionally punctuated the sand-colored walls. The doors never opened. Mayla always wondered where they led.

Ten years ago, she had planned to explore Paris with Thiago. Neither had been there before. All the places they had never seen, she had hoped to experience together. For weeks, she had pored over guidebooks and websites with him, planning the Perfect Parisian Tour. She had thought they shared the same goals. Back then, she believed perfection was possible. She knew better now.

She knew the city, now, too. Every time she visited, she spent hours—days—walking the streets and alleys of the various *arrondissements municipaux*. Every time, she discovered something new. Every time, she told herself she didn't need Thiago's company to enjoy the city. Every time, she knew she lied.

At Place d'Iéna, she saluted the giant green statue of George Washington riding a horse that graced the center of the traffic circle. Though it was easy to find fault with Washington's equitation— the rider's legs were too straight and he appeared to be bracing himself against his steed; the horse's mouth gaped open from the leverage of a harsh bit— Mayla loved the texture and nuance of Edward Clark's bronze craftsmanship. Washington's clothing, from breeches and boots to waistcoat and epaulettes, was so realistic, she could almost see the fabric move.

The text on the statue was her favorite on any monument in Paris: "gift of the women of the United States of America in memory of the brotherly help given by France to their fathers in the fight for Independence."

Picking up her pace, she was soon jogging along the right bank of the Seine, with the river on her right and the unending wonder of the Louvre to her left. She crossed over to Île de la Cité at Pont au Change, wishing, as she always did, that she could go back in time and see the grand bridge in the seventeenth century, when it was the widest one in the city, featuring two rows of multi-level houses.

Once on the island, Mayla stopped at a café. Her ultimate destination wasn't yet open. No need to rush. Nibbling on breakfast, she watched the parade of people passing by. She took her time, savoring the fresh herbs in her omelet, breaking off tiny pieces of the best bread on the planet, and doling out hummingbird-sized sips of black espresso.

Shortly after nine o'clock, she made her way to the Conciergerie, the medieval palace turned prison, and from there, to Sainte-Chapelle. She purchased her entry ticket and hurried inside, entirely avoiding the lower level, with its tacky tables of souvenirs skirting the walls of the area originally allotted for Louis IX's palace staff to attend services.

Slipping through a modest doorway, she made her way up a spiral of ancient stairs, emerging into the jewel of the upper level. There she stood, awestruck.

Fifteen enormous stained glass windows surrounded her on three sides, each one fifty feet high. A giant rose window depicting apocalyptic scenes filled the western wall. The morning sun shone in, setting the thirteenth-century chapel ablaze with a kaleidoscope of rainbows. Swaths of color—rich red, blue, green, and gold—sparkled on the floor, the walls, and the visitors. Though she had been unable to get away yesterday, Mayla had visited the day before, after discovering the loss of the foot mallet. When in Paris, she took every opportunity to come here. It never grew old.

She stood motionless, soaking up the lush hues as if her soul were a sponge. Her heart longed to share this experience with Thiago, but her head questioned the wisdom of doing so. This was her sacred space. It was the one place, other than astride a horse, where she truly felt at home. She didn't want to bring Thiago here if he was toying with her; that would taint the site, profane it, and she didn't want to risk losing the peace of this haven.

Mayla walked the perimeter of the chapel, keeping to herself as the tourists came and pointed and babbled in a hundred different languages and went away again, hurrying to "do" Paris in a day or two. They would go home and look at their selfies with the enormous rose window in the background, perhaps even including the vaulted ceiling with its gilded stars speckling a midnight sky. "Where was this?" they would say. "Noter Dame? Or that Saint Eustace one?" And they would puzzle over the question for half a second, then shrug and post the picture on social media. "Yay, Paris!"

Mayla ignored them. Their chatter that bounced and echoed in the space bounded by stone and glass was so much easier to quiet than the thoughts of Thiago lurking in her mind.

She remembered how he held her last night, confident, assured, and real. She had spent years building a wall around the soft, vulnerable part of herself that she had once allowed to trust him. Sainte-Chapelle took seven years to build in the thirteenth century. The wall around her heart had taken a decade. She had thought her defenses strong. But one evening—one dance—had reduced her wall to rubble.

She could no longer feel Thiago's hands on her as she had when they danced together. But that didn't stop her from fantasizing about his touch.

After nearly half an hour of soaking in the light of medieval stained glass, Mayla left to head back to her flat.

Squinting as she emerged into light unfiltered by colored windows, she ran her fingers through the hair at the nape of her neck. She broke into a jog. Though she'd had a haircut in London a few weeks ago, a trim was warranted. Best to get a move on. After all, she had her polo students to teach. And it would soon be time for Valentin to meet Monsieur de la Foret.

18

Valentin

MILAGRO FOLLOWED THIAGO AROUND like a puppy, nosing pockets for the peppermints he knew were there.

"Sorry, son, but you're in the way." Thiago blocked the horse with his shoulders as he picked the stall clean.

A door to the shed row opened. The horse pricked up his ears, distracted for the time being.

Bruno came down the hallway carrying a bucket full of grooming supplies and a bag of rolled polo wraps.

Milagro snorted in disgust and resumed his search for treats.

"The great Calvo," Bruno said, his words dripping with disdain. "I saw you last night: the dancing fox poking around the American's hen house."

Thiago saw no need to dignify the comment with a response. But Bruno took his silence for an invitation to stay and chat.

"They mock us, putting a woman on their team." Bruno raised his lips in what he must have thought was a conspiratorial smile, though it reminded Thiago of a rabid baboon.

"Maybe. I've seen her play. She's good."

Bruno snorted. "Women are good for many things. Making babies. Warming your bed, if you don't mind having your damn ear talked off. Polo isn't one of them."

"Bruno Carrizo, some might call your views primeval."

Bruno preened as if complimented. "It's a fact: different people were put on the planet for different purposes. Women are soft. Pliable. That is their purpose. Not racing around on the playing field. Makes the men look bad."

"Mayla Alvarez has the same handicap as you do."

"In America maybe." Bruno hocked and spit a glob onto the floor. "Women have everything handed to them."

Milagro stretched out his head for a friendly sniff. He drew back in alarm when Bruno smacked his muzzle away.

Thiago felt his hackles rise. "I take it you don't think much of the American players. I thought you played over there."

"Years ago. But I play to win. And the Americans, they have too many rules. We parted ways." More spit splattered in the aisleway. "If you're half as good as Sergio claims, I'm glad to have you on the team. We'll destroy them. You'll see."

⚜

Mayla sat astride Widdershins, a fast little mare who loved the repetition of drills as much as she loved actual play. She held an assortment of mallets in her hand, doling one out to each student.

"Every player has her own stick preference. Some like them whippy. Some like them stiff. Personally, I like mine half and half, more flexible near the head, but firmest near the handle."

She crossed her arms. "Anyone feel compelled to make risqué remarks, now's the time. I'll wait…"

"Aww," said Doreen. "That sucks all the fun out of it."

Mayla smiled. *Mission accomplished.*

"These are for training purposes. They may or may not fit you correctly, which is fine for our use today. However, when you go to get your own stick, there are a few things you should know.

"First, grasp the handle." Mayla demonstrated, hefting a mallet high.

"How will we know it's the right size?" Proue asked.

"Most players prefer a medium or large," Mayla said. "If the handle is too small, it will spin in your hand when you hit the ball."

"Do they come in extra small?" said Yvonne.

"I'm sure they do. Make sure you insist on a good fit when you get your own," Mayla told her.

"Next, check out the length. Since these are all my personal mallets, they are between fifty-one and fifty-three inches long—or a hundred twenty-nine and a hundred thirty-five centimeters. The one I use depends on which horse I ride.

"To determine the ideal length, sit on your horse and swing as if you are hitting the ball, but stop with your hand pointing toward the ground. The mallet should just reach."

Several of the horses skittered sideways as the women practiced swinging. Proue's Andalusian rolled his eye at the stick by his side.

"I don't know if this is such a good idea," Doreen said as her mare raised her head and considered bolting for Spain. "She's played before, but not with me. Maybe I'm not cut out for this."

"That's OK," Mayla told her riders. "This is why we train. Today is all about the horses—helping to make them comfortable with these new things we're asking of them."

She swung her mallet beside her like a pendulum. "Our first exercise involves doing an impression of a metronome."

As the session progressed, the horses gradually learned to accept the swinging sticks. At the end of an hour, Doreen's mare held her ears at half-mast, nearly asleep, while her rider whirled a mallet over her head like a helicopter.

Mayla checked her watch. Almost time for Valentin to make an appearance.

"Keep learning. Keep improving," she told her students. "Never hold a horse's inexperience against it. Instead, look for teaching opportunities.

"Aside from a flea in fluorine, a horse is the most reactive creature in the world. It naturally wants to run from things that frighten it. And when it's young, everything frightens it. So we create situations where we show the horse that something it would normally be frightened of isn't worth freaking out about."

"Look at Giselle!" Doreen said, her curls bouncing as she whipped her mallet in circles. "Even if she never plays a single game, this will be worth it. At the very least, she will be less inclined to leap in the air when something startles her."

Laudine looked at the calm, quiet horses. She weighed the situation, taking everything in. "Again, I am struck with how easily one can desensitize an animal to anything if you pick away at it long enough."

She spoke quietly, musing to herself.

Mayla wondered why the woman's comment on something so positive filled her with such foreboding.

⚜

De la Foret was punctual, Thiago mused. And his custom-made riding boots showed signs of real use, so perhaps the next hour wouldn't be wasted.

"This is Ibby." Thiago double-checked the saddle's overgirth. "She'll take good care of you."

He held the stirrup on the off side as the big man clambered up on a mounting block and heaved himself aboard. Ibby, sturdy as a tank, but able to turn on a pin, stood gamely for her rider.

"You already know the basics," Thiago said. "Each team has four players. Each player has a handicap. A team's total handicap is the sum total of the players. Here, in France, beginning players start at a negative four handicap. Top handicap in any country is a ten."

"Is that what you are?" de la Foret picked up the reins in both hands.

"Someday." No point in mentioning there were fewer than twenty-five ten-goalers alive. "Today, I'm an eight."

De la Foret shot him a knowing look. "Moving up soon, though, I hear."

Thiago showed the man how to hold the reins in his left hand and mallet in his right. "The Number One player is the front man. The forward."

"Offense."

"Right. Number Two is One's wing man. He has to mark the best player on the opposing team: Number Three."

De la Foret's attention flickered for a fraction of a second as he noted the number "3" on Thiago's shirt. The man was sharp; he missed very little. Again, he reminded Thiago of his father.

For the first time since last night, a tiny pin-prick of misgiving made Thiago wonder if he had made a miscalculation in setting up today's lesson. If things went badly, he suspected the big man—like Calvo, Sr.—would fail to find humor in the situation.

"So Four is defense? The goalie?" De la Foret hefted the mallet and swung it experimentally.

"To a point," Thiago said. "Four plays back. But he may also advance the ball whenever possible. Your purpose isn't to maintain your position, it's to identify the line the ball is on and join it."

He smacked a polo ball with his mallet and sent it away from them.

"When the ball is hit, envision the line from where it was to where it goes. The line of the ball is the most important thing in the game. Find it. Follow it. But do not cross it. It's somewhat oversimplified to say 'as long as you follow the line of the ball, you have right of way,' and I am happy to argue the nuances of the game with you later, but for now, it's true."

"And if someone hits the ball and changes its direction?"

"Then the line changes and your right of way is no longer valid."

"So: find the line."

"*Si.* Equally important is sticking close to an opposing player until you have the advantage. Then you can hit the ball toward your goal."

"Which changes," de la Foret said.

"Yes. Every time a team scores, they switch goals. Simple!"

De la Foret squinted at the goal posts nearly two hundred and seventy meters apart, flanking opposite ends of the ten-acre field. He said nothing.

Tough customer, Thiago mused.

Aloud, he said, "Remember: man, line, ball. Stay with your man—"

Off to his right, a rider on Zoelie appeared, cantering easily toward them.

Words failed Thiago, but his heart leapt at the sight. He broke into a grin he couldn't have contained even if he wanted to.

"Ah," he said. "Here's Valentin!"

❧

Mayla had spent the better part of the past half hour transforming herself beyond all recognition. Instead of a sports bra, a compression bandage bound her breasts, flattening them to her body. She wore the purple and gold of an old Calvo Estates polo shirt. Heavy leather knee pads disrupted the contours of her legs. Dark sunglasses hid her eyes while a polo helmet with full faceguard obscured much of her face. The *coup de grâce*, however, was the wispy mustache decorating the top of her lip.

What sort of a stunt was Thiago playing at?

More perplexing: why was she so willing to play along?

Moments ago, when she had gone to Thiago's row of stalls to tack up, she had intended to ride Milagro, her old friend from her days as the Calvo groom. But the realization that Sergio's peerless Zoelie was a legitimate choice for her mount hit as she entered the barn. Of course, Thiago's groom would have equal access to all of his available horses. She couldn't pass up this opportunity; it would never arise again. If Sergio pitched a fit and Thiago left her on her own to deal with the fallout— well, she would survive. She had experience with that sort of thing.

As she prepared to mount, her phone buzzed with a text from her realtor in Kentucky.

Looks promising. Land perked. Structure and foundations of house and barns fine. No other offers being entertained. Word is the owners will probably accept. More info soon.

With heart pounding as much at the possibilities of her future as at her present situation, Mayla directed Zoelie toward the two men. It took little more than a thought to guide the mare, who moved like a queen gracing them with her presence.

The lesson was already in progress when she arrived.

Mayla bit the inside of her cheek to keep from laughing at the combination of disbelief and amazement that registered on Thiago's face when he saw her.

"There are a few basic shots you need to know before you play," Thiago told de la Foret. "Valentin will demonstrate each one, and I'll talk you through the technique. Ready, Valentin?"

Nodding curtly, Mayla threw herself into her role. Thiago's swift smile was full of the good humor she had always loved in him.

"Let's start with the offside forehand." Thiago mounted his horse. "Mallet up. Arm straight back. Then let gravity take over and bring the mallet down to the ball." Mayla demonstrated proper form as Thiago coached his student.

After a few practice hits, the billionaire contemplated the long, flexible mallet. "This thing could do a lot of damage. Especially at speed. Get it tangled in a horse's legs and you could break them." He shuddered at the thought.

Mayla stayed mute, so as not to blow her cover, but she was relieved to hear Thiago reiterate the Cardinal Rules of Polo: absolutely no dangerous riding.

"No excessive whipping or spurring. In fact, many players ride with neither whip nor spur. No coming into contact with another horse behind the saddle or at too great an angle. No using your mallet as a weapon. Remember you have a responsibility to gauge both course and speed so you don't endanger any lives—horse or human."

As the session progressed, "Valentin" and Thiago provided an introduction to the wild, wonderful game they loved. To Mayla's surprise, the big businessman was a fair rider. He handled his horse well and adapted quickly to both one-handed steering and handling the mallet.

At the end of the lesson, their student's face was redder than ever. He wiped his brow and brought his horse up short. He grew still, as menacing as the quiet before a thunderstorm.

With unnerving focus, he looked Thiago in the eye. "OK, *gros bonnet*. What sort of scheme are you two up to?"

Mayla's heart hiccupped.

Alarmed, she licked at the hair on her lip, making sure it hadn't dislodged. Had her disguise failed and given her away? She looked to Thiago for how to play this.

"I beg your pardon?" Thiago said, ignoring Mayla's glances.

"This game! This was the best time I've had in years," de la Foret boomed, so loud that Zoelie turned her ears away from the noise. "An hour ago, I thought it was sillier than engraved horseshoe nails. But now, thanks to you, I'm going to have to endanger my life and risk looking ridiculous in yet another riding sport."

He rode alongside Mayla and clapped "Valentin" on the shoulder. *Wham!*

Mayla was certain her teeth rattled. She sidled Zoelie out of reach.

"Good man! Helluva rider! Whoo!" De la Foret dismounted heavily. "Quiet, though." He handed Ibby's reins and his mallet up to her.

Mayla glanced at her watch. Time to prepare for the tournament. She touched the brim of her helmet in what she hoped looked like a farewell salute and turned the horses away from the men.

"Hold up, there."

Mayla stopped. Waiting. A feeling of dread seeped into her stomach.

"Let me say a proper thank you. Come to dinner at my club tonight." De la Foret mock-bowed to Thiago. "You can tell me stories about life at the top of the polo pile. And you—" he wagged a finger toward Mayla, "we'll get some cognac in you and hear you speak a word or two."

Mayla shuddered, envisioning the inevitable disaster.

"We would love to," Thiago said. "But Valentin will be cleaning tack. And I have plans with a beautiful woman."

"You do?" De la Foret was crestfallen.

He does?

Mayla wondered if her irrational dismay showed on her face. She immediately berated herself. He had a life—a rich, full, successful life—that did not include her. Why wouldn't he? And why should she care?

She felt Thiago's eyes on her, so she met and held his gaze, even though doing so made her feel as if someone had dropped a toaster in her bath.

"Yes," he said, watching her, but speaking to de la Foret. "You remember my dance partner from last night?"

Rochelle? How? Wha—?

"*Mais oui.* That tango: memorable."

Thiago looked away, severing their connection. "*Pardon. Non.* I was speaking of the salsa."

"Ah! The American player." De la Foret wobbled his head in what he must have thought was a suggestive manner. "Scoping out the competition, yes?"

"Something like that."

Mayla bit her lip to keep from spilling all the exclamations rushing through her head. With a final nod of farewell, "Valentin" left the men behind.

She abhorred surprises—and Thiago was full of them. Did they have a date tonight? Was he trying to get out of an awkward dinner? Or was he simply having a little fun at her expense? And why—*why*— did a thrill go through her at the thought of experiencing Paris with him? Had she learned nothing since they were together?

As she jogged the horses back to the barn, she shook her head, hoping to clear her thoughts.

Very soon, she would meet Thiago on the playing field. Now was not the time to dither over his plans for the evening. Nor would she let him mess with her head and throw her off her game. For the foreseeable future, it didn't matter whether he was single or taken, charming as a prince or crass as Bruno.

She exhaled sharply, trying to rid herself of all the tension and deception of the past hour. With a steady hand, she peeled the faux mustache from her lip and steeled herself for battle. Right now, all that mattered was that when she rode against him, she played to win.

19

Game On!

ROCHELLE HAD THE HORSES GROOMED and their tails tied up when Mayla arrived at her row of stalls. "You just missed Carson and Moe," she said, picking debris from Cantata's hooves. "Meet in the Team Room in ten—"

She straightened up, got a good look at Mayla, and clamped a hand over her mouth in an unsuccessful attempt to keep from laughing.

"Not one word," Mayla said. "Just keep a lookout, in case anyone comes."

She ran to the tack room where she had stowed a duffel bag full of her game clothes, then ducked into a corner of the stall, unwrapped the compression bandage, shrugged into her sports bra, and got dressed in her team polo shirt with the big "2" on it.

"The date, it went well?"

Mayla rubbed the top of her lip, still raw from removing "Valentin's" mustache. "Very. I think polo may have a new patron."

"And?"

"And I think I'm going out with him tonight."

"The patron?"

"Thiago."

"You think?"

"I know."

"Good," Rochelle said.

But Mayla realized she couldn't say for sure what she knew. In the past twenty-four hours, everything she thought she had known had been thrown out the window and was currently free-falling through a fog of confusion.

She hurried to the Team Room and listened as Moe reiterated everything he had said yesterday during the coach's chalk talk: teamwork; sportsmanship. Day one of a three-day series. Bring your best, but pace yourself; we've got two more days to play. Make it look good for the ticket holders.

Then Carson spoke up. "Just a few notes. Remember to watch out for their Number Four. That Bruno, he's a brick wall with a mean streak. Be careful: he's the master of the stealth foul and he cheats every chance he gets. Also, as you know, with Sergio out, they've brought in an assassin: Thiago Calvo. I don't need to tell you the man is top-notch."

"But jet lagged," Mayla said.

"Beg your pardon?" Moe asked.

Carson twitched an interested eyebrow.

"He's exhausted. I don't think he's slept in two days. Don't get me wrong. He's still an amazing player, but he's never ridden with this team before. I think we can make that work in our favor. Also," she lowered her voice, whispering as if conspiring, "he has a weakness. It's small, but—"

As one, the entire team leaned forward to hear what she had to say.

Thiago adjusted the protective sleeve on his arm as he rode out with Team South America. His mount, a nimble gelding with a top-notch right lead but a slightly sticky left, played with the bit in his mouth, ready to run.

All through the opening festivities, the singing of the national anthems and presenting of the teal and orange Parisien flag, he reviewed what he knew of Team North America.

The two teams were well matched; each had a total handicap of twenty-two. Though Thiago had been happy to remain at home in Buenos Aires and play there, he was well aware of the elite players in the sport. He had played against eight-goaler Jerrol Morgan, for instance, when Team North America's Number One had visited Argentina. The man was a focused, fearless hitting machine. Both Captain Carson and their Number Four he knew by reputation. Both had unerring instincts.

And then there was Mayla. When he knew her years ago, she had been good but untried. After she quit working for his father and went pro, he had watched every available video he could find online of the games she played in. He had seen her grow as a player, steadily improving, until now, when she was among the top-ranked women in the world.

A mental image of "Valentin" made him smile. She was still the same Mayla. Dedicated. Bold—practically reading his mind, not only willing to play along with his little scheme, but also snagging the opportunity to ride Zoelie while she was at it, knowing he would say nothing so as not to ruin the charade. And she was as passionate about the game as about everything she loved...

Without warning, thoughts of how Mayla responded to what she loved overwhelmed him. His stomach tightened with feral force. His hands missed the feel of her. His mouth starved to taste her.

Thiago's horse shook his head, doubtless picking up on his rider's tension.

Stop it! Clamping down on all extraneous distractions—including thoughts of Mayla—Thiago forced himself to come back to the present. Right here, right now, the game was all that mattered.

"Top players from Argentina, Chile, Uruguay, and Brazil have come together to form Team South America," blared the loudspeaker.

The crowd, sizeable for any French gathering on a Friday afternoon in late July, applauded. As the announcer stated players' names, countries of origin, handicaps, and positions, Thiago and his teammates moved forward. Riding abreast, they picked up a canter and took an easy lap around the field. Team North America followed.

Thiago settled into the familiar pre-game routine and concentrated on what was to come. When the game started moments later, he was ready.

Play started fast and got faster. Nothing mattered but the game. No longer tired or distracted, Thiago charged after the ball.

With Mayla hot on his heels, he and Carson followed the line of the ball. Shoulder to shoulder they rode, leaning out of the saddle, their horses pressed up against each other like half-ton tanks, trying to push each other out of the way.

Thiago spied the ball, a bright spot on the dark green field, waiting for him to knock it through the goal. He drew back his arm, prepared to swing, and dropped the mallet toward the ball—

Out of nowhere, Mayla hooked the mallet, destroying his shot.

Fast as a pit viper, Carson flicked the ball toward the North American goal. The game turned and Thiago turned with it, speeding to the opposite end of the field.

⚜

At the end of the third chukker, Mayla jumped on Cantata, handing the reins of her tired gelding to Rochelle.

"You're sticking to Monsieur Calvo like a rumor on a politician," Rochelle said. "Like you can read his mind."

Mayla laughed because she knew she was supposed to. She didn't want to admit, even to herself, how much she wished Rochelle's words were true. She would give anything to know what the man was thinking.

Playing on the field with Thiago again brought back even more memories than she had feared. Memories of early morning stick-and-ball drills. Of practicing various shots till her thighs and shoulder burned. Of warming up his horses. She remembered the hours spent watching him ride, shadowing him, chasing after him.

All that was well and good. It afforded insight into his strategy, allowing her to take appropriate countermeasures. But the memories of riding with him brought baggage along with them that set the stage for other, more personal pieces of their past.

She remembered how he sang along to the radio, deliberately getting the lyrics wrong because it made her laugh. Remembered his breath on her neck. The exhilaration of being enfolded in his arms. Though it had been ages since she had rested her head on his warm, solid chest, she still remembered the primal joy of hearing his heart beat in rhythm with hers...

What had he meant when he said they had plans for tonight? During this brief hiatus in play, Mayla's thoughts spiraled into speculation. Every time she shut down one tangent, more questions arose to fill the void.

How dare he assume she would go out with him? *Did* he assume such a thing? Was she engaging in wishful thinking, hoping he would ask her out? Or had he merely invented their nonexistent date as an offhanded way to get out of dinner with de la Foret?

Offhanded. That reminded her...

"If I could read his mind, I'd learn how he does his offside tail shots," Mayla said. "They are textbook perfect."

"Perhaps if you ask *verrrry* nicely, he will tell you all of his secrets." Rochelle said, her undertone making it clear she wasn't talking about polo.

"I don't know why I keep you around," Mayla laughed.

As she rode onto the field for the throw-in, she heard Rochelle call out, "Go get him!"

Mayla brooded on the words. Is that what she wanted to do? Forgive him and forget their past? Did she value herself so little? Even if she could start afresh with the Thiago of today, rather than the young man she once knew, would she?

Chewing her lip, preoccupied, Mayla stepped onto the field. She took her position, marked her man, and kept her eye on the ball.

Then the ball dropped. Her mare blasted forward as play started. And the only thoughts of Thiago crossing Mayla's mind were strategies to keep him from scoring.

This—THIS—was why she loved the game. She and Cantata worked as a single unit, whether sticking with their opponent or joining the team train chasing the ball down the field. They darted first left, then right, pulled up short, then raced ahead again, senses soaring.

Mayla knew she had a silly grin pasted on her face. She didn't care. She had never played better. If Thiago thought she was going to go quietly along and worship at the shrine of his greatness, he had another think coming.

She watched for the giveaway—a minuscule shift of his weight a fraction of a second before he swung. Then she moved heaven and earth to get there first. Thiago might hit harder. Faster. Stronger. But she knew his tells. They had become more subtle since she last played against him, but they were there.

Chukker after chukker, play after play, she harried him like a gnat. Every time he tried to take a shot, she snicked the ball away.

At the end of the final chukker, with Team North America ahead by two goals, Mayla was exhausted, but exhilarated. She trotted over to Rochelle and dismounted, both she and her horse puffing from exertion.

"Glowing with glory!" Rochelle stripped off the saddle while Mayla removed her helmet, catching her breath. "Perhaps Monsieur Calvo, he is not as good as he thinks he is."

"No," said Mayla. "He's better. I have a feeling we just got lucky today."

20

Making Plans

BRUNO SLAMMED THE DOOR of the tack room. His face twisted in disgust when he saw Thiago leading horses down the aisle.

"Bah! The revered eight-goaler. The American girl rode circles around you."

Thiago ran his hands down each horse's legs, checking for any signs of heat or soreness before he put the animal in a stall. Thoughts of Mayla sporting that ridiculous mustache ran through his mind. He laughed at the memory.

"You find it funny?" Bruno swore. "You scored only four goals the whole game. Sergio is sick and he could have done better."

"Perhaps, but my four were three more than yours," Thiago said quietly. "Don't forget, she held you off, too."

Bruno snarled. "Count on it. I will not forget." He stalked off, muttering in anger.

Thiago closed the last stall door. He leaned against it, rubbing his neck. Every time he blinked, his eyes tried to remain closed.

Though he had high hopes for the evening, all he could think of at the moment was getting some rest. Squaring his shoulders he set out for his guest house. On the way, he texted Mourad, hoping his request made sense.

Once inside, he showered off the sweat and grime from the game. Then he collapsed on the bed.

Belatedly, he realized he had neglected to lock the door. He really should remedy that, his brain tried to tell his body, citing Bruno's penchant for dropping in unannounced. But it argued in vain. Within moments, he was sleeping so soundly that Bruno could have crashed through the door on an elephant without waking him. And as he slept, he smiled as he always did when he dreamed impossible dreams of a long and happy life with Mayla.

⚜

Mayla leaned close to the delicate yellow tuberoses and inhaled their citrusy fragrance again. And again.

Mmmm...

A tumbler full of water on the tiny table acted as a makeshift vase. She reread the note that had accompanied the flowers:

> *As I recall, you don't like surprises. I have saddled you with far too many since we met. From this point forward, I am transparent. To be clear: I hope for nothing more than the pleasure of your company. Please do me the honor of accompanying me into this beautiful city for dinner tonight. Mourad, my trusted friend, will call for you at five.*
> *Yours,*
> *Thiago*

It was, perhaps, the most charming note she had ever received.

It also sounded nothing at all like the Thiago she knew. Had he changed so much since they were together?

She checked the time on her phone. Four fifty. The flowers and the note had arrived shortly after the game. One more surprise in a day full of them.

Dinner with Thiago. Did she want to eat with him, sit across the table from him, order appetizers, debate over entrées, and wonder if the waiter would approve of the wine she chose? The answer to that question changed several times a minute.

Mayla's stomach rumbled, reminding her that she was ravenous, regardless of whom she dined with. Raiding the tiny fridge yielded nothing but an elderly carrot and a half-finished container of yogurt. Grabbing a scrap of paper, she wrote "buy food!" and skewered it onto a hook intended for keys. For the briefest of moments, she considered running out to a boulangerie and to G20, taking long enough with her shopping to avoid the awkwardness of a date with Thiago.

Even as the thought occurred, she banished it. Experience had proven that running away wouldn't solve any problems. Truth be told, no woman in her right mind would run from Thiago if he asked to spend some time with her. That's all tonight was. Spending some time with an old friend. An old flame. Nothing more.

A series of raps on her door made her jump.

Carson cracked the door open and poked his head inside. "We're going swimming at the Pontoise tonight. Then: wine bar. You two want to come with?"

"Come in," Mayla invited. She scanned the empty hallway as Carson settled into the flat's sole chair. "The whole team's going?"

"Hardly. Moe's going to Crazy Horse. The other guys are going with him to make sure he gets home in one piece this time."

"Who's 'we,' then?"

Carson's smile could charm a cobra. "Piotr. We met last night."

"That wouldn't happen to be the handsome server circulating with a tray of bottomless champagne… "

Such a happy cobra.

Mayla crossed her arms and looked down at him, severe as a drill sergeant. "All due respect, O Captain, my Captain, but I find your motives suspect."

"You suspect nothing!" Carson exuded offended innocence.

"I suspect you know Rochelle went dancing on Rue de la Huchette. I suspect the last thing you want is me—or anyone—crashing along on your date. And I suspect you may have heard that I have my own plans tonight."

Carson leaned forward, a spy with a secret. "Word on the street is you're sleeping with the enemy."

"Nobody's sleeping with anybody," Mayla spluttered, her heart jumpstarting at the thought of sleeping with Thiago. "We just have a date, that's all."

She didn't know what surprised her more: her falling for Carson's bait, or the thrill that seared through her, painting intimate portraits of Thiago with an Old Master's attention to detail on the canvas of her mind.

Carson held up his hands, obviously enjoying himself. "So it's true. Who are you infiltrating?"

Before Mayla could respond, explain to him she was merely reconnecting with an old friend, Carson took in the flowers and the name on the note propped against them. "Señor Calvo? And you're wearing *that*?"

"Yes, to both," Mayla informed him, refusing to feel self-conscious about her breezy, comfy summer dress. She pulled him from the chair and propelled him toward the door. "This interview is over."

"I'm going. I'm going. Sheesh."

Carson opened the door to leave, revealing a quietly confident man in an impeccable suit, his hand raised to knock.

"Good evening," the man inclined his head, conveying a reserved bow. "I am Mourad, Monsieur Calvo's trusted and assured driver. May I escort you, Mademoiselle Alvarez, to the car?"

"Looks like you're in for an interesting evening. I expect to hear all about it tomorrow," Carson said.

Mayla smiled, sweet as a canary-eating cat. "Expect to be disappointed, then."

Mourad's eyes lit up with recognition as Carson sauntered away. "That was Captain LeVallier! The great Canadian eight-goaler."

"Not to mention leader of the fashion police and relentless investigative reporter," Mayla said.

As they walked down the hallway, Mourad blurted, "I, a devoted fan, am most honored to meet you. And to think I have the distinguished joy of introducing you to my beloved city."

"Thank you," Mayla said. "But I have been here before. Many times."

"With all respect, revered American lady, you do not know Paris until Mourad himself has introduced you."

Mourad and Mayla emerged from the cool interior darkness of the residences to stand blinking in the afternoon sun.

He escorted her to a sleek car parked as if it owned the club and held open the rear passenger door for her as if she were a princess. Her stomach rumbled so loudly she feared it wanted its own podcast. Mortified, she got in as quickly as possible.

When Mourad took his place in the driver's seat, she leaned toward him to ask where Thiago was.

Before she could speak, she saw him.

He moved toward the car with feline grace. His dark hair was just long enough to hint at curling. A light gray shirt clung to his body; muscles molded the fabric into a visual feast, a moving work of art that made Mayla itch to peel the shirt off and toss it to the ground so she could see the real masterpiece it covered. An expensive, exotic aura enveloped him.

Mayla smoothed her skirt, insecurity niggling at her. The opulence of the car... the clothes... the man himself gave her second thoughts about the evening ahead. Clearly, Thiago was no longer the twenty-year-old boy who worshipped his father, wore his heart on his sleeve, and thought the best use of his family's fortune was purchasing impulsive gifts such as vintage evening gowns. He was a man of the world, with a self-assurance few men ever attain, packaged in a body every woman would want.

Perhaps Carson had been right. Perhaps she should have worn something more chic...

Then she saw his watch. Her father's old military watch. Thiago had been fascinated that she carried it with her even though it no longer worked. Within a week of her arriving at the Calvo Estates, he had taken it to a jeweler and had it fixed.

Nothing else came close to conveying what she felt for him, so she had given it to him on his twentieth birthday. His fervent, heartfelt embrace, crushing her close, breathing words of love on her had been the prelude to one of the most passionate, memorable nights of her life. She had hoped to enjoy loving him like that for a lifetime, but it was not to be. Still, the sight of him wearing her watch warmed her heart. And it erased any worries she might have had about what she was wearing.

Mourad got out of the car to hold the door. Thiago slid into the seat next to her, electrifying the atmosphere like a lightning strike.

They gave each other a quick, awkward hug, hampered as much by the physics of sitting in a sedan as by their history.

"Thank you for coming," he whispered in her ear, his voice rich as his grandmother's *dulce de leche*. "You know I could never enjoy Paris without you."

Sitting next to him, with ten-year-old memories dancing in her head, Mayla realized that though she had been starving moments earlier, she was no longer hungry.

21

New Beginnings

MAYLA SMELLED LIKE HOME: an indefinable *bouquet garni* that made Thiago's mouth water and his blood roar.

When he had texted Mourad after the game (*Tired. Ask Mayla to give me the benefit of the doubt and go out with me this evening.*), he had been surprised at the speedy answer (*The lady is delighted. It is her fondest dream. I shall escort her to the car at five. Permit me the distinction of being your agreeable and discreet guide.*) but too drained to question it.

After waking from a sleep that left him south of refreshed but north of exhausted, he reconsidered Mayla's response, wondering if Mourad had been an unwitting target of her legendary sarcasm. He knew damn well he had long ago destroyed any dream of Mayla's that included him.

He had half expected her not to show up. When he saw her in the back of the car, alert as a lead mare, he was hardly able to restrain himself from breaking into a trot to reach her sooner.

As he entered the vehicle, he slipped a tightly folded piece of paper—one of his most treasured possessions—into Mourad's hand. For reference. For safe-keeping. For luck.

The car's engine purred to life. Thiago found himself at a loss for words as Mourad navigated off the grounds of the Parisien, through the leafy green woods, and into the city.

Mayla, too, was silent. Though the quietude was more companionable than contentious, fingers of tension kneaded Thiago's stomach. What if the two of them discovered they had nothing more to say to each other?

"You must be hungry. But not too hungry, so early, yes? I have the most superlative of excursions planned." Mourad made eye contact with Thiago in the rearview mirror, nodding almost imperceptibly.

Mourad was a godsend. Thiago relaxed as much as possible. Somehow, Sergio's sickness had caused him to win the cosmic lottery and given him a second chance. He intended to make the most of it.

"But first, a detour through the very chic Passy, then a quick and delicious stop in the Quartier Latin for world's best tapas."

"Outside of Spain, you mean."

Mourad shrugged. "If you say so."

They drove south into the sixteenth arrondissement. Soon they were winding through an upscale neighborhood of quiet beauty.

"I never thanked you for the flowers. They are lovely," Mayla said quietly.

Flowers? Thiago tried to hide his confusion, but she knew him too well.

"Ah," she said. "I see. Well, that explains a few things. I didn't think the note sounded like you." Her smile highlighted the sadness in her words.

"Mourad, did you send Mayla flowers?"

"The very aromatic, very romantic flowers are from you, sir," Mourad said.

"What about the note?" Mayla asked. "Did you write that?"

"But of course. As instructed."

"What did you say to her?"

"Words that brought you together tonight. Were they inadequate?"

"No," Thiago had to admit, "they were perfect."

Without benefit of turn signals or advance notice, Mourad veered to the right, parked the car, and jumped out, disappearing down a cobblestone sidewalk.

What the hell?

Mayla turned to Thiago, every bit as mystified as he.

"Was it something we said?" she asked.

He laughed, more from confusion than humor. Mayla joined in, coasting along with the oddness of their situation.

Their laughter cleared the air. All tension dissipated, leeching from his neck and shoulders, draining any worries from his mind.

He was with Mayla again. As little as two days ago, he would have never believed it possible. Now, here she was, within his reach; her calm, bemused presence had re-entered his life. He could think of a thousand worse things than being stuck in a car with her in Paris.

They people-watched for a bit. Some pedestrians walked dogs. Others toted bags from exclusive shops, visiting with each other and window-shopping down wide alleys of beautiful nineteenth-century Haussmannian buildings, all topped with an array of red clay chimney pots. Before the scenery grew old and they began to wonder what to do next, Mourad returned.

"I ask a thousand apologies," he said, gently placing a white box on the passenger seat beside him before pulling out into traffic. "It is a surprise."

"Mayla hates surprises," Thiago said.

"A thousand more apologies, then, Mademoiselle Alvarez. I do not wish to offend."

"It's fine," Mayla laughed. "Maybe before you leave us next time, we discuss it first? Something like: 'I'm popping off for a bit to visit my good friend Fred' would do."

Mourad nodded. "I am guilty. And chastened."

"Not at all," Mayla said, leaning forward to pat the driver on the shoulder. "You are a treasure."

When Mayla sat back in her seat, Thiago's hand moved as if on its own accord, drawn to her like iron to a magnet. He covered the back of her hand with his palm the way he used to do when they were driving into town or to a match. The moment they touched, a wave of warmth washed over him, bringing a rush of memories with it.

Her thumb moved, stroking the base of his wrist. His heart raced as it never had with any other woman. Long ago, the first time she ever did that, her quiet response to his impetuous advance had taken him so by surprise that he had squeezed harder than he intended. To her credit, she hadn't pulled away—and later that evening, she had taught him much about the benefits of restraint.

Back then, he thought matters of the heart were so easy: find the girl who makes your heart act like a two-year-old colt turned loose in pasture; feel superhero-strength whenever she was near; see everything through the filter of Her; expect to have her and love her forever. Back then, he liked to say he lived his life with no regrets. He wished he could say that now.

He wanted to reach across the seat, pull her to him, and gather her in his arms. He wanted to watch the pulse dancing just below her ear. Wanted to trace the life cycle of her smile. Wanted to hold her and tell her a decade's worth of prayers and dreams. But he knew better.

It gratified him to realize that he could still read her. Right now, her stillness belied the fact that she was poised for flight—a bird on a branch. If he let his body control his brain, moving toward her like a freight train full of heat and hunger, she would fly away, building walls around herself in the name of self-preservation.

He must be careful. Take his time. This was his chance—his one, his only, his miraculous chance—to try to repair the damage he had done. Outwardly calm, he thrilled anew every moment this bird in his hand chose to stay.

22

Going Up

THE CAR STOPPED NEAR THE TROCADÉRO.

Mayla reluctantly pulled free from Thiago's gentle touch, though the memories it had unleashed continued to haunt her thoughts.

Mourad got out and opened the doors, escorting first Mayla, then Thiago, from the vehicle. "The light, it is perfect," he announced. "The Palais du Chaillot has wonders to show you. A short walk takes you across Pont d'Iéna. I shall attentively await you at Quai Branly."

He bowed as if ushering them into a magical kingdom, got back in the B7, and drove away.

"We have been given our marching orders," Thiago said, gesturing for her to lead.

Together they walked onto the enormous esplanade that separated the two neoclassical wings—the only remnants of the original Palais du Trocadéro—arcing off to either side. Under their feet, like a giant quilt, tiles formed a grid of forty-nine large gray squares, each with smaller concentric squares of varying shades of gray and tan. The afternoon sun blazed off the eight golden statues that flanked the square, towering above the crowds on concrete plinths.

Mayla caught her breath at the sight.

Ahead of them, the Eiffel Tower reared into the skyline, looking as if it perched at the end of the terrace instead of standing a kilometer away.

Mayla wasn't a crier. Her mother, God rest her opioid-addicted soul, had always had a cistern of tears ready to trickle free at a moment's notice. But aside from the opening number of musicals, which, inexplicably, made Mayla weep, she remained dry-eyed. She usually took a sort of perverse pride in remaining tear-free. Now, however, she was so full of happiness, she envied the release a little crying would provide.

Without thinking, she reached for Thiago's hand. Her fingers interlaced with his, completing this moment. Clarifying it. Anchoring it in her memory forever.

Enchanted, they walked the length of the square and descended a wide gray staircase.

The somber stone yielded to the lush grass and spraying water of Trocadéro Gardens. People lounged on the green slopes lining the Fountain of Warsaw. Hand in hand, Mayla and Thiago followed a rose-colored walkway that skirted the gardens.

Keeping her eyes on the Eiffel Tower before her, burnished and bronze against an impossibly blue sky, Mayla filled her lungs with the warm Parisian air. She breathed in again, deliberately, as they stepped onto the Pont d'Iéna that had bridged the Seine for over two hundred years.

Above them, sculptures of two nearly naked soldiers standing beside their horses flanked the bridge's entrance. One, an Arabian warrior, wore a long, flowing head scarf and a discreetly draped cloth. He gazed at his steed with pride, one hand on the elaborately arched crest. The other, a Greek fighter, had never heard of discretion. With an arm over his ill-tempered horse, he sported a flamboyant beard, helmet, and cape which unfurled over his shoulders, leaving nothing to the imagination.

Thiago shook his head in mock dismay. "Bare feet near hooves," he shuddered. Mayla squeezed his hand in silent agreement.

At the other end of the bridge, on the Right Bank, they passed between statues of two more horsemen.

"Looks a little bit like Zoelie," Mayla said of the high-headed horse prancing next to a Roman soldier.

Thiago indicated the other: a barrel-chested, wildly bearded Gallic man standing with brazen arrogance beside a massive warhorse. "And that, I'm sorry to say, looks a lot like Bruno."

Mayla laughed, her heart so light she thought she might fly.

Soon, they stood at the base of the Eiffel Tower. Thiago led the way past a long line of people waiting for tickets to a sign that declared "Welcome to the Eiffel Tower" in three languages. There, with a magician's flourish, he produced two tickets to the second tier.

"It appears Mourad has been busy this afternoon," Mayla said as Thiago escorted her into the red double-decker elevator that angled upward on the north leg of the tower.

Thiago feigned wounded innocence. "You caught me."

"I've learned. I'm no longer a young thing who is beguiled by your adorable charm."

"I'm adorable?"

"No. Not at all."

People crowded around them, pushing her close to him. When she inhaled, his nearness, his scent, the warmth of his body, overwhelmed her senses.

The spectre of their past reared its ugly head, reminding her of what he had done, of why this ride they had planned together had never happened before. But she banished all dark memories to the basement of her consciousness before they could taint her happiness or infect the moment. She couldn't forgive him, even if he asked her to. His actions had proven to her that his words meant nothing. It pained her even now to admit that when push came to shove, she could not rely on him to have her back. For the moment, however, she didn't care. Her body overruled her mind, craving the chance to be near him, to share this with him.

She leaned against him, every cell singing with joy, as the doors closed and the lift began to ascend.

⚜

Thiago's heart lurched in his chest. He was a king, with all of Paris spread out at his feet, but his racing heart had nothing to do with standing at the top of the Eiffel Tower.

A summer breeze blew through the wire mesh protecting the people on the platform, bringing a welcome break from the summer heat. Thiago's arm wrapped around Mayla as effortlessly as breathing. She leaned into him, accepting him. Welcoming his touch. With every movement she made, his heart pounded with more enthusiasm. They were like two halves of a larger whole. When he was with her, he was stronger, smarter, braver, better than when she was missing from his life.

How he had hated her missing from his life.

To the north and west wound the blue ribbon of the Seine River, with a magnificent view of the esplanade, gardens, and bridge they had walked across a few minutes earlier. People scurried around below like ants. The carousel near the base of the tower was small enough to fit in his hand. To the southeast, the Champ-de-Mars rolled out like a long, green, grassy carpet, fringed with hedges and trees, all the way to the rather severe military school at its far end. Behind the school, a little over three kilometers away, loomed the rectangular gray tower of Montparnasse, the only skyscraper in the city—a modern anomaly in an old-world setting.

A smiling couple in front of a pink sign declaring "Kissing Place" took selfies while obeying the sign's directive. Thiago took his cues from Mayla and pretended not to see it.

"Ugh." A round American woman with a green plastic sun visor and a bulging fanny pack gestured toward Montparnasse. Her voice carried far past the ears of her associates. "Look at that thing. It doesn't belong there. It completely ruins the view."

"You are not alone." Mayla's quiet words caught the woman's attention. "But it is. After it was built, the city put a moratorium on anything so high. Rather than ruining the view, however, I think it is the best place to see Paris."

Fanny Pack scoffed, but Mayla held her ground. "When you think of Paris, what do you see in your mind's eye?"

"The Eiffel Tower, of course."

Mayla nodded. "Which you cannot see from here. From there, you can."

Thiago leaned his chin lightly on Mayla's head as the Americans clucked to themselves about the truth of her insights. Her hair smelled like lavender and vanilla. His stomach tightened with a hunger no food could satisfy. She was his Tour Montparnasse. His anomaly. She didn't come from his culture or his country. Everything in his life was full of old-school tradition until she showed up: a sleek, modern woman whose drive, charm, and humor towered over every other person he knew.

That, of course, was the problem.

When he was younger, he had thought everyone would acknowledge the merits of growing, of evolving, of changing with the times. Just because something had been done one way for years didn't mean that was the right way or the only way to do it. In both his head and his heart, he had believed this to be true. Yet, when he had the opportunity to stand up and defend the dreams of the woman he loved, he had chosen to fall into the safety net of tradition rather than risk his father's wrath. God help him, he had dismissed her ambitions as if they were somehow less important than his own.

He had instantly recognized his mistake, but the damage had been done, breaking the bonds of trust that had once brought them so close together they practically inhabited each other's thoughts.

Tonight, when he heard that Mayla had said spending the evening with him was her fondest dream (a phrase he now suspected originated with matchmaking Mourad), he knew that was an exaggeration. She was already living her fondest dream without him.

In spite of him.

He would have been content to stand there for hours, breathing in the rich scent of heaven. Instead, he reluctantly drew apart from her and escorted her to the elevator for the descent.

He had dreams of his own that included her. And he had a plan, a crazy scheme to try to show her how much she had meant to him. How much she still meant. But he needed to act quickly. If those dreams stood a chance of coming true, he and Mayla needed to find their way back to earth—and to Mourad—soon.

23

Signs and Wonders

MAYLA COULD NOT REMEMBER when she had enjoyed a meal more. She stood next to Thiago in the narrow galley of a packed tapas bar. In lieu of menus, they consulted the ceiling, where wine bottles hung from ribbons and scores of banners fluttered, each bearing the picture, name, and price of a different food option.

Her stomach had been a knot of nerves from the moment she and Thiago had embarked on their date. When Mourad dropped them off outside this unassuming establishment in the Latin Quarter, promising he would return within the hour, Mayla had been certain she would be unable to eat a bite.

How happy she was to be proven wrong.

Savory macaroons, seared *foie gras*, roasted peppers, croquettes, a platter of beef carpaccio, and a deep bowl of crispy *fromage frites* took away the hunger that had plagued her earlier. In its place, a deeper hunger prowled, taunted by Thiago's warmth, his smile, and the forced togetherness of the busy place.

It was the ideal location for a first date: many interesting things to look at, delicious delicacies, but far too loud for any real conversation.

Which was perfect.

Though she wanted to talk about their past—pretending it had never happened was as pointless as pretending she was an Amazon queen—she doubted she could do so without sounding as if she blamed him.

Of course she blamed him.

She had ignored the signs that clearly pointed toward their downfall. Thiago's devotion to his father. His eagerness to learn the family business, to make the old man proud of him. She had thought such things were evidence of his love of family. Instead, they were harbingers of his Achilles' heel—the small but fatal weakness that destroyed them.

She had believed the lie that "love would find a way." Love could overcome many things, but it was impotent in the face of tradition.

That lie had hamstrung her emotions, preventing her from moving on, for thoughts of Thiago still dominated her dreams. After all these years, she still compared him to every man she met. No one else ever came close. If love couldn't find a way for her to be with the man of her dreams, she had no use for it during her waking hours. It would simply lead to more heartache.

No: talking about anything of substance would only open the door for more disappointment, more regret. Better to eat bites of this delectable sugar-dusted waffle and keep that door shut. For now.

"Wish I could try everything, but it would take a week!" Thiago said.

"At least," Mayla agreed. "But it would be worth it!"

Thiago checked the time. "We should go. Don't want to be late."

Late for what? Mayla wondered. Aloud, she said, "You still have the watch," ignoring her own keep-the-door-shut rule.

"It is the only one I wear."

His eyes, open and unguarded, met hers, as intimate as an embrace. For a moment, everything in her world was a little brighter. A little warmer. A little more optimistic.

While Thiago settled the bill, Mayla finished off the last of their dessert, her heart still tap-dancing, her mind racing.

They went outside and walked northwest, past the water-spewing dragons of Fontaine Saint-Michel, toward Île de la Cité, with Thiago confidently choosing the way.

"So... do you come here often?" Mayla said.

"Never," he confessed, taking her hand and matching his stride to hers. "But Mourad gave me directions, with strict instructions to make sure we don't miss this."

Mayla accompanied him, intrigued. Not until they crossed Pont Saint-Michel did she realize, with a mixture of joy and dread, that he was taking her to Sainte-Chapelle.

As she entered the church for the second time that day, something new infused the essence of the place. Hidden somewhere in the dark recesses, a string quartet played Vivaldi's *Winter*, filling the air with ethereal tones. A lump of emotion formed in Mayla's throat at the combination of music and mystical beauty in the company of the man she once loved.

She would allow the chapel to determine whether or not she should continue their time together. Thiago's reaction to it would be the deciding factor. If he remained unmoved, she would accept that as a literal sign from God that too large a gulf separated them. In that case, she would cut the date short and go home. If, however, the place spoke to him on some level as it did to her, that would be her sign to keep stepping forward in faith. And, perhaps, to start looking for answers to a few questions.

The afternoon light did not show the Lower Chapel at its best. The low vaulted ceilings rose twenty feet overhead, but their blues and reds were dark, rather than vibrant. The gilded fleurs-de-lis dotting the ceiling like stars were lost in the dim lighting.

Even so, Thiago stood and stared, transfixed.

It was a sign. A good sign.

Anticipation mixed with dread held Mayla in its grip as if she were in an airplane preparing to skydive for the first time. Taking Thiago's hand, she led him through the shadows toward the small staircase to the Upper Chapel.

⚜

Thiago followed Mayla up a gloomy set of stairs to emerge into a glorious riot of color. The afternoon sun illuminated the windows with such vibrant intensity that they seemed almost alive. Blues, reds, golds, and greens danced like living flames, speckling the bodies of the few people in the room.

Haunting strains in F minor eddied in the chapel's bright acoustics, sending shivers up his spine. The music seeped into gray cracks and crevices. With melancholy mystery, it swirled in the corners, beguiling as a siren at sea. For a moment, Thiago forgot himself, so caught up was he in the strange beauty of the place.

But he could never forget her.

Her.

A slim, strong arm slipped around him. Mayla nestled against him, her eyes sparkling.

She still fit like his personal missing puzzle piece. How he had missed her. He could have done this—should have done this—ten years ago. His heart constricted; his chest physically ached as the bittersweet realization weighed on him.

Together, they moved through the airy space, taking in the exquisite workmanship that illustrated several millennia of sacred stories in glowing glass.

They were the last to leave when the chapel, still aglow with splendor, closed to the public at seven. Outside, Thiago blinked as he rejoined reality.

He took Mayla's hand and led the way according to the landmarks Mourad had provided. Neither spoke, though he knew they both had things to say to each other. Some of the mystery of the chapel still surrounded them. He didn't want to be the first to break the spell.

They paused in the shade of the trees of Place du Châtelet. A stone column loomed sixty feet above them. Atop the column, a gilded Goddess of Victory held laurel wreaths in her outstretched hands. Mist from the fountains gushing from four sphinxlike creatures cooled them.

"What are ye wearing?"

On the periphery of the little park, a young blonde struck an elaborate pose, preening and pouting at the edge of the greenery. "Trainers by Me-N-Myself. Tights by Something Borrowed. Supe spanking cami by—" Her voice, full of edges and angles, shot like a thrown blade through the air to stab the ears of all who heard it.

As Blondie itemized the origins of her eclectic, expensive outfit, her waiflike friend documented it all on her phone.

Ignoring the vloggers, Mayla swirled a hand in the water pooling at the base of the monument. "How is your mother?"

Dread clenched Thiago's jaw. This simple question was the opening act. It would invariably lead to questions a part of him—the tiny, cowardly, defensive part that had tried to bandage over an old wound of his own making—would rather not answer.

He stood next to her, staring up at the wings of Victory.

Time to tear the bandage off and kick anything cowardly to the curb.

"She's well," he said. "Still involved with her foundation. Had a breast cancer scare a few years ago—"

"I'm so sorry," Mayla said.

He heard in her voice how much she meant it.

"—but she fought it. And she beat it."

He stared straight ahead, but his peripheral vision registered Mayla's nod of relief.

Thiago's senses sharpened as they did before a game. He watched the waif and Blondie switch roles and places. More concerned with getting a shot of the fountain than with safety, Blondie backed into the busy road. Car horns meeped at her. The sounds of the city clarified. Instead of quiet background rumbling, he noticed distinct birdcalls and revving engines.

He braced himself. He knew what was coming.

"And your father? How's he?"

Such an innocuous question. So loaded with land mines from a former war.

He almost answered, "Dad will never change. He's as stuck in his old ways of thinking as he was when he kicked you out. He hates surprises even less than you do, remember?" But he knew it would sound glib. It would slam the door on any further conversation. And there were already enough barriers between them.

The words crowded his mind, pushing and shoving, trying to find utterance, hoping to be heard. He held them at bay, though he wanted to say:

"I know I let you down. I caved to Dad when it counted. What you don't know is that I did stand up to him. I just did it a day too late.

"He accused me of deceiving him; I blamed him for you leaving. But I knew I had no one to blame but myself.

"We argued, loud and vicious as a dog fight, until I left in a rage. We didn't speak or see each other for months, until Mom showed up at my place in Recoleta nearly incoherent with worry: Dad had a minor stroke. I'll always believe I had something to do with it.

"I went back to help with the horses and the business. He's happy... as happy as he ever is about anything... that when he retires in a few years, Calvo Land Development will continue.

"Our disagreement is still a sore spot, though we never talk of it. My stupid, snap decision all those years ago hurt every person I love. You most of all.

"I tried to tell you. But I couldn't get in touch. You changed your number. Blocked my emails. Sent all my letters back unopened. Standing up to my father was the second hardest thing I've ever done in my life. The hardest was losing you."

Instead, he said, "Oh, you know Dad. Some things never change."

❧

Mayla heard an undertone of unspoken words in Thiago's voice. His response to her question cracked open a door leading to a deeper, more difficult conversation. Taking a breath as if she were ready to dive underwater, she chose her next words carefully—

"Catch me! He's wearing Vevier. Juju, he's—oh my god oh my god! Juju! Come here! HURRY UP, YOU USELESS COW!"

A screeching bundle of British energy appeared on the other side of the fountain as if conjured by a fashionista genie. With fair hair flying in all directions, the young woman rushed at them, clutching a bag that cost as much as one of Mayla's horses. Maybe more. Carson would approve. A small mouselike girl—Mayla assumed this was the useless Juju—scurried behind.

"You're Thiago Calvin, aren't ye?"

Mayla had never seen eyes so round and wide. Those eyes fixated on Thiago with a disciple's devotion.

"HURRY UP, JUJU!"

As the hapless Juju finally arrived, the first interloper reached into her bag and pulled out a rolled-up tabloid: *CECI*. Ignoring Mayla completely, she thrust it toward Thiago. "That's you, innit?"

Mayla peered around Thiago's side and bit her lip to keep from laughing. On the cover of the little rag that focused on all things famous and fashionable in Paris this week, Thiago and Rochelle tangoed in living color.

"Oooo! Can we take a selfie, Mr. Calvin? Pleeeeaaase! Our fans will love it! 'Cause we love you!"

Blondie clutched at Thiago's arm in supplication.

"Ooo!" She sidled closer to him, rubbing his bicep. "Keeps himself in shape, don't he now?"

She feigned twisting her ankle, faux-falling. Thiago, ever the gentleman, reached out to steady her.

"*Merci beau cul,*" she vamped.

Oh, hell no. Enough of this nonsense.

Mayla cleared her voice and stepped into the midst of the fawning fray. The two girls stared at her as if she had magically materialized. So fixated had they been on Thiago, it was quite possible that they literally had not seen her. Their mouths dropped open like hooked trout.

"Agent," she said. "One photo. Then Mr. Calvin has to leave."

Mayla held a hand out to the blonde leader, demanding—and getting—her cell phone. She set up the shot and captured the moment: Thiago in the middle; a grinning, quivering bundle of nerves on either side.

With both girls squealing giddily behind them, she and Thiago left Place du Châtelet, all possibility for a serious conversation long gone.

They crossed Avenue Victoria and arrived at Saint-Jacques Tower, where a few stone creatures kept watch atop all that remained of a sixteenth-century church destroyed during the French Revolution.

Mayla kept a straight face for as long as she could. Which wasn't long.

When she looked at Thiago, she saw him struggling for decorum as well.

"Juju, you useless cow," she whispered.

His easy laughter filled her ears, making it impossible for her not to join in.

At first, she had resented the girls' intrusion into their privacy. Now, she was grateful for it. She hadn't heard Thiago's laugh for so long, she had forgotten how it struck a sympathetic chord with her, causing every part of her body to resonate with gladness.

She knew without a doubt that if they had continued their earlier conversation, neither of them would be laughing now.

"All I know," she said, "is Philippe is going to be mad as hell he blew his chance to be a cover story."

"You handled those fans well," Thiago said.

"They appeared out of nowhere!"

"I never know what to do when they spring like that with no warning. I don't want to be an asshole, but they're so...intense." Thiago leaned close, as if sharing a deep secret. "I believe you scared them into submission."

"I'm not you. I can get away with saying things to your fans that you can't."

"You should be a judge. Or a general. Or—scarier still—a teacher."

"I'm not scary."

Thiago reared back, pretending to be shocked. "You're terrifying. Did you not see them shut up and shape up? Where did you learn that?"

Mayla lightly smacked him. Then, as if her body had a mind of its own, she linked her arm around his, soaking up his warmth and strength as they walked.

"I don't know," she said. "The only teaching I do is giving clinics to new polo players."

Thiago took this in stride. "I guess there's a certain amount of authority that comes with telling people how to stay alive till the end of a game."

He led the way a bit further north, zig-zagging a short distance through picturesque narrow cobblestone streets until they came out at the whirling, whimsical, oddities of Stravinsky Fountain. A psychedelic snake spiraled and spouted near a spinning skull and garish parrots. Water spewed from red, oversized lips. The fountain bridged the gap between the severe sixteenth-century Gothic Church of Saint-Merri to the south and the modern human hamster run of Pompidou Centre to the north.

Mayla leaned into Thiago and took a selfie of them in front of Saint-Merri. When he wrapped his arm around her and pulled her closer, she snapped another. And another. No matter what happened between the two of them, this perfect moment would live on.

24

Talking Points

"I HAVE A REAL PHOTO SHOOT at the d'Orsay after the game to-morrow," Thiago said when Mayla finished selfie-snapping. He edged them toward Rue du Renard. "I'd like it if you would come with me. Then dinner afterward?"

A cloud of butterflies erupted in Mayla's stomach, set aflutter by the electric energy in Thiago's touch and his invitation. She tried her best to calm them down, but it was a losing battle.

Of course, she wanted to spend more time with him. Every moment they shared counted among the happiest of her life. But the things they needed to talk about weren't things one discussed during fashion shoots. Or while ambling down Rue Saint-Merri toward the bus stop where Mourad waited for them in an illegally parked car.

Once, she thought their relationship was built on the bedrock of open communication and shared goals. Instead, it had disintegrated in the quicksand of empty promises.

Really, what did she think would happen between them? He was a man, not a god capable of rolling back the years. He had already betrayed her trust and sold her dreams short. Reconnecting with him would only reopen old wounds. What purpose would that serve?

When they were young, when she thought they shared the same dreams, they had planned a future together. Now, though, they literally lived on separate continents. Traveled in different circles. Lived very different lives. Where was the future in that?

She felt the welcome weight of his arm around her. His singular spicy scent made her mouth water with an age-old hunger.

Mayla knew she would hate herself if she ignored the rubble of their past and swanned around for a few days in a frenzy of games and dates before rejoining her Thiago-free life already in progress. It might seem tempting now, but she would regret it later. And regrets were bad. Weren't they?

Thiago's eyebrows scrunched together. He looked at her...waiting.

Belatedly, she realized she had never answered his question. The photo shoot! Right...Dinner. A date—

"I'd love to," she said, grateful that her voice sounded stronger than she felt.

She rationalized her decision as he ushered her into the welcome coolness of his car, telling herself that when life came around asking her to make good choices, in this case, and this case alone, she would send her regrets.

⚜

Thiago had wanted to ask Mayla to join him tomorrow, but blurting it out in the middle of their date wasn't how he had planned it. He had intended to wait till later in the evening, to see if there was any animosity between them, any strain. But being with her was so freeing, so galvanizing, the only strain was in keeping his hands to himself.

He knew he could never make up for what he had lost. The clock's hands only turned in one direction. But he also couldn't argue with the fact that he was at his best when he was with her. She inspired him. Challenged him. Made his blood simmer with what his *abuelita* would deem "impure thoughts."

Paris paled in comparison to her. All he wanted to do was take her in his arms and hold her so tightly he never lost her again. He wanted to taste her. To tantalize her. To transport them both on a shared adventure of the senses that drained them both and made them desperate for more.

When she unbuckled her seatbelt and slid over next to him, laying her head on his shoulder, thoughts of how they could best use the back seat of the car so filled his head, he felt like a teenager again.

"You're stuck now, Mr. Calvin," Mayla said, her voice low and lucid. "*Si?*"

"There's a whole game between now and your shoot. If I clean your clock the way I did today, maybe you won't want me around."

He rested his chin on the top of her head. "Juju, you worthless cow," he whispered.

He would always want her around.

They drove westward down Rue de Rivoli. On their left, stretching block after block, the arched windows and brown stone of the Louvre formed an imposing wall.

Mourad turned suddenly, darting down a narrow stone archway to emerge on Place du Carrousel, the cobblestoned roundabout at the entrance to the largest art museum in the world. A perfectly groomed box hedge blanketed the center of the circle while the warren of the Louvre's many wings rose up around them. Between them and the structure, a glass pyramid rose up out of the ground like a massive cut jewel.

Mayla sat up straight, leaving his shoulder colder and his side empty. Damn.

"I know what you are thinking," Mourad said.

Thiago doubted it.

"You are thinking there isn't time enough tonight to experience the mysteries of this, the mistress of museums."

No. That wasn't it at all.

"Well, my friends, this is true." Mourad slowed the car and crept around the roundabout. "For over six hundred years, this place has collected treasures. Many days it takes to explore. Several lifetimes would be required to comprehend the beauties it holds. Yet, when we are here, we must at least say we visited.

"And when we visit the greatest of all museums, we may be forgiven for indulging in the greatest of all creations, *n'est ce pas?*"

Mourad took the little white box from the seat beside him and passed it back. Thiago opened it to discover four small wooden spatulas and four perfect meringues, each slightly larger than a golf ball.

"Mourad, you are *merveilleux!*" Mayla said. She reached for a confection covered in white chocolate, dipping into it with a spatula and scooping some into her mouth. With a look of delirious rapture, she turned toward Thiago. "Edible art. Mmmm."

Thiago tried one covered in dark chocolate. The crunchy meringue melted on his tongue, chased with a sweet cream infused with hazelnut and cappuccino. Heavenly.

With a smile as guileless as a child's, Mayla took his hand in hers.

As they returned to Rue de Rivoli, Thiago's mind raced. He could think of no better way to spend his days than sharing heaven with Mayla.

⚜

With Thiago at her side, a perfect postcard of Paris unfolded before Mayla in a whirlwind tour as the setting sun dyed the sky. The Louvre…Palais Royal…Jardin des Tuilleries…

While driving away from Tuilleries Gardens, she saw Mourad consult a folded piece of paper in his hand. The handwriting on the paper jarred her. She recognized it. It was her own.

But she didn't remember writing anything like that…

And then, suddenly, she did.

Like a sonic boom, it hit her: ten years ago, she had written out her dream trip to Paris on that piece of paper. Today, they were following the tour she had planned. The one she and Thiago had never taken.

Emotion clogged her throat for the second time that afternoon. As recently as yesterday, she would have blamed Thiago for the naïveté of trying to regain lost time. Right now, however, she was so enchanted by the city and overwhelmed with his thoughtfulness that her capacity for resentment was at an all-time low. Their plans must have meant a lot to him if he had kept her original notes so long.

She considered saying something about their itinerary, but decided against it. What purpose would it serve?

She leaned against Thiago's side. His chiseled arm hugging her shoulders was as close to a dream come true as reality allowed.

At the Arc de Triomphe, where the wind never ceased blowing no matter how calm the day, they paid their respects at the flame burning over the Tomb of the Unknown Soldier. Then they proceeded to the top of the arch, climbing a never-ending spiral of narrow stairs until their legs burned.

"Now I know what it's like to be trapped inside a conch shell," Thiago said.

At the top, a hundred and fifty feet above the ground, they looked out over the city.

The arch held pride of place on the enormous roundabout of Place

Charles de Gaulle. Beneath them, twelve streets radiated in all directions into the city like spokes of a wheel. White and yellow streetlights illuminated the various avenues.

"*Quelle heure est-il?*" a deep voice asked nearby.

"Almost ten," came the reply.

Mayla nudged Thiago and indicated the Eiffel Tower rising in the south. As if on command, white spots of light began dancing on the tower like a jubilation of fireflies. *Ooohs* and *aaahs* and applause greeted the display.

"It would be so easy to believe the city is showing off just for us," Thiago said, articulating Mayla's private thoughts.

He shifted to stand behind her and wrapped her in his arms like a human security blanket. Mayla sighed with contentment, relaxing her spine to melt against him.

Here, at the top of Napoleon's monument to himself, everything coalesced into a gleaming, golden moment. Thiago holding her, practically reading her mind as he used to do. Paris spilling around them. The last tints of a spectacular sunset painting the sky. She wished she could stop time. Freeze it. Make this one fragile experience last indefinitely...

His breath warmed her temple. His rough-shaven cheek pressed against her ear. Every nerve awoke, shivering with winter-fresh anticipation. When he lowered his head and kissed the side of her neck, hungry and deliberate, the embers of her heart that had laid banked and cool all evening flared into flames. Mayla closed her eyes as her temperature rose.

She turned to him, wove her fingers into his hair, and kissed him with an old fever that had only grown stronger in the time they had spent apart.

But kissing him was not as she remembered.

When she knew him, he had been young. Eager. Coltish. Overflowing with wild potential. Any intimate contact with him had filled her with excitement and granted her access to his never-ending supply of energy. Then, they had come together like two candles to burn with one flame. But now—

Thiago's kiss consumed her like a wildfire, igniting and engulfing every part of her in an instant. His raw potential had matured into contained power. The hands that held her moved with a gentleness that belied their strength. Every place he touched flared with new awareness as if awakened from a lifetime asleep. She clung to him, not trusting her legs. He was an elemental force; a sculpted god come to life.

When they drew apart, she opened her eyes to gaze into his. The naked emotion she saw there seared her soul.

"I. Missed. You."

Mayla nodded, not trusting herself to answer.

He kissed her again. Her hands trembled as fires raged.

"Stay with me tonight," Thiago whispered, his breath hot on her ear, scorching her spine. "Come home with me."

Oh yes yes yes yes, her body cried. To her, home was not a matter of geography, attached to a place. It was a matter of proximity—anywhere he happened to be.

Her imagination soared with visions of Thiago and her together, skin to skin, nothing between them. A shiver of anticipation raced through her.

A night with him all to herself was what she needed. No need to make plans that would never materialize. No need for commitment. No need for a future.

But even as she thought these things, she recognized them for the lies they were. At one time, she had planned a life with this man. Every time she touched him, every breath she drew near him, reminded her of how those plans had died. Spending the night together wouldn't resurrect what they had. In all likelihood, when he left after this weekend—this time, for good—it would drive the final nail in the wall around her heart.

The sparkling tower before them blurred, fading into the background. Mayla's focus shifted, instead, to the unsettling army of tall metal spikes surrounding the perimeter of the platform on which they stood. Rather than making her feel safe from falling, the sudden awareness of being fenced in filled her with foreboding.

Once, they had a relationship based on the rich depth of shared emotion. But Thiago's cavalier attitude toward her dreams had destroyed their love. If she was willing to push the past aside to spend a single night with him, didn't that prove how right he had been to discount her ambitions?

The thought terrified her.

⚜

As soon as he spoke, Thiago sensed the change in Mayla. The desire he had tasted was still there, but it was masked by something new flickering in her eyes. Not anger. Or resentment. Those he would have understood. It took him a moment to place it.

Fear.

The concept of Mayla fearing anything was so foreign that he blinked, surprised. In that split second, the strange emotion he had sensed in her vanished so completely, he suspected he had imagined it. Sadness reigned in its place.

Mayla took his hand in hers, her melancholy smile so pure it hurt him to breathe.

She was going to leave him. He could see it in her eyes. It took every iota of self-control not to tighten his grip in an effort to anchor her there with him.

"We planned on forever, once," she said. "Every night was ours. But a night together isn't a way I can play What Could Have Been. It would just serve to remind me of what never was."

She walked away, disappearing down the dark staircase while he stood rooted to the spot, as unable to move as if he were carved out of stone. Conversations and comments swirled around him, but all Thiago heard was the roar of regret pounding in his ears.

The Eiffel Tower dimmed. The lights no longer danced. The magic was gone.

25

Nightmares

THIAGO FOLLOWED MAYLA down the spiraling stairs from the arch, but her head start, the crowds, and the traffic conspired to keep him from catching up to her. When he reached the car, he discovered she had told Mourad she'd take a bus home.

In silence, they rode back to le Parisien. Mourad held the car door for Thiago to exit. Then, nodding with a solemnity usually reserved for deathbed visits, he drove away. Thiago slogged to his cottage. He had been so full of energy when he was with Mayla, but when she left, it all left with her.

Traffic hummed in the distance. Nearby rustlings betrayed the presence of night creatures. Here, away from the city lights, stars dotted the sky.

The night was perfect.

So was Mayla. Not "perfect" like a princess enshrined on a pedestal to be idolized and objectified. Perfect for him. Driven, competitive Mayla, who would plan life to the final breath, if possible, had her flaws. He knew that. But he had a few as well. Somehow, when they were together, an alchemy of sorts transformed even their dullest traits into something dazzling.

Usually.

Unless he did something dazzlingly stupid. Like suggesting they have a quick, cheap hookup.

Of course she didn't want a fling. Neither did he. His moment of weakness a decade ago had haunted him every moment since, mocking him for his short-sightedness, taunting him with the tattered remains of the plans they had made together. Now, Mayla was back in his life. For the next two days, he had a narrow window of opportunity to reverse the finality of his mistakes. Asking her to stay with him had been such a rookie move. At the time, caught up in the mystique of Mayla, all he could think about was how much he wanted her. But he had failed to articulate how much he *always* wanted her.

As Thiago entered the house, he kicked something across the floor. While he was out, someone had slipped a copy of *CECI* under his door. The picture of him dancing with Mayla's groom had been defaced as if by a juvenile delinquent. One look at the revolting, borderline illiterate message scrawled across the cover confirmed who the culprit was: Bruno.

Way to build team camaraderie.

Thiago refused to let the vile man ruin his night. He pitched the tabloid into the trash—then snatched it out again, folding it back to better see the page that had fallen open when it fell.

Tough Guy scowled at him in living color, surrounded by several of Paris's finest. "Notorious Jewel Thief Apprehended at Polo Fête!" the headline trumpeted.

"Police, acting on an anonymous tip, successfully apprehended international jewel thief Jakub Nekovar exiting the chic Monde du Polo party (see p. 3) Thursday night.

"Nekovar is charged with the robbery of several notable partygoers, including Dr. Aristide Boisselot, Dean of Flambeaux University, and beloved socialite Mme. Estelle Delacroix (pictured below, in vintage Chanel). Authorities place the combined value of the items Nekovar succeeded in liberating at an estimated €1.4 million. Thanks to the anonymous tipster, all items stolen have been recovered and returned.

"Nekovar, however, has neither recovered his freedom nor been returned to the streets to prey upon Parisian society. Having traded his hand-tailored cotton seersucker suits for prison garb, he awaits trial. He is also wanted by authorities in Prague for his alleged roles in other, more successful, high-profile thefts there in April."

Thiago replaced the publication into the bin where it belonged.

So his eyes weren't playing tricks on him. He hadn't imagined seeing his traveling companion last night.

He spared two seconds to wonder if Swizzle Stick had also been caught thieving. But the longer he thought about her, the more vividly he could still feel her hands on him. A tiny, involuntary shudder slithered through him. Perhaps she had successfully evaded Nekovar's clutches and had avoided the inevitable result of a life of crime. He doubted it.

He splashed cold water on his face and hands until he felt clean, and was soon in bed.

He considered getting up and pouring himself a drink.

Then he thought better of it. If he was honest with himself, a drink wasn't what he wanted.

He wanted Mayla.

The memory of her kiss filled him, more warming than cognac. He reached for it, trying to hold it close, experience it again, but it eluded him—flitting through the chambers of his consciousness, systematically shutting the lights out, dooming him to fall into a dreamless sleep.

The dream was always the same. Though it hadn't haunted Mayla in months, tonight it struck with a vengeance. She slept, but found no rest as history replayed in graphic detail, every element glaring and hyper-focused.

Nighttime. Ten years ago.

She had been up since four a.m. exercising the Calvo polo ponies, feeding them, mucking stalls, grooming, cleaning tack, and training. Twenty-hour days were easier to handle when one was twenty-three. Though Señor Calvo, Thiago's father, didn't approve of female polo players, he had no problem with female grooms and trainers.

"Girls work harder for cheaper," he was fond of saying.

Young Thiago would cringe and cover his eyes with his hand. "Dad. Stop. You're embarrassing yourself."

But nothing ever embarrassed Señor Calvo. Why should it? Everyone knew what he said was true, including Mayla, who leapt at the opportunity to train and groom for the Calvos. If she'd had any money, she would have paid for the privilege to learn from the best polo players in the world.

In two days, Thiago—the hotshot Argentinian up-and-comer—was headed to France for a charity match. Though Mayla was accompanying him as his groom, everyone knew the two were inseparable.

They lounged in the tack room, sipping *Fernet con Coca*, cell phones out, a crazy quilt of guide books to Paris, maps, and notes all around them. For weeks, Mayla had planned where they would go when they reached the city. She had memorized bus routes and metro lines. Neither had been to Paris before. She could not wait to go on this adventure with the man she adored.

Around midnight, Señor Calvo stopped by, his wide shoulders

blocking the moonlight shining through the doorway. "Nicolas Pérez called. He needs some players for a match tomorrow."

"I'm in," Thiago said.

"Me too," said Mayla.

"Oh, I don't think so." Señor Calvo's condescending laughter hid a razor's edge. Reaching toward her, he tweaked her long ponytail. "The men would run all over a pretty little thing like you."

Upon seeing his indulgent smile, she should have stopped and let the matter drop. Should have held her tongue. Should have just let it go.

In her waking hours, as she relived these events, she often wondered if she could have lived with herself if she *had* stopped.

But she hadn't. Instead, she'd said, "I'm good enough to work, but not play?"

The smile vanished. "What are you aiming for, Girlie?"

With the enthusiasm of youth, she spoke her goals aloud. "I want my own breeding and training farm. Someday. But first, I want to go pro."

"Pah!" Señor Calvo waved her ambition aside as if it were nothing. "Polo is a man's game." Shaking his head at her naïveté, he left, refusing any rebuttal.

"Don't cross Dad," Thiago said, petting her, running his hand up and down the curve of her spine as she shook with anger. "He can be...difficult."

Well, so could she, Mayla decided. She would show them both how much her dreams meant to her.

The next day, while Thiago warmed up, Mayla approached one of the team captains.

"I hear your forward broke his foot," she said.

"*Sí.*"

"Who is replacing him?"

He indicated a stringy-looking man who rode like an ungainly bird, elbows flapping, legs flopping. "Lautaro. My cousin. A no-goaler. From the city." He shook his head in despair.

"If you have the horses, I know a two-goaler who'd like to play."

"*¿Quién es?*"

"Me."

The hope that had sparked in his eyes died. Unimpressed and uninterested, he turned away, muttering.

"I'm sorry. My Spanish, it isn't what it should be," Mayla said, shocked at her own audacity. "His name is Valentin. My, er, brother's college roommate." She bit her tongue to make it shut up.

The rival captain turned to her and smiled, his hope reincarnated. "A two-goaler, you say?"

Mayla nodded. "He would love nothing more than to play today. Do you have a shirt? I'll take it to him."

With her heart threatening to pound through her ears, she hurried back to the Calvo trailer, where she cut off her ponytail, used a stub of eyeliner to smudge her upper lip enough to suggest a mustache, and bound her breasts with polo bandages. Within minutes, she was wearing an oversized polo shirt with an enormous "1" on it, mounted on a nervy black gelding, waiting for the game to start.

The game in her dream played out as it had in real life, in a whirlwind of excitement. Up and down the field they raced, stopping and turning and making a hundred decisions every second.

Valentin was immediately accepted as a valuable member of the team. No one questioned his judgment. No one made crude comments about how he looked in the saddle. No one reduced Valentin to the sum of his body parts or suggested that his place was anywhere but on a horse.

Mayla played her heart out, reveling in the joy of the game. When her team won, for a brief, shining moment, she was on top of the world.

But the higher you are, the farther you fall.

It takes very little to warp a dream into a nightmare.

When Señor Calvo approached the opposing team to congratulate the winners, he became apoplectic when he discovered Valentin's real identity.

"How dare you mock me! Go against my orders!"

Grabbing Mayla by the back of her shirt, he dragged her off the horse as everyone—including Thiago—stared, stupefied.

"I forbade you to play. You defied me."

Mayla shrugged out of his grasp, so angry that silver shooting stars twinkled at the periphery of her vision. "All due respect, sir, you do not own me. You told me polo was a man's game. I proved to you that it's for everyone."

A crowd gathered, drawn to the drama like flies to manure. Señor Calvo, whom she had idolized as an employer, whom she had adored as a mentor, erupted, turning into something monstrous and unfamiliar before her eyes.

"Gold-digging bitch! As if my son would ever align himself with someone so unladylike. So untrustworthy. Get out!"

"What?" On some level, Mayla honestly thought he was joking.

The man towered over her, rage smoldering in his eyes. "You heard me. You're fired. I will be home in two hours. You will be gone before then." Turning on his heel, he left her behind.

Thiago wouldn't let this happen, Mayla told herself. She waited for him to say something, to stand up to his father. But as his stunned son reeled in surprise, Señor Calvo grabbed him by the collar and dragged him away.

Every time she relived that moment, Thiago's silence broke Mayla's heart.

Brreeeng!

A text alert dinged on Mayla's phone just as the dream reset and began again. She sat up in bed, groggy and still tired, her sheets moist with sweat.

The message from her realtor in America energized her:

Looking good. Should hear something definitive by Monday. Though offer is lower than they want, I expect they'll accept it. No one else has considered the property. Owners are antsy to sell. Don't break open the champagne just yet, but OK to chill it. Salut!

Sleep vanished. The pall of her dream disappeared. In the darkness just before dawn, Mayla climbed out of bed and got dressed. Time to get her head out of the clouds, stop thinking about Thiago, and start planning for her future.

26

Runaway

A THIN, GRAY MIST of early morning fog blanketed the grounds of the Parisien. Thiago inhaled, breathing in the cool air heavy with the scent of mown grass. Few things in the world smelled as invigorating. Mounted on Zoelie, with two horses on his left and another two on his right, he made his way away from the barns to the exercise track.

Nothing compared to riding at sunrise. Birdsong greeted the day with a fanfare as the sky glowed like fire. The horses trotted together side by side around the wide dirt track. Zoelie moved easily, snorting in time to her footfalls, a sound more soothing and regular than a metronome. Thiago's muscles limbered up and his thoughts wandered, coalescing to a single focus.

Mayla.

Last night, the whole time they were together, he kept expecting her to bring up their past. To clear the air. Or to accuse him. Or to drive home a point. But aside from her references to his parents, it was as if their history had been erased. They had continued on with their lives, chasing their individual aims, moving ever apart from each other.

Yet, after all this time, she still moved him. When they touched, the indefinable frisson of chemistry still sparked. And when they kissed, everything else paled, fading in importance until only ghostly outlines remained. With Mayla nearby, nothing else mattered.

His horses pricked their ears at the sounds of hoofbeats some distance ahead. Soon, indistinct equine shapes appeared in the misty morning. As if his thoughts had taken tangible form, he recognized Mayla riding Cantata in the middle of her little herd.

Thiago trotted on. Exercising horses was one of the most mundane of tasks. It didn't involve active training or fancy riding. All it required was the basic skill to keep a few ponies moving together in the same direction, yet he knew if given the opportunity, he would be content to watch the woman ahead of him ride in endless laps, indefinitely.

The sky lightened; the fog began to dissipate. As Mayla and her charges neared the barns, they veered off toward their shed row, their exercise over. When she left, however, Thiago saw he was not alone on the track. In addition to a few grooms, he recognized several others. On the other side of the dirt oval, Carson rode with perfect, show-ring equitation. And ahead of where Mayla had been, Bruno had his hands full with a high-spirited bay gelding.

As Thiago watched, Bruno jerked on the bay's lead rope trying to correct him and bring him under better control. The animal threw his head up at the heavy-handed treatment. Suddenly, the horse flung himself sideways in a frenzied dance of hooves and legs. With an explosion of power, he reared up and pulled back, ripping the line out of Bruno's hand and taking off.

Bruno bellowed with impotent fury.

Thiago understood the dilemma. He faced it too. He couldn't simply drop the lines of his horses and ride to help, but there was also no way to maneuver his little herd quickly enough to head off the loose gelding. Nor was there a place to stop and tie up the extra horses.

Bruno tried to swipe at the halter as the horse raced by. He was hardly a calming presence. The bay darted to the left, easily avoiding him.

Swearing like a line cook in the middle of the dinner rush, Bruno dragged his remaining horses toward the barn to put them up so he could go after the loose one.

The bay whinnied, shrill and loud. He bolted around the track, kicking up dust, making mad rushes toward the riders, but never coming close enough to catch. The other horses, feeding off his nervous energy, became antsy and began pulling at their own leads. Blowing through wide nostrils, the gelding bucked like a bronco, then bounded away, racing like a thing possessed—off the track toward the open gate along the road.

Mayla appeared in the doorway of the barn. She took in the situation and ducked back into the building's shadow—but not for long.

Within moments, she appeared, shaking a small can of grain.

Instantly, every horse pricked up its ears.

The crazed bay changed course. With head and tail held high, he trotted over, nickering happily at the thought of breakfast.

Mayla gave him a handful of feed, then caught the rope. "Easy," she said, patting the wet, dark neck.

Thiago drew near, but Bruno got there first.

"What do you think you're doing?" Bruno demanded. He shoved Mayla away from the bay, scarcely grabbing the rope in time to keep the horse from taking off again.

Without conscious thought, Thiago reached down from the saddle and caught hold of Mayla's arm, saving her from falling.

"I think I'm helping you catch your horse," she snapped. "Maybe keep it from running into traffic, getting splattered?"

Without a word of thanks—without uttering a single civil syllable— Bruno took the bay and stomped away.

27

Power Play

AFTER EXERCISING THE HORSES and feeding them breakfast, Mayla headed out for her morning run.

As she trekked through the wooded footpaths, thoughts of La-May Farms—her own place, her own broodmares, her own training facility—inspired her. Thirty-five acres on the outskirts of Lexington. Surrounded by a high stone fence, with a clear river running along the northern border, it held enormous promise. But the barns and paddocks needed a significant amount of work; neglectful owners had allowed leaky roofs, termites, dry rot, and vermin to compromise the structures. The main house also needed upgrading, though the foundation was sound. The necessary improvements would be both extensive and expensive, forcing her to make such a lowball offer. But as Mama had been fond of saying, she had grown up pinching pennies to pay attention.

She repeated her realtor's text from this morning over and over: "I expect they'll accept it...Don't break open the champagne, but OK to chill it..."

Her own home. Hers. She had never had a permanent residence—a place no one could force her to leave.

Her heart beat with anticipation as she imagined her place fully renovated and open for business. Intercollegiate scrimmages on summer evenings. Arena tournaments in the winter. Bridle paths for leisurely hacks. Freshly painted house and barns. Acres of strong, safe fencing. Foals frisking in the fields.

And Thiago.

The thought was so unexpected, she increased her pace, but the memories of last night followed her. Thiago holding her hand. Thiago holding *her*. His touch. His laugh. The way his kisses burned like bourbon and made her thirst for more.

The trees blurred. The path became a featureless ribbon unrolling beneath her feet. She ran until her lungs burned, until her legs felt like jelly. But she couldn't outrun the visions in her head. Every step underscored the fact that any home she dreamed of included him.

Back at the flat, Mayla showered in record time, cleaning up enough to be presentable for her clinic.

Her stomach grumbled, reminding her that breakfast was the most important meal of the day, but a quick glance into the cupboards and mini-fridge yielded nothing portable but a baguette. She tore off a hunk of the heel, crammed it in her mouth, and charged out the door.

Laudine and Yvonne arrived early while Mayla was still tacking up.

"Mademoiselle Alvarez?" Laudine approached, holding a bulky black duffel bag. "Do you have a moment? I wanted to show you something before the rest of the class arrives."

Mayla finished winding the polo wrap around Widdershins's leg, then left the mare in her stall while she followed her student outside.

A few yards from the shed row, Yvonne sat on her leggy chestnut, holding Ombré, Laudine's handsome buckskin gelding.

Laudine patted the caramel-colored neck as she took her horse's lead rope. She ran her fingers through Ombré's long black mane.

"I'm not sure I can bring myself to shave this off," she confessed. "I think it is beautiful."

"It is," Mayla said.

Laudine sighed. "But it is not, perhaps, what makes *him* beautiful. He is a good horse. A good horse, with or without the mane, which will certainly grow back if I should shave it off."

"You're in the lesson stage at the moment," Mayla reminded her. "You have just begun to dip your toe in the water—and polo is an ocean. There is no need for you to take the plunge, as it were, and roach Ombré's mane off right away."

"Oh, I'm not. Not today, anyway. But as an artist, this is making me do some soul searching about my beliefs on the definition of beauty."

Setting her bag down, Laudine reached into it and drew out the same clippers that had caused her horse so much consternation a few short days ago.

Oh no. Here we go. I don't have time for a full-blown learn-to-tolerate-the-clippers lesson today. Plus, it wouldn't be fair to the other students...

"Wait—" Mayla said.

But Laudine didn't wait. She flicked the switch.

The clippers buzzed to life.

The buckskin switched his tail with half-hearted enthusiasm.

As Laudine lightly held the lead in one hand, she ran the clippers over her horse's bridle path, shearing off the three inches of mane immediately behind his ears so the halter and bridle would fit better.

Ombré stood quietly, basking in the sun. He didn't even nicker at being left alone when Yvonne turned her horse and rode away.

"That is amazing!" Mayla said when Laudine had finished. "I am entirely impressed! He was a basket case on Tuesday. What did you do?"

"I took your advice."

Laudine put the clippers away. "I thought: here is a horse that is terrified of anything buzzing on him, especially around his face. And who can blame him? He's an animal on the wrong end of the food chain, whose instinct is to run away from things that threaten him. I wanted to test your teaching. I wanted to see how readily he could be taught to overcome his instincts. So I have used the desensitizing techniques you showed us."

"Good for you. It worked!"

With a wave of a calloused hand, the woman brushed off her accomplishment as if it were no more noteworthy than taking out the trash. "Oh, that's nothing. If you would be so kind as to hold him… "

Yvonne established a vantage point some distance away. She spoke to a few of the other students who had arrived with their horses. They, too, stopped and watched from afar.

Laudine handed Mayla the lead. She rummaged in her duffel and pulled out a small chainsaw.

Apprehension flooded Mayla with a blast of adrenaline. She took an involuntary step backward.

"Laudine. I'm not sure this is a good ide—"

Laudine pulled the starter cord. With a damp burp of oil-rich gas, the chainsaw roared to life.

Brmmm-brmmm-brUMMMMMMM! Laudine revved the motor like a ten-year-old boy on a minibike.

Without so much as cocking an ear at the noise, Ombré stood like a statue.

"IT AMAZES ME," Laudine said over the racket. "THIS COULD LITERALLY DESTROY HIM. HE SHOULD RUN FROM IT. IT'S NOT IN HIS BEST INTEREST TO STAND THERE. BUT HE HAS LEARNED NOT TO CARE."

She walked around the buckskin, moving the chainsaw as she went. She held it high and brought it low.

The horse stood still.

She moved it near enough to cause serious damage—a severed artery, a shattered leg—if he moved.

He didn't.

Laudine shut the machine off and put it back in the bag. "You have opened my eyes," she said. "I have learned more from you than I ever thought possible."

"You did some amazing work in a very short time." Mayla handed back the lead. The watching students joined her in hearty applause.

"It didn't take long at all," Laudine said quietly. "Just a few days."

"Imagine what could happen if you kept up this level of training over a period of years," Mayla said.

"Just imagine," Laudine echoed.

⚜

Thiago had spent the early morning hand-walking Sergio's horses and grazing them on the outskirts of the field. Ibby and Zoelie were his last customers. As he let the mares nibble some grass, two of Mayla's students passed him on their way toward Team North America's shed row.

A sparrow-small woman mounted on a sprightly chestnut chattered with animation, maintaining a stream of mostly one-way conversation with her more substantial companion, who walked with genteel dignity alongside a buckskin.

"I'm not saying you shouldn't, you understand. Not my place. But you shouldn't. It's not safe."

The matronly woman said something too low for Thiago to hear.

"I know. I know," Sparrow twittered. "I'm your friend and I'm worried about you, but whatever you decide, I support you a hundred thousand percent. Is there anything I can do to help?"

"Yes," came the quiet reply. "Hold Ombré while I go inside."

When Mayla came out and joined them, the morning sunshine lit her as lovingly as if she were Hollywood royalty. The rays rode her curves, highlighting her assets, inviting his appreciation.

How he wished he could take a snapshot. Preserve the moment in high-definition. He could study her forever and never grow tired of the view.

He forced himself to blink. The last thing he needed was for Mayla to think he was some leering Lothario. He tore his eyes away and looked at his horses instead.

But the vision remained indelibly imprinted in his mind.

He gripped the lead rope, remembering how she had pressed her body against his last night. Every plain, every hill, every valley of the landscape that made her *her* was etched in his memory, right down to how the contour of her arm had felt when he helped her maintain her balance this morning.

Though tense with anger at Bruno for shoving her, Mayla hadn't shaken off his help. That meant something, right?

All it means is you rank higher than Bruno in her estimation. To be fair, a donkey's arse probably ranks higher than you do as well.

This might be true, but after Mayla's decade-long avoidance, he chose to view it as a positive development.

28

Basic Training

AFTER EVERYONE HAD WARMED UP, Mayla surveyed her students. "Today, we're going to focus on one of the key tenets of polo: taking a man," she said.

"Well, it's about time," Doreen cracked.

"Taking him where?" Yvonne said.

"The older I get, the less it matters," Doreen said.

"I'll take *him*, please and thank you." Proue nodded toward the shed row.

Several students seconded Proue's comments.

Mayla followed their gaze.

Thiago led two horses through the shed row's green door. His wide shoulders—shoulders her arms had encircled last night as she pulled him closer—tapered to strong, narrow hips. The morning sun danced over his body, gracing him with an aura of vibrancy that shone even at this distance.

Mayla's breath stuck in her lungs as if she had stepped into an icy pool.

Of course Proue and Yvonne and Doreen wanted him. Every woman with a pulse would want him. And she'd had him all to herself last night. She had laughed with him, held onto him, blended her breath with his—right before she let him go.

Even now, she wasn't sure if she was proud of her choice or if she regretted it. Regardless, it was the right one and she would make it again, if given the opportunity.

Probably.

Almost definitely.

"Can we take him now? Or do we have to wait?" Doreen said.

Mayla reminded herself that she had made a reasoned decision. An adult decision. And as a reasonable adult, she certainly wasn't going to stand idly by while other women ogled the man of her dreams. Even if those dreams were her nightmares.

She moved Widdershins to stand parallel to Yvonne and her horse, head to head, side by side.

"Ahem." Mayla waited until she had regained her students' attention. "To 'take a man' is not a kidnapping or an abduction. It means when you play polo, you never ride alone. When you're on the field, find an unguarded opponent and see to it that he—or she—has a shadow. A close, aggressive, determined shadow."

"How close?" Yvonne twisted her hair.

Rather than answer her student, Mayla nudged her mare to move sideways, crowding Yvonne, bumping against her horse.

"Ooop! Hey!" Yvonne yelped.

Yvonne's horse stepped away. Mayla and Widdershins followed.

"On a rideoff, you'll get close enough to bump your opponent—"

"Ooof! I'm your opponent?"

"For now. Out of the way and out of play."

"It's so... personal," said Yvonne. "Like bumper cars on horseback."

"Ideally, you can maneuver so you get your knee ahead of your opponent's. Like this," Mayla demonstrated. "Then you can steer them and control where they go."

"Hallelujah," said Doreen.

"We're going to practice, but be careful," Mayla said. "All joking aside: no surprises. It's essential that you don't smack into anyone at a sharp angle. You want to ride your opponent off the line of the ball, not blast her to the ground."

"So that is taking a man." Yvonne said, adjusting her reins and re-settling in her saddle.

"Not in my book." Proue chewed her bottom lip, still looking toward Thiago in a way that left no doubt in Mayla's mind what the woman would say had he invited *her* to spend the night with him.

⚜

Thiago couldn't wait to talk to Mayla and discuss her training philosophy, for though he continued to rack his brain, he couldn't for the life of him determine the purpose of the earlier chainsaw drill. Even from their vantage point many yards away, neither Ibby nor Zoelie had appreciated it.

He watched Mayla trot Widdershins out, giving encouragement and instructing her students as they practiced mallet desensitizing and did a few warm-up drills. Most of the women taking the class could ride well enough, but their polo skills left much to be desired.

They hit the ball too early. Or too late. Too close to the horse. Or too far away. They twisted in the saddle when they should stay straight, sat in the saddle's seat when they should stand in their stirrups, and hit with all the accuracy of a drunken golfer in a hurricane. God forbid they should ride with chainsaws.

"Time to go in, girls," he said. "I don't think I can take much more of this."

As he led the horses to the barn, he had the curious sense of being watched. Without turning around to verify his suspicions, he knew he was a focal point of the class's attention. Did they know who he was? Did they care? Were they aware of his history with their teacher?

Zoelie discovered a patch of grass near the shed row entrance that merited closer attention. Thiago indulged her while Ibby relaxed her lower lip and snoozed in the warmth of a sunbeam.

A woman whooped behind him. "Hey!" she squawked with the shock of a lesson learned.

The grazing mare snorted.

"I agree," Thiago patted the flat, strong neck.

Mayla had a soft spot for people who wanted to learn to play and a knack for finding their hidden talents. Her unbounded empathy was one of the things he most admired about her.

He rarely worked with new players, and for good reason: the ratio of his rapidly thinning patience to a novice's skill level was never in favor of anyone enjoying the lesson for long. That's why he had needed her help yesterday with de la Foret.

And she had helped. Not only in bringing de la Foret on board as a potential patron, but also in easing much of the weight of reproach Thiago had carried around all these years. With any luck, today they could continue to repair their relationship. If he dared to let his thoughts run free, it wouldn't take much to envision reconciliation. Forgiveness. A renewed alliance that formed the foundation of a bright future together.

Careful, a little voice of self-preservation whispered. *You're getting ahead of yourself. You came here to play polo, not play with Mayla. Let her in your head too much and your game will suffer. First things first.*

Thiago set his shoulders, shook off the feeling of being watched, and took his horses into the barn. Time to grab a bite to eat while attempting to do the impossible: put Mayla out of his mind and get ready for today's match.

When Mayla returned to her flat after her lesson, the heavenly aroma of scrambled eggs, bacon, and fresh brioche greeted her as she opened the door.

Dripping with sweat, her stomach snarling with hunger, she nearly tripped over Carson. Perfectly dressed and groomed as always, he and Rochelle thumbed through *CECI* over the remains of their breakfasts.

Mayla grabbed a piece of bread and loaded it with the fluffy eggs awaiting her in the skillet. "Lifesaver!"

"We're officially out of food," Rochelle said.

"Which is why I'm here," said Carson. "All I had was wine."

"In other news: your boyfriend made the front page."

"Frolicking with the help." Carson ducked as Rochelle aimed a playful slap at his head.

Mayla refused to acknowledge them while she beelined for the restroom, but when she returned to the kitchen a few moments later, both turned to her expectantly.

Carson toyed with the glass of tuberoses still on the table. "How was your date?"

"It was good. We ate. We walked. We came home early."

"Alone," Rochelle said.

Mayla piled a plate with more food. "Mmmmmm...How was yours?"

"Lost my trunks swimming, drank a wee bit too much absinthe, got locked in at Disneyland, then couldn't find a bus to bring us home till a ridiculous time this morning."

"So: typical."

Carson shrugged modestly.

"Same here," Mayla said.

Two pairs of eyes asking silent questions that made her defenses rise. "What?"

"We need details," said Rochelle.

"Lots of them," Carson added.

Mayla laughed. "Not going to happen, sports fans."

If she closed her eyes, she could relive every moment of her date, including the kiss.

Especially the kiss.

But she wasn't about to share her time with Thiago with anyone. She cleaned her plate and went back for more, resolutely refusing to talk about last night.

"Saw you catch Bruno's pony this morning," Carson said. "I hear he couldn't even bring himself to say 'thank you.'"

Mayla poured the last of the coffee from the French press. "I'm pretty certain someone kicked him when he was a puppy. He was in a foul mood."

"He's always in a foul mood. Someone needs to wash his mouth out with soap," Rochelle said.

Carson grew uncharacteristically serious. "Watch yourself out there. I mean it. He's a piece of work. Been booted off more teams than I can count. He plays rough."

Mayla waved her hand through the air as if clearing a bad odor. "We held him off yesterday. We'll do it again. Piece of cake."

She had no idea how wrong she was.

29

Cut and Run

GAME TWO WAS NOT REMOTELY CAKE-LIKE. From the get-go, it was full of gritty, dusty, hot, hard-hitting guerrilla warfare. Things only escalated from there.

Mayla raced down the field chasing the ball, several tons of horse-flesh thundering behind her. Everything about the game had changed since yesterday. Twenty-four hours ago, both teams had competed with the good-natured zeal of rival high school football teams. Today, the prevailing atmosphere was one of gladiators in battle. Plays were more intense, the aim deadly accurate.

Now that Thiago was rested and his teammates more familiar with his style, they advanced down the field with all the hallmarks of a tactical strike, holding their mallets high like lances. Steel bits flashed in mouths full of teeth and foam. Hooves pounded, tearing great clumps of turf from the field and flinging it like shrapnel into the air. This team was completely different from the one that played yesterday; this one rode hard, shot harder, and advanced with military exactness.

Thiago was an unstoppable force of nature. He rode like a god, head held high, shoulders wide, moving in perfect harmony with his horse. Every shot he hit sailed true, drawn like a magnet toward his team's goal.

On the first play of the game, Mayla approached him at an angle, expecting to exploit the same weakness she had taken advantage of in yesterday's match. She waited for his telltale weight shift before he dropped his mallet to hit the ball—

It never came.

Instead, he moved his horse sideways, blocking her before she could compensate and alter her swing.

The crowd cheered, but pounding hoofbeats drowned out their voices.

Subsequent plays mirrored the first as the game unspooled, chukker after chukker, with frustrating repetition.

Gone were the minute tells that telegraphed Thiago's intentions. To make matters worse, Mayla discovered that every time she prepared to take a shot, he was there to destroy it, swooping in to capitalize on any weakness and turn it to his advantage.

Get your head together! Mayla chided herself as Thiago emerged victorious after yet another rideoff.

Anger at allowing herself to be dispatched so easily lurked at the edges of her thoughts, threatening to come out of the shadows and interfere with her judgment. But anger was a game-killer. It made you reckless. It destroyed your timing. It blinded you to potential dangers and pitfalls. Above all, it did a great disservice to both your horse and your team. Riding angry meant you lost before the first play.

She patted Cantata, toying with the few wispy strands of mane at the mare's withers, drawing strength from the horse's calm reliability.

In an instant, her focus realigned.

Her man, the opposing team's Number One, was wide open. So was the ball.

Banishing her unprofessional ire, Mayla and Cantata raced down the field. The gray mare sped along, scarcely touching the ground. As they neared their target, Mayla shifted her weight back, checking her horse, slowing a bit before she hit the ball—an easy shot—

Out of nowhere, a black horse loomed, charging toward her like a frigate, with Bruno urging it on.

A sharp angle collision was inevitable. If she pulled up, Bruno's horse would hit Cantata's head and neck. If she turned Cantata aside, they would be off-balance when their opponent struck. Both actions carried a high possibility of knocking them to the ground.

Mayla braced herself.

Bruno's big black horse smacked into them: an obvious, deliberate foul.

Cantata never wavered. Though the tough little mare was knocked off-balance, she staggered, flinched, but recovered and stayed on her feet.

The moment they came into contact with each other, Bruno leaned forward and attempted to hit the ball via a neck shot.

His mallet missed the ball entirely, but the momentum of the swing bent the flexible cane shaft of the mallet. The wooden head at the end of the shaft traveled under the neck of Bruno's horse and under Cantata's neck, briefly yoking both together as it continued to whip around toward Mayla's face.

Only a sixth sense of self-preservation saved her. Mayla instinctively ducked her chin toward her chest, lowering her head, using her helmet to block the blow. The mallet slammed against her helmet with so much force it made her ears ring.

The ringing grew louder; the umpire's whistle denounced the foul.

Mayla pulled Cantata to a stop, vaguely aware of a pain in her leg. A horizontal slice slashed into her thigh. Blood seeped out, staining her whites. Looking behind her leg, she discovered that Cantata had blood on her haunches. No wonder the mare had flinched on impact.

The anger that had threatened earlier erupted now in pyroclastic fury.

She wanted to vent and spew: *What sort of scumsucking liver fluke jeopardizes not only his opponent and her horse, but his horse as well? That wasn't even a spectacular play, unless you count its spectacular ass-shattery. Of all the vile, troll turds in the world, he—*

But she knew better. Even though she had been deliberately fouled, the strict rules of sportsmanship forbade her from giving Bruno a piece of her mind.

To keep herself from spewing a stream of profanity that would solve nothing and would only earn her a penalty of her own, Mayla ground her teeth together until she heard her jaw creak.

Play stopped while she left the field to change horses.

"Vet's on his way over," Rochelle said in response to Mayla's mute rage. "I thought we'd have to bring in the ambulance."

"I'm fine," Mayla said, waving off the two young men running toward her from the medical van.

Still seething, she went back on the field.

Her head throbbed, a portent of an epic headache in the near future. She blocked out Bruno's sneer of disgust, Thiago's worried eyes, and her teammates' barely concealed outrage as she maneuvered into position for her penalty shot. Breathing deeply, intentionally, she experienced a random moment of regret that she had neglected to do any yoga this morning.

Imagining that the ball was attached to a critical part of Bruno's anatomy, she swung at it with all her strength, sending it sailing through the goal.

It wasn't enough.

As the final chukker limped to an end, Team South America won by two goals. Normally, Mayla hated losing. Today she didn't care. The only thing on her mind was getting to Cantata and seeing how badly her mare was injured.

⚜

Thiago wanted nothing more than to drop Bruno down a deep pit with a short ladder. He had never felt so powerless as when he watched the hit on Mayla take place. Her riding had been impeccable. Few other riders would have managed to keep their seat and continue playing after getting steamrolled like that.

He pitched in to help the grooms immediately after the game. The mundane tasks of unwrapping horses' legs, rubbing them with liniment, rinsing sweaty bodies with cool water, and scraping coats dry helped dull his anger. With so many capable hands helping, taking care of the ponies' needs didn't take long. When all chores were done, Thiago went searching for Bruno.

He found the wretch in the center of a knot of people congregated near the Team South America tack room. They spoke in quiet, earnest tones, outwardly so civilized. However, it wasn't difficult to see that Bruno was on the defensive; he stood with his arms crossed, a scowl etched into his face as two Monde du Polo officials and Captain Remigio grilled him about his riding. Carson and Moe from Team North America fumed on the periphery, making an official complaint to a league representative.

Thiago's inner caveman itched to smack Bruno until that scowl disappeared, but the rational, evolved part of him knew that wouldn't solve anything. It would only land him with a hefty fine.

His hand clenched into a fist anyway.

It would be worth it.

"For the last time," Bruno said, irritation amplifying the gravel in his voice, "I have no idea how the horse got hurt. Maybe a buckle scraped it or something."

"This is not a slash-and-dash bush league. The horse required veterinary attention." The league official's posh, cultured tones belied the steel beneath the surface of his words.

Captain Remigio drove the point home. "The foul was deliberate. Inappropriate at any time, but especially out of line in a goodwill exhibition game."

"I want an exhaustive examination of everything that sumbitch wore," Moe said, gnawing on a well-chewed toothpick that poked out of his mouth.

Bruno grimaced in what he must have thought was an ingratiating manner. "I apologize for the poor judgment. A bad hit, *si*." The picture of wounded innocence, he showed Moe and the authorities his boots and kneepads. "But I am at a loss as to how the injury happened. Look: I don't even wear spurs."

Thiago heard Bruno's words, but didn't believe a single syllable. From the expression on Moe's and Carson's faces, neither did they.

He started walking toward the stalls where Team North America kept their horses. Thanks to his teammate, Mayla was down a horse until Cantata healed. He knew she operated on a different revenue stream than he. Leasing a horse for the interim would be a very costly undertaking, provided she could find one suitable. Seasoned ponies that could play high-goal polo were never easy to come by.

He wanted to do something for her; something that would both aid her current situation and help bridge the gap between them.

A solution, perfect and poetic, presented itself.

Thiago pulled out his phone and began texting. So absorbed was he in his conversation, he didn't realize anyone was near until a shadow blocked out the sun.

"You were amazing. Amazing!"

Thiago looked up in surprise. "Monsieur de la Foret, how nice to see you again."

"It was eye-opening," the big man boomed. "Exhilarating! After seeing today's game, I wouldn't play unless I was in a tank, but you were fearless."

De la Foret paced beside Thiago, beaming like a man caught up in a religious awakening. "Mesmerizing. Absolutely mesmerizing. I don't care for that goalie of yours, though. A rogue trader if ever there was one."

Thiago smiled in what he hoped was a noncommittal way, though he privately agreed with Bruno's character analysis.

"That little lady I met you with the other night, she's pretty good," came the businessman's considered opinion. He wobbled his head. "She can play; holds her own out there. She's not a bad little rider."

Thiago bridled.

He tried not to take offense at the comment.

He failed.

"That 'little rider' is one of the best, most knowledgeable equine professionals I have ever met," he said.

"Maybe so. Maybe so." De la Foret shrugged. With a shrewd side-eyed glance, he said, "I daresay she's no better than that Valentin fellow."

He may be a rich, privileged, out-of-shape businessman, but he's no fool.

Thiago tipped his head in admiration. "Touché."

De la Foret smiled, his good humor infectious. "Ah, *Monsieur*, since last we met, my life, it has turned upside down. I blame you."

"Oh?"

"*Oui.* Did I not tell you? I've become a patron! *C'est vrai!* After yesterday's match, I went home with all the energy of a man half my age! I stayed up half the night watching the last five World Finals online. My Sofie accused me of watching the pornography. She does not understand my latest obsession."

"Perhaps we should get Sofie on a horse and show her how much fun she could have."

De la Foret's explosive laughter echoed through the halls and stalls. "My Sofie!" he barked. "On the field with an animal like your Number Four? Ha!" He wobbled his head in wonder at the suggestion of such lunacy.

"But seriously," he said, "I am exhilarated. I feel better than I have in many years. I want to thank you."

Thiago placed a hand on the man's shoulder, genuinely touched. "I am glad you found the same joy in the game as I do. There is no need for thanks."

"Not so. Not so. A token of my appreciation is already on its way."

As they neared the North American team's stalls, a tiny kitten mewled. The mewling continued, shrill and insistent. Thiago stopped short, looking for the little creature.

"Heh," said de la Foret, pulling out his phone with some embarrassment. "When my Sophie calls, I answer." With solemn formality, he executed a fluid, unexpectedly charming bow. "*A bientôt*, my friend." He swiped right and the mewing stopped.

❧

Mayla tried to harness her anxiety and refrain from hovering while the veterinarian sutured Cantata's cut. Under the influence of a local anesthetic, the gray mare stood patiently munching on hay.

The vet's neat mustache, tweed coat, and round, wire-rimmed glasses made Mayla feel as if she had slipped through a hole in time and emerged a hundred years earlier. Fortunately, the man exhibited a twenty-first-century competence.

"She'll be fine," he said. "Clean cut. Not too deep. No muscle damage. Keep her quiet for a few days, then some easy exercise to keep her in shape. It should heal completely, but it will take time."

Mayla nodded. She tried to pay close attention, absorbing most of what the vet said: watch out for excessive swelling, heat, signs of infection, fever, or separating stitches. But a part of her brain spun on an endless hamster wheel, reminding her that in addition to being down a horse, the unexpected vet bill was not in her budget.

"How are you?"

The smoky baritone rolled over her, a balm to her raw nerves. The question wasn't the typical off-the-cuff space filler. Its harmonics of genuine concern soothed her.

Mayla turned away from Cantata's injury as Thiago neared. He searched her face, empathy furrowing his brow, worry quirking his mouth to one side.

"I'm OK," she said. "So's she."

He leaned closer, looking deep into her eyes. "Do you have a headache or feel dizzy? Blurred vision?"

Gently, she pushed him away. "As I said: I'm fine. No concussion. Doc checked me out the second I dismounted. And he insists on a recheck tomorrow before he'll clear me to ride."

Thiago relaxed. The veneer of objectivity vanished. His relief at her safety was so complete and so candid, it brightened Mayla's day as if a cloud had moved away from the sun.

His eyes darted to the thin line of blood staining her white jeans. Mayla crossed her arms, defiant, waiting for him to say something. He must have read her mind, for he clamped his mouth shut and gave her a thin smile.

As the stitching progressed, Thiago inspected Cantata's wound, muttering a string of curses against Bruno.

Mayla's hamster wheel churned on.

There is literally no food in the flat. If you buy the farm, how are you going to pay for Cantata's vet bill, deal with her recovery time, and still eat?

Trying to ignore her worries rather than succumb to them, Mayla stood next to Thiago, resting her chin on his shoulder as she watched the vet work. Every breath she took was full of him—his latent power, his quiet authority. How she wished she could infuse herself with some of that calmness and strength.

"Take Zoelie," he said, the words little more than a whisper inches from her ear.

The hamster wheel froze.

"Beg pardon?"

Mayla knew what he had said. She just needed some time to process it.

"As your replacement. Till you find a horse to lease."

Reaching around him, she hugged him tightly, pressing him close to her heart for a moment before stepping away and reclaiming her own space. "You and your extravagant gifts," she said. "Sergio would have your head—and mine—on a platter."

Wordlessly, he pulled out his phone and showed her his most recent text exchange. "I asked. Serg' said 'yes.'"

"Thanks, but no." Mayla said. She gestured toward Cantata's injury. "If something like this happened to Zoelie or any of his horses, Sergio would never forgive me. Frankly, I'd never forgive myself."

Two league officials, one willowy and aristocratic, the other compact, with a telltale hitch of arthritic hips, appeared in the doorway. The duo walked purposefully toward them.

"This should be interesting," Thiago said. "I just saw them having a tête-à-tête with Bruno."

"Mademoiselle Alvarez," the aristocrat said. "We have finished our preliminary inquiry into today's unfortunate event and determined that though the foul was both reckless and dangerous, it was unintentional."

Thiago bristled with anger. "How can you possibly—!"

As happy as Mayla was to hear him come to her aid, this was not his mess to fix. She touched his arm, silencing him. "I can fight my own battles."

Stay civil, Mayla reminded herself. She clenched her teeth to keep from snapping. "What cut my horse?"

The tall official cast a jaundiced eye at Cantata's wound. "A fine has been levied against the offending player."

"That doesn't answer my question."

"We don't know," the other official admitted. "But we have inspected his equipment: he has no dangerous buckles on his boots or kneepads, carried no crop, and wore no spurs."

"Accidents do happen. 'Tis not a sport for the fainthearted," the first official said.

"Do I look fainthearted to you?" Mayla locked eyes with him. She held his stare, refusing to blink, until he looked away.

30

Family Feud

THIAGO WATCHED THE LEAGUE OFFICIAL look down his long nose at Mayla as if suggesting this whole debacle were all *her* fault. She stood, feet apart, shoulders squared, hands clenched as if ready for battle.

Fines be damned! He drew a sharp breath, intending to set the man straight and knock him down a peg or two.

But a subtle shake of Mayla's head stopped him, defusing him completely.

The officials said nothing more. They left as the vet finished his stitching and began to dress the wound.

Thiago's blood surged through his veins, spoiling for a fight. He marveled at Mayla's poise and composure.

"What an ass," he said.

She shrugged, but did not disagree.

"I have to run," he told her. "Shower. Shoot starts soon. But I can cancel—"

"No," Mayla said, her voice firm. "You have a commitment. I understand. There is no need for you to stay."

He didn't like the sound of that. "You sure you're OK?"

A long look passed between them, but he could not tell what she was thinking. No poker player was more inscrutable, or more unreadable.

She nodded. "I'll see you later."

He wanted to ask her to promise that would happen.

He wanted to tell her that when the accident occurred, every event in his life appeared ashen. Without her in the picture, both light and color faded from his world. He wanted to talk about last night and ask forgiveness for old sins. He wanted to shower her with gifts, protect her from all the world's *patánes*, utter vows that would never be broken. But here, in the hallway of the barn, both of them crusted with sweat and grime, not to mention blood, such things seemed incongruous.

Instead of saying anything, he brought her hand to his lips and kissed it. Then, silently cursing the timing, he left.

Outside, on the way to his cottage, he saw Rochelle leading Bogo to turnout.

"*Bonjour,* Monsieur Calvo," Rochelle said. "You are looking for Mayla?"

"I just left her, thanks."

I just left her. He didn't like the sound of that, either.

Struck with a brainstorm, he veered in Rochelle's direction. Perhaps he could convince her to talk Mayla into using Zoelie as an interim mount.

As he drew near, before he could say anything, Rochelle's phone rang. "Ah. Poor Philippe." She swiped left, ignoring the call.

He pulled up short.

Rochelle arched an eyebrow. "You think me harsh, *non?*

"Nooooo."

"*Vraiment.*" She tossed her head. "If I am not good enough for him before he sees me dance, I am not interested in him afterward."

"As it should be."

Rochelle turned the red horse loose. He dropped his nose to the ground and trotted in two tight circles before dropping to his knees and rolling from side to side, grunting with happiness.

"I'd like to talk to you about Mayla," Thiago said.

But before he could mention Zoelie, Rochelle regarded him with unnerving frankness. "You love her, don't you?"

"Always."

The word rolled out of his mouth without thought, without reserve. It came from his core, steeped in truth.

As if on cue, the light breeze that had been blowing all day stilled. The birds quieted. The world around him held its breath, causing the hairs on Thiago's forearms to raise up and pull at their roots.

The conviction that he stood at a pivotal crossroads struck him. For some reason, this conversation, right here, right now, was critical. Maybe he couldn't say what he had wanted to in the barn, surrounded by the seriousness of Cantata's injury and Mayla's worry. Here, however, he could speak.

"I made a huge mistake," he said. "Years ago. I was young and dumb. I tried to apologize so many times. But I couldn't. Calls, texts, emails… She wouldn't hear me."

"Like I won't hear Philippe?" Rochelle's quiet voice belied the icebergs in her question. "I should give him a second chance, yes?"

"No," said Thiago, though the admission was like an arrow to his heart. "He does not deserve it."

Bogo, done with his roll, leapt to his feet and shook. Then, with a mighty buck, he raced to the far end of the paddock.

Rochelle softened a bit. "You tell me these things. Why not tell her?"

"I haven't had the right time."

"There is no right time. There is only now. Or not now."

She turned to walk back to the barn. Their conversation was over.

The breeze blew again. The stillness vanished. Something shifted in the pit of Thiago's stomach. A sense of missed opportunity—of irreparable loss and loneliness—nearly overwhelmed him. If only there were a way for him to show Mayla the depth of his devotion to her.

"Wait," he called after Rochelle. "A small favor. Please?"

⚜

The sweat and blood and dirt from the game had disappeared down the drain some time ago, when the water was still hot. Though Mayla had scrubbed herself clean, she remained in the shower hoping to relax. Instead of quieting, however, her thoughts churned, dredging up worries about Cantata, her finances, the Kentucky farm, and Thiago to cycle in a dizzying parade.

To stop her agitation, she practiced abdominal breathing. With eyes closed, shutting out all distractions, Mayla focused on the technique. The chaos of her thoughts resisted, but she persisted. Though progress was slow, each new breath brought a grain of peace.

The spray grew colder, but she stayed until the reserves in the tiny water heater were depleted. By then, she had corralled her thoughts, controlling them and arranging them in a way that brought equilibrium: Cantata would heal. The injury was neither deep nor serious. In the long run, it was unlikely to affect her health or her soundness. All that could be done for the mare had been done. Worrying about her was an exercise in futility.

Worry also wouldn't add a single euro to her finances, but skill might. The league paid each player a bonus for every goal he or she scored. The goals she made today would pay for Cantata's medical bills. Time to up her game rather than wallow in financial fear.

The farm she wanted would happen. She had to believe the sellers would accept her offer and let the deal go through. This, of course, would spark additional anxieties about other things, but at the moment, the ball was in her realtor's possession. Fretting over the situation wouldn't change it. For now, she could let that particular worry go.

And then there was Thiago.

She tried to tell herself she could let him go, too. It shouldn't be difficult: aside from the occasional sleepless night, he hadn't been a cause for concern in years. She presented a reasoned, rational argument that the past two days had given her some much-needed closure, enabling them to reconnect in a way that would allow both of them to move on when they went their separate ways.

But the deepest part of her refused to buy those lies.

⚜

"You bought *what*?"

As Mourad drove away from the club, Thiago held the phone away from his ear and turned down the sound. Even with those precautions, his father's voice blasted through the car, indignant and angry.

"Is this why I worked myself to an early grave, all these years? For you to throw everything away?"

"Pa, to begin with, you're not dead."

"Yet."

"You're not in the grave. And you won't be for a long time."

"*No le llega agua al tanque*," Pa mumbled.

"I can hear you," Thiago said. "I'm not an idiot. I'm your son."

"My son the idiot."

Thiago closed his eyes, blocking out the scenery as they left the tree-lined roads of the *bois* behind and entered the sepia tones of the city. He tried to picture his father's face. Weatherbeaten skin. Hard-earned lines of learning around eyes that never admitted uncertainty or regret. Even his stroke couldn't keep Pa down. If anything, the fact that he sometimes moved slower now than he once did only further infuriated the man. And when Señor Calvo was unhappy, mere mortals trembled.

Once upon a time, Thiago, too, had ceded to Pa's rages.

Not anymore.

"I am throwing nothing away. I'm making an investment. Like you taught me."

"Then I have failed if I taught you no better than this. It's bad business," his father shouted. "You're a fool, son, on a fool's errand. Forget this 'investment' of yours."

"Pa, you know I can't do that. It's already done. Even if I could reverse it, I wouldn't."

"I didn't grow my company to have my son throw it away!"

"You are well aware the business is worth at least three times more now than when I got involved," Thiago said, ignoring the older man's bitter growls. "As you are also aware, the money I used was from my personal account."

"A decision made in an instant brings regret for a lifetime."

"I know."

Señor Calvo must have heard the steel in Thiago's voice. "It is a mistake. One day soon, you will see."

"Papa, I've told you before, and I'll tell you again: you are wrong."

⚜

The shower grew colder, but Mayla did not move from under the spray. Seeing Thiago warmed her in ways she had never expected to experience again.

Seeing him again—being with him again—was like replacing a part of her body that had been surgically removed. The life she had learned to live without him was one handicapped by resignation. For years, she had thought it a permanent part of who she was. Now, she recognized it for what it was: a mere prosthetic. An imperfect replacement. A shallow placeholder for the depths of emotion she experienced with him.

Thiago was like her own personal power pack. His voice energized her soul. Her heart beat with more verve when he was around. Each breath brought more clarity. Every touch fanned dormant embers into flame, rekindling nerves that had been cold for so long, she had feared they were dead.

And his kisses...

When their lips met, she tasted the passion that fueled him. It teased her with the promise of things to come, tempting her to experience the raw surge of surrender when they breathed as one and their bodies fit so perfectly together that, for a moment, nothing separated them and they became two equal parts of a larger, blessed whole.

Stop it!

The rational part of her mind loomed, fencing off her fantasies, dousing them with cold, hard orders.

Pull yourself together! Quit acting like some lovestruck kid.

Berating herself, Mayla rounded up the thoughts of Thiago roiling in her head. What was the point of encouraging them? Though just being near him made her body crave his heat, made her hands ache to hold him and her mouth hunger to explore him, their relationship wasn't a long-term prospect. She knew that.

She had to think of her future. A future that did not include him.

31

Shoots and Letters

THE ONLY WAY MAYLA WAS HERE, now, at Musée d'Orsay, was if she had found a way to manipulate time. Thiago knew this. He knew she had her hands full dealing with her horse and the vet and the league officials in addition to the normal things that took up one's time after a game. Yet a part of him—the six-year-old-at-heart part—hoped to see her already there when he arrived.

As Mourad navigated the complicated nuances of Parisian parking, Thiago indulged himself in whimsical thinking, mentally fast-forwarding through the next few hours until the photo shoot was history. Then he could give Mayla her present and they could start planning their future. Together.

A massive bronze horse installed outside the Musée d'Orsay brought him back to the moment. Thiago gazed, awestruck. Everything about the statue commanded attention and respect, from the wrinkles in the crest of the noble arched neck, to the powerful legs ready to launch the horse forward, to the individual hairs on its body. A harrow made of a series of wicked-looking spikes threatened to puncture the animal, but unlike Cantata, the horse remained unscathed.

Before Mourad turned off the engine, the Vevier crew materialized, virtually conjured out of air to usher Thiago into a side door as if he were some sort of celebrity.

While they hustled him to the fifth floor of the converted train station, he had a vague, general impression of high, vaulted ceilings overlooking a space as glassy and airy as a conservatory. The Orsay housed the world's largest collection of Impressionist and Post-Impressionist art. Rodin. Gauguin. Daumier. Manet. Monet. Cézanne. Renoir. Van Gogh. Hundreds of works of art invited closer contemplation. Yet his viewing of the museum's collection was minimal and hurried; they rushed him through so quickly, the sole piece that registered in his mind was a too-short glimpse of a marble boyish satyr lying on his stomach, laughing at two baby bears.

He itched to move, to walk around, to explore, but he was here to work. The job began immediately. As soon as Thiago arrived, wardrobe, hair, and makeup professionals swarmed him like an army of expensively dressed, creatively coiffed ants.

Throughout the preparations, Mathieu, the Vevier photographer, moved like a stop-motion character made of clay, taking quick steps forward, stopping, crouching down, remaining nearly motionless, then rising and moving sideways in a blur of speed. His long, dark, flowing forelock reminded Thiago of a Friesian horse. Mathieu might be the most acclaimed fashion photographer in all of Europe, but Thiago had no idea how the man could see.

With all the makeup artists (it took the girl with shocking silver hair over forty minutes to attend to his eyebrows), wardrobe wranglers, security guards (a king's ransom of jewelry demanded their presence), models, scrim holders, and assistants—not to mention Mathieu himself—the Vevier shoot commandeered a significant portion of the Orsay's fifth floor.

In addition to the professionals, a small gaggle of fashionistas hung about on the periphery, lounging in one of the blobby brown leather seats or lining the red and gray walls. They *oooh*ed and *aaah*ed over each piece of jewelry, worshipped the models, and took surreptitious photos on their phones. Their presence almost, but not quite, drowned out the dismayed comments of tourists when they encountered the red ribbon that cordoned off the photo area and discovered the photo session barred their access to the clock.

"We saved for years for this trip to Paris, mate," a sunburned Australian with a barrel of a beer belly complained. "Stood in line for hours to get in here and you're telling me we can't get to the clock?"

A middle-aged woman holding a creased guidebook pulled his arm. "It's no bother, Howie. Don't make a fuss. Come with me and see the nudes."

Howie went, grumbling. Guiltily, Thiago watched him leave.

Mourad sat on a small folding chair, taking everything in.

"You're free to go," Thiago told him. "It's going to be a long afternoon."

"And I shall spend it here, your grateful and well-compensated driver, in this beautiful place, with these beautiful people."

Thiago envied Mourad's contentment. He fought the urge to prowl. The forced inactivity inherent in any still image shoot always made him restless. Still, he would stay here and fulfill his contract. In a few hours, when the shoot was over, he and Mayla would be free to wander the rooms together and examine the museum's treasures in detail. He could wait. It wouldn't be long now.

"At least take a break," he said. "Go look at the artwork."

"It is spectacular, yes, but I have seen it all before, Monsieur. Many times." Mourad peered down the hallway Howie and Ms. Howie had just taken. "Even the nudes." Smiling like a rogue, he turned his attention to the models and their attendants. "However, I find this new exhibition riveting."

A statuesque Ethiopian goddess and a red-headed Irish siren sat patiently while aestheticians applied their faces and stylists arranged their hair.

Conversation was hushed, private; the atmosphere as rarefied and subdued as a cathedral. Exuding blasé detachment, the models stared at their phones, their twitching, scrolling thumbs the only indication hinting at life.

A pouty French girl with skin so pale it was translucent joined them. Ignoring the stylist's greeting, she stared into an empty middle distance. She carried a vintage guilloché perfume flask with vivid rose and periwinkle enamel set into a silver body—a stunning piece that would have been at home on display among the museum's treasures. From time to time, she raised the flask to her perfect lips, taking tiny, hummingbird-worthy sips.

A fourth model remained hidden behind the privacy screen set up for a changing area. Occasionally, her thin, bronzed arms were visible, waving like antennae above the partition.

When she emerged, sleek and chic, Thiago recognized his personal pickpocket from the plane.

Mourad gave a low murmur of appreciation. "I see her and I hear beautiful musics." He moved his hands as if playing the piano.

"Keep your eye on your wallet with that one," Thiago advised.

Swizzle Stick strolled past, looking up at him through long lashes. "*Hola*, lover."

"You know her?" Envy and wistfulness colored Mourad's voice.

"We spent some time together. Your musician is a felonious drunk."

The driver shrugged. "And yet who can tell the heart who makes it sing?"

A vision of Mayla, molding her lithe, limber body against his, hit Thiago like a furnace blast. He didn't want to argue with Mourad, but his heart wasn't the part of his body that wanted to make music with the woman he loved.

⚜

The heavy backbeat pounded as Mayla tidied up their little flat. She loved these musicians; their vaguely Latin sound fused with Celtic overtones that played with a nod toward old-school stadium rock. Their music flipped some switch in her head and made her feet move in a trippy, happy dance.

The minuscule flat took no time to clean. The song lasted longer than it took her to go from "dishes washed" to "floor swept," but it reminded her of the best thing about this band: when played at high volume, their music overpowered all thoughts. Even thoughts of Thiago.

The door opened, admitting Rochelle, who crept in with all the enthusiasm of a parent venturing into a delinquent's den.

"What. The hell. Is that?"

Mayla flushed with guilty pleasure. Not everyone shared her musical appreciation. "*Los Buzones* have a new EP."

"Evidently recorded during a hog butchering. Imagine my joy."

Rochelle darted for the shower while Mayla found her earbuds.

"*EEeeee!*"

"Sorry!" Mayla said. She meant it. For even music pumped directly into her ears couldn't drown out Rochelle's squeal when she discovered there was no hot water.

Mayla's phone vibrated, alerting her to an email. Perhaps her realtor had sealed the deal...

But it wasn't from him.

Dear Mme. Alvarez,

I hoped to speak with you after the game, but didn't want to bother you while you were with the veterinarian. I pray that you are unharmed and that your horse makes a full recovery.

Thank you for your patience with me these past few days. I learned so much more from you than I ever dreamed possible. Regrettably, I will be unable to attend your last session tomorrow. I am grateful for everything you have done to help me learn about polo. Your courage, confidence, and skill are admirable. I wish I shared them.

Few fly,

Laudine Rochambeau

Mayla read the message twice, unable to articulate what, exactly, bothered her about it. It sounded so fatalistic. So final. So sad. It stood in such contrast to the bubbly, vibrant, chainsaw-wielding woman she had spoken to a few short hours ago.

She read it again, unsure of how to respond, but certain that something was wrong.

32

Stolen Moments

SWIZZLE STICK HANDED MOURAD her half-empty bottle of water as if he were a second-rate waiter clearing away trash at a third-rate restaurant. Holding the bottle with reverence and beaming with joy, he skirted the room, taking pains to stay out of everyone's way as he returned to his place on the shapeless leather ottoman.

Mathieu arranged his subjects, clustering them close to Thiago, draping their fat-free bodies over him until he enraptured himself with the results. Only then did the photo shoot progress.

Thiago was well aware that wearing top quality clothes while surrounded by beautiful models and a king's ransom in jewels was the literal definition of "living the dream." He wasn't complaining; he recognized the role that privilege played in his life. Even so, he envied the unabashed pleasure Mourad took in the proceedings. He wished he shared it.

"Something has changed," Mathieu's voice echoed through the clock tower of the Musée d'Orsay. "I turn away for a moment—thus—" he flung his face to the side with great theatricality, dislodging the black hair draped over his eyes, "and when I return, something… Something…"

The Vevier photographer's gaze roved over the assembled people, a maestro assessing an orchestra, looking for the player of the false note.

He consulted his camera, checking it against reality.

"*Le Gotthard*! It has disappeared!"

Mathieu pointed at the Ethiopian model. Her hands flew to her bare throat where her necklace had been; her movements fluid and graceful even when she was alarmed.

"No one move," Mathieu announced, reviewing the images on his camera as murmurs of confusion susurrated through the fifth floor.

Swizzle Stick took Mathieu's instructions at face value—she lounged beside Thiago, her hands still resting on his shoulders.

Thiago remembered the piece: a moonstone pendant with a green so otherworldly it made one believe in magic, suspended in a platinum ring encrusted with spectacular green diamonds. He didn't know how long it had been missing, but he had an idea how it had disappeared.

"My rings, they are gone!" the French girl pouted.

"'Tis like Prague," the Irish model said. "'Twas an incident this spring. Things went missing. Whoever ye are: may the cat eat you and the Devil eat the cat!"

"You've been busy," Thiago kept his voice low, for Swizzle's ears alone. "When were you in Prague?"

She laughed, a deep, sensual sound that sang with seduction. So full was it of art and artifice that rather than turning Thiago on, it left him cold.

"I see you lost your handler."

"Nobody handles me." She turned her head and breathed in his ear. "Unless I let them. You want to, yes?"

"No."

Mathieu clapped his hands, ensuring he had everyone's attention. "It pains me to say this, but prepare for security to search you."

"You better confess. They will arrest you," Thiago said.

"You insult me. I have nothing to hide and no place to hide it." She pressed her body close and rubbed against him. "You see? They will find nothing on me. I worry about that funny little one, however. His pockets run deep. So I hear."

She jutted her chin in Mourad's direction. Spikes of hot anger stabbed Thiago's heart as the man's face brightened, basking in the knowledge that beauty noticed him.

Of course Mourad hadn't pinched the jewelry. Swizzle Stick was the only model he had approached since they had been here.

Still, Thiago knew firsthand how light the girl's touch was. Eiderdown, chaff, spiderweb silk—all deferred to her. He hadn't known his driver more than a few days. Hardly long enough to give a credible character witness. Further, if he spoke up now, the theft would be laid on his shoulders, with Mourad considered an accomplice.

Swizzle snorted. "Those guards could not find their heads if they were stuffed up their own arses. The tall white one with bad skin and worse hair, he spends his days rooting through ladies' purses and shouting rude things at elderly men. As for the wide dark one, he exerts all of his energy kissing up, following every rule, so he is not accused of being a terrorist."

"You aren't afraid of getting caught?"

She *tsk*-ed in his ear, but did not dignify his question with a response.

⚜

Dear Laudine,

I am sorry to hear that you won't be joining us tomorrow morning. We will miss you. You are a wonderful student: capable and curious. You have been an invaluable contributor to our training sessions.

I sincerely hope you continue to progress in developing your polo skills. With your drive and determination, you can do anything you set your mind to.

It's always an honor to teach new students. It was my privilege to start you on your polo journey. You are braver than you know. In the game of life, may you continue to play with boldness and grace.

Best,

Mayla

Mayla hit "send" and checked the time. Scarcely more than an hour and a half since she had seen Thiago. He had asked her to the photo shoot, which would likely take all afternoon. She could make it there with time to spare, but...

Did she want to go?

Oh, yes.

Should she?

Probably not.

They weren't kids anymore. They were adults. And as an adult, she was mature enough to realize that going to the shoot would be irresponsible. It would encourage her to indulge herself at a time she needed to practice restraint.

She took the jar of wine from the fridge, poured herself a glass, and sipped. Still good. This was exactly what she needed—

Then she checked herself. Even when she was stone-cold sober, Thiago wreaked havoc with her thoughts. Though her self-control was currently fully operational, anything that dampened her ability to think clearly might change that. She didn't want any reason to doubt herself or to rationalize her actions. She was a grown-up. She needed to act like one.

Rochelle emerged, blue-lipped and shivering, toweling her hair dry.

"I poured you a conciliatory glass of wine," Mayla said. "Sorry I used all the hot water."

She put the rest of the wine away and grabbed a bottle of water from under the sink.

Adulting sucked.

⚜

"I have no time for this! No patience! None!" Mathieu pulled his hair in frustration. His outburst caused a stylist to scurry across the floor, heels clicking like tap shoes, to pat the errant locks back into position.

While the photographer paced in fits and starts, grumbling at the delay, the guards started searching the hangers-on in the gallery.

As they approached Mourad, Swizzle Stick tensed. Lurking behind Thiago, she watched, taking it all in, a cat in front of a mouse hole, waiting for the guards to pounce.

Étienne! His good friend Étienne Trabert could vouch for Mourad. As soon as they discovered the pieces in his possession, as soon as they could move, he would contact Étienne...

Mourad held his hands high while the tall guard patted him down. They found nothing.

A quiet growl rumbled behind Thiago. He could practically smell Swizzle Stick's confusion.

"Something wrong?" he asked. But he knew the answer: things were not turning out as she had expected.

Before the guard moved away, Mourad said something that caused him to hesitate. Mourad carefully drew his phone out and the two men conferred, looking at the screen, their heads close together.

Sensing that he was no longer the most important part of this event, Mathieu edged closer, flinging his forelock from his eyes and peeking over the guard's shoulder.

"*Mon Dieu!*" the photographer groaned, clapping a hand to his chest with a theatricality that ensured he was again the center of attention. The buzz of conversation stopped.

Mourad offered the bottle of water he had received from Swizzle. The guard reached for it with gloved hands and placed it in a plastic bag.

A quick consultation with the shoot manager led the guards to a particular bag in the holding area for the models' personal things.

"*¡Qué mierda! Ya fue,*" said a quiet voice behind Thiago. Swizzle Stick's hands left his shoulders. He sensed, rather than heard, the girl backing away.

Within moments, the bag yielded three elegant rings and the green moonstone necklace—all of which were placed in plastic evidence bags, in spite of Mathieu's protestations.

As the tall guard took photos and documented their findings, the other guard moved with a speed surprising for one of his height-to-weight ratio. He blocked the entrance as Swizzle Stick approached.

In short order, with far less drama than one might suspect, she was detained and put in handcuffs. As the guards led her away, she neither protested her innocence nor shouted curses. Rather, she held her head high and kept her mouth shut, her smile as unrepentant as any of the portraits on display in the Impressionists Gallery just down the hall.

Mathieu clapped his hands. "*Ça va*, people. My heart has stopped. First from shock. Now from boredom. *And* I am desolate: they have taken *Le Gotthard* for evidence."

He tossed his hair as if it were a war pennant capable of rallying the troops. "Yet we must... we must soldier on. For Vevier! For *la Collection!*"

Thiago desperately wanted to speak with Mourad and get his story, but a small crowd mobbed the man.

After a quick drink of water, Thiago resumed his place. Mayla hadn't come yet, but she was sure to arrive soon.

He practiced patience, scanning the faces of the crowd for Mayla as Mathieu and his assistant strategically repositioned the female models around him. In addition to giving her his gift, he wanted to tell her what had happened this afternoon. He couldn't wait to see her. Everything was better when he shared it with her.

❧

Wearing her comfiest yoga pants and a slouchy top, Mayla grabbed her purse and walked to the door.

"You're wearing that?" Rochelle pushed her empty wine glass aside and peered over the screen of her laptop.

"Now you sound like Carson."

Rochelle's wide-eyed, thin-lipped smile held a dash of disapproval. "Bold choice for a fashion shoot."

"I never said anything about—! I'm just running out to get us some food." Mayla crossed her arms. She knew doing so made her look like a defiant child. She crossed them anyway.

"Uh huh. You're not... going anywhere else?"

Rather than reply, Mayla stood her ground, waiting.

"I spoke with Monsieur Calvo," Rochelle confessed. Pink spots flushed her cheeks.

"I can't get away from him!" Mayla groaned, but she cut it short when she saw her roommate's look of solemn confusion.

"Why would you want to?"

"Why? I'll tell you. Our story is over. It's history. But every time I see him, I get lost in the past."

"So let the past go and start again."

"To what end?" Mayla paced the tiny flat: five steps one way, four another, then back again. "When I saw him, after all this time, I was angry. I had been mad at him for years."

"And now?"

"I don't want to fight. I don't even want to rehash what happened between us. Now, I just see what we've both lost out on."

"You two have history. And you have chemistry. Those were my two favorite classes in school. The very pretty Monsieur Calvo likes you. How is that losing? There are worse ways to spend an evening in Paris than going to a glamorous photo session and then enjoying dinner with a gorgeous man who rides as well as he looks."

"I hardly think the world of the rich and privileged is my thing," Mayla said.

Rochelle closed her computer and gave Mayla her full attention. "I know you. You're going to dither over this whether or not you go see him. If you don't go, a week from now, you'll be second-guessing yourself. If you do go, a week from now—"

"I'll be second-guessing myself."

"*Oui!* So you see, there is no escaping destiny. Furthermore, if you don't go, you will eat by yourself tonight. I have a date."

"Don't tell me it's Philippe?"

Rochelle pretended to blow her nose. "God forbid. I met a lovely man last night who chatted me up for half an hour before the dancing started. Yes, it is taking a chance. But he is worth seeing where things lead." Rochelle shot Mayla a meaningful look.

"Fine. I'll go."

"*Bien!*" Rochelle regarded her critically. "Monsieur Calvo asked me to tell you the photo session is on the fifth floor of the Orsay. Your name is on the list. La di dah." She held out her pinkie finger and mimicked drinking a posh cup of tea. "He offered to send you his driver—?"

Mayla frowned and shook her head.

"This is what I told him. You can find your own way there. But first, you're going to change, yes?"

"Change nothing! Nothing!" Mathieu's voice echoed through the tower.

Thiago stood at one of the clocks that graced the grand old Beaux-Arts style building. Twenty feet in diameter, with stark black wrought iron numerals against its clear glass face, the clock was a huge north-facing window. Through it, he could see boats on the Seine. Across the river sprawled the formidable fortress of the Louvre and the greenery of Tuileries Garden, and behind that, far off on a hill in Montmartre, glinted the white dome of Sacré-Cœur Basilica.

Here he was, on display before Mathieu's lens, as if he were more important than the masterworks around him. He knew better, of course. No one but Bruno had accused him of believing his own press in a long while.

Bruno. Son of a flaccid fishmonger...

He fought to maintain a neutral expression. Though in his mind, he rained down curses on Bruno—a perpetual sour note in any song—he didn't want his dislike of the man to show up on camera and taint the results of the session.

Better, instead, to think of Mayla, a much more appealing subject than his pig of a teammate.

Today, he would take steps to make up for lost time. He would bare his soul to her. He would say the speech he had spent years planning and perfecting. The future stretched before him, limitless and free, so it didn't matter that—for the moment—he was packed into this little alcove to parade at Mathieu's whim.

"That glance! Pensive. *Passionné. Oui!*"

Mathieu's words scarcely registered.

As the photographer darted around, Thiago thought again of the gift he had for Mayla—a small token of his feelings for her. Though he felt like grinning, he did not; Mathieu had made it abundantly clear that he did not approve of smiling subjects.

Still, the prospect of giving his gift invigorated him. If Superman were real, Thiago mused, this is how he would feel when he flew.

"Saxxy! More saxxy! *Oui-oui-oui!*"

Mayla had been out of his life for so long, but she had never been out of his thoughts. He wanted to tell her everything. How visions of her haunted him when he rode at dawn. How his mind tricked him into imagining he heard her voice every time it rained at twilight. Seeing her again had reclaimed a part of him he had feared lost to the past. And he didn't want to face the future without her.

Thiago stood behind the three-foot tall iron VII and gazed outside, thinking.

A horse's future is in its foundation. With no foundation, the animal is dangerous. Untrustworthy. Worthless. When training, you can't avoid the basics. The better the basics, the better the horse, for they form the basis on which the horse's entire life is built.

As far as he was concerned, Mayla was his foundation; the essence of any future worth living.

She was his first love. His only love. Any thought of family or legacy always included her. She challenged him in the best way possible. He never knew exactly what she was going to do. He could happily spend the rest of his life being surprised by her.

You are all the present I need. The only future I want. He would whisper those words to her, his mouth just below her ear, while his hands slowly traveled along her body, lingering, teasing, every time her breath caught in her throat. He knew, after last night, she still responded to his touch.

His hands pleaded to hold her. His body begged for her. Heat rose in his core as for the first time in a long time, he let his imagination run wild.

This indulgence was partly out of self-preservation. The pouty French model at his side reeked of whiskey. When interacting with her, Thiago mentally put Mayla in Pouty's place. As they came together, he envisioned Mayla in his arms, her eyes bright and dancing with depth and humor, rather than bleary and bloodshot.

Thoughts of Mayla infused him like an elixir. Electricity crackled in his veins. Never before had he felt stronger, bigger, or bolder.

Mathieu ran and stopped in fits and starts. "My head, it is exploding. It is too much—*Non! Non!*" he yelled, as Thiago turned to him, concerned. "Keep the saxxy! Give me more! Give me... " he paused dramatically, waiting until all whispering in the nearby galleries had ceased and everyone present hung on his next words. "*Le Grand Oui!*"

Thiago had no idea what The Big Yes was or how to give it to anyone.

He scanned the crowd, looking for Mayla. He was as excited as a child at Christmas to tell her what he had done. It would make her day. When she smiled, it would make his.

She wasn't here.

Yet.

But he had faith that Rochelle would be as good as her word and persuade Mayla to come. And when she came...

33

Museum Sights

MAYLA GOT OFF THE METRO at Concorde Station. She walked under the vaulted ceiling and arching walls covered with nearly fifty thousand black and white tiles spelling out the Declaration of the Rights of Man of 1789 in individual letters unbounded by spaces or punctuation.

As she walked, she played search-a-word, looking vertically and diagonally as well as horizontally. Once she had found "Carson." Both "Bogo" and "Cantata" were there. Rochelle swore her name was here, but Mayla had never been able to find it.

Then, arching overhead, she saw T-H-I-A-G-O, cascading vertically. She stopped in the middle of the platform to better see it. Her mouth fell open when she also saw M-A-Y-L-A, running diagonally, with the final "A" in her name also being the "A" in Thiago's.

She took out her phone and zoomed in to be sure. Instead of snapping the photo, though, she put her phone away. She wasn't in junior high anymore, looking for signs of things that were Meant To Be.

Lost in thought, she went up the stairs and emerged at Place de la Concorde, near the American Embassy. During the trip, she had decided upon her best plan of action: focus on the history she and Thiago shared. Have a ten-year reunion of sorts. Talk about old times. Remember old friends. Reminisce about great horses. They would have a few drinks, have a few laughs, make a nice, anchoring memory, and then they could both go their own way.

She crossed the street paved with cobblestones arranged in arching patterns and walked onto Paris's largest public square.

To the west began the magnificent Champs-Élysées—beneath which her subway had just traveled. The green trees of Jardin des Tuileries decorated the eastern side of the *place*. In the center rose the three-thousand-year-old Luxor obelisk. The dark granite finger stabbed seventy-five feet into the air, each side covered in hieroglyphs detailing highlights from the reign of Ramses II.

She knew she stood on the site of over thirteen hundred executions, including Marie Antoinette and Louis XVI. But it was such a peaceful place, full of camera-toting tourists gawking at the obelisk, the two magnificent fountains, and the imposing statues of eight women denoting France's largest cities. Every time she visited, she tried to picture it dominated by a guillotine and filled with a furious crowd of revolutionaries. Every time, she failed.

She turned southeast at the end of the *place* and walked along Quai des Tuileries, bordered by stone fences and trees on her left, with the afternoon sun glinting off the Seine on her right.

At the Passerelle Léopold-Sédar-Senghor, Mayla crossed the river. Her footfalls, and those of the other pedestrians, sounded like horse hooves clopping on the exotic Brazilian hardwood that formed the bridge's walkway.

She missed the multicolored, ever-hopeful "Locks of Love" that once graced the bridge, when lovers affixed padlocks to the fence lining the sides of the walkway, then threw the key into the water, symbolizing their eternal love. But she understood why the city had removed the locks from this and all other Parisian bridges: their sheer weight had damaged the integrity of the Pont des Arts and threatened it with collapse. Perhaps that was the hard truth about all grand gestures of love—they made a pretty show at first, but ultimately dragged one down.

At the entrance to the Musée d'Orsay, she passed the esplanade featuring the *Six Continents*: striking, greenish-black statues of seated women, one for each of the inhabited continents, which were originally displayed at Trocadéro for the 1878 *Exposition Universelle*.

Mayla tipped her head toward the sculpture of the regal, indigenous woman representing her part of the world.

"Stunning. Simply stunning," said a middle-aged woman with glasses so thick they magnified her eyes to owlish dimensions. She leaned in closer to examine North America's finely detailed feathered skirt and bear-claw necklace.

Mayla agreed. "It's a miracle they are here," she said. "They ended up thrown out with the trash."

The owl's eyes blinked solemnly as the woman patted North America's bare foot. "Happens to the best of us, doesn't it, dear? But we survive."

Mayla walked through the glass entrance doors, pensive, contemplating her survival instincts.

Inside, she traversed the long main hallway with decorative arches on both the ceiling and the supporting walls.

A nine-foot tall version of Bartholdi's *Statue of Liberty* greeted her, indoors at last after over a century in the Luxembourg gardens. Alabaster-white figures of transcendent beauty dazzled against walls of vivid aubergine, tangerine, and red. Carpaux's intricate, exuberant *Dance*. Pradier's lyrical, suicidal *Sappho*. She visited one of her favorites: Fremier's *Pan and Bear Cubs*. The impish enthusiasm of the faun had always put her in mind of Thiago. Today, however, the rough intensity contained in Bugatti's *Walking Panther* made her think of him on a baser, more visceral level. Everywhere she looked, masterpieces invited her to linger, to look, to stop, to absorb. But she pressed onward, upward, to the clock tower on the fifth floor.

She heard Blondie before she saw her.

"We was online, posting to our fashion vlog."

The girl spoke to a young man with so many piercings he looked like his face had been attacked by a riveter. He recorded her conversation, hanging on every word, listening as gravely as if she were unveiling a scientific breakthrough.

"We're vloggers. I'm a vlogger, yeh. We saw him yesterday, scouting locations. And I told Ju it was a sign. 'It's a sign,' I said. Of what? Well, of more, you know. And I was right! In the catacombs of the comments, past the trolls, someone dropped that there was a Vevier shoot today. So we did a bit of spying to find out where—and here we are!"

While Blondie gave her interview, Juju hung about on the sidelines, half listening, craning her neck to see—

Thiago.

Framed by the clock, every muscle, every plane lit to perfection, he dominated the room. He was the apex of creation; the crowning culmination of what artists wrestled to achieve with marble and clay. A living, breathing sculpture chiseled by the hand of God. Even if Mayla wanted to, she couldn't take her eyes off him.

But she didn't want to look away.

She never wanted to look away.

There was so much more to him than she had known. Last night, he had been tired and jet lagged. Everything about him had been a little more accessible. But now—

The lighting, the makeup, the attendants. All conspired to elevate Thiago to a completely different realm.

The tiny hairs on the back of her neck prickled, responding on a cellular level to his magnetism. There was no way this man in front of her was part of her past. At no point in her history had she ever seen anything quite like him.

Her eyes feasted on him, letting him pour into her, liquid and alive, obliterating stray thoughts, filling her to overflowing. She stood motionless, caught in the amber of the presence that filled the room.

The more she watched him, the smaller she felt.

The scratch on Mayla's leg twinged a bit as she shifted her weight. Something shifted in her thoughts as well. The models draped over Thiago, with their perfect pouts and luminous skin, made her acutely aware that a few hours ago she was sweaty, covered in dirt and blood, and getting whacked upside the head with a wooden mallet.

"Polo is a man's game. Not for a woman. Even one so unladylike as you!" The words snaked through her brain, their contempt echoing in her head. She remembered Thiago's father shouting at her. And she remembered that Thiago had not spoken up in her defense.

The polo field was so far removed from this that it could have existed in another world. She belonged in that world. She did not belong in this one.

"Magnifique!" cried the photographer, hopping about like a frenzied squirrel. *"Trop parfait!"*

What a delusional fool she had been. All afternoon indulging little daydreams as if *she* had the upper hand. As if she were the one to say "no" to him.

This was a man in his prime—the sort of prime with which few men are ever gifted. He was unescapable.

Unforgettable.

Dangerous.

Irresistible. And completely out of her league.

She had thought she could relegate him to the past. That was impossible.

Twenty-year-old Thiago no longer existed, any more than the majestic stallion Faustino was the gangly, headstrong colt she had once known. She had seen Thiago's potential years ago. Now, however, he more than fulfilled his boyish promise. He filled the place.

He held the stick-thin model in his arms, staring at her as if she were a banquet table set just for him. He held her close to his chest, coming within a breath of ravishing her. When he breathed, her body moved with him.

The model swooned.

Blondie fainted.

The photographer snapped, ecstatic, caught up in the electric current of unbridled desire emanating from Thiago and swirling around everyone within fifty feet of him.

Mayla realized she was a witness to greatness. All this time, she had thought the connection they shared was something unique—something almost magical. She had always thought the spark that smoldered in Thiago's eyes was for her.

Now she knew better.

The spark that flared there was *him*. All him.

"Mademoiselle Alvarez?" A young woman stood near Mayla's shoulder. Her dark hair was pulled back into a chignon so artful, it could have been one of the d'Orsay exhibits. Chic, rather severe glasses perched on her nose. Something about her ensemble must have been noteworthy, for behind her, Blondie grabbed Juju's arm in paroxysms of joy. "Monsieur Calvo has instructed me to look for you. If you will come this way? I have a chair for you. May I get you a beverage?"

Mayla was so still, she could feel her pulse pounding. Though Rochelle had finally approved her clothes, she was acutely aware that few others in the room wore anything off the rack. "Thank you," she said, "but I'm afraid you have the wrong person."

The Thiago she knew was long gone. On some level, she had realized that last night. Now, however, it was as transparent as the glass in the old clockface. He had surpassed her long ago.

She was no model. She couldn't compete with those women.

She backed away, fading into the shadows.

Mayla wasn't coming.

The realization crept into Thiago's consciousness on felted cat feet, advancing by inches, until it pounced.

He had been looking forward to seeing her so much, it had never occurred to him that Rochelle wouldn't be able to convince her to join him.

He had hoped to be able to give her a gift of his time, of himself. But she wasn't here.

They would not investigate the museum's treasures together. Nor would they share a quiet dinner. Not only would he miss seeing the joy in her eyes, but he would miss everything about her tonight. Her sense of humor; her companionship; the way she made his blood run wilder than Bruno's horses.

Yes, they needed to talk. He knew that. He looked forward to the conversation they must have to clear away the murk of the past. But they couldn't clear anything if she stayed away from him.

The day, which had been singing with expectations, suddenly rang hollow.

"*STOP!*"

Full of pique and privilege, Mathieu's command bounced off every flat surface.

The photographer shook his head to dislodge the forelock obscuring his eyes. He stood immobile, examining the last few frames. "It. Is. Finished." he sighed with excessive theatricality.

The assembled onlookers mumbled among themselves, little moues of surprise on their hungry faces.

"That's it?" Thiago said, checking the outrageously expensive watch on his wrist. Things were wrapping earlier than he'd expected.

"Oui. C'est tout."

Mathieu, to whom personal space was simply an idea floated by uninspired people, walked over and stood so closely that it became a matter of personal pride for Thiago not to take a step backward. The photographer stood on his tiptoes, peering into Thiago's eyes long enough for Thiago to concoct at least four ways of permanently dispatching him.

"Something has changed. The saxxy, it is gone."

Mathieu backed up and looked at the images on his camera again. "It is the sorrow," he announced. "The sorrow, it has fallen all over you. And the sorrow, it does not sell."

34

Surprise

THE MAELSTROM OF EMOTIONS Mayla experienced in the past two days had dispersed. In its place was nothing but a hollow, empty hole.

Outside the Orsay entrance, she stood near the base of the pedestal which displayed Rouillard's *Horse with a Harrow*. Usually, viewing the statue gave her a sense of dread and set her teeth on edge, so real was the imminent danger to the horse. Today, though, she saw it for what it was: a majestic animal escaping something designed to hold him back.

Her stomach grumbled, telling her that if she wasn't going to go to dinner with Thiago, could she kindly find a good restaurant in which to conduct the rest of her moping?

She wandered along Rue de Lille without a specific destination in mind. A delicious aroma, heady with the scents of cardamom, cinnamon, mace, anise, oregano, and hinting at exotic Moroccan spices she could not name, tantalized her.

Her stomach rumbled again, emptier and more insistent, so Mayla followed her nose.

It led her to a plain, unassuming door that opened into a clean, quiet establishment, scarcely larger than her flat at le Parisien. Intricately carved self-standing panels formed decorative islands behind bright tam-tam drums with hide tops and small bases.

A discreetly placed door opened, ushering more enthralling aromas into the air. A dark head sporting a wispy beard peeked out.

"*Bonjour.* Am I too early?" Mayla asked.

"To the contrary," the man said, "you are simply ahead of the rush."

Mayla took a seat on a long, low, upholstered bench. Though she loved France, she had never learned to love eating the main meal of the day late at night, like most Parisians—indeed, like most Europeans—did.

She ordered *tagine aux sept legumes*, served with a flourish in a red earthenware dish with a conical chimney for a lid.

"Seven vegetables," the waiter said, bowing while serving her as if she were a queen. "For luck. Very lucky. You'll see."

Mayla dug into the food, savoring the different textures and flavors. It was the best thing she had eaten in weeks.

Images of Thiago flared in her mind like strobed stills. Detailed recollections flashed into her thoughts with shocking clarity. How his hair curled at his temple. How the corner of his mouth creased before he smiled. How his eyes made promises only his body could keep.

Though such visions fed her fantasies, entertaining them would ultimately end in emptiness. Time to close the lid on Pandora's box and get on with the business of living in the real world.

Mayla ordered *nous nous* to finish off her meal. Her drink arrived shortly: equal parts hot milk, frothed to perfection, and strong espresso, served in a tall glass tumbler with two cubes of sugar on the side.

While she sipped and savored, she pulled out her phone and opened an app containing all the notes, photos, and sketches of plans for her farm. She reviewed where the polo field would go, where the most practical location of the exercise track would be, and played around with sketches of stall placement.

She reviewed her finances for the umpteenth time. Though it had taken practically all the money she could scrape together, she had her downpayment and was pre-approved for the mortgage loan. But the margin was so tight that, try as she might, she could not find the funds to lease a horse to replace Cantata.

She entertained the offer of Zoelie—for about ten seconds. In less time than it took for the sugar cube to dissolve in her coffee, she knew she wouldn't be using the prize mare, though she marveled that Thiago had secured Sergio's blessing. No. She wasn't a charity case. She would simply have to suck it up and finish the next five weeks of competition with one less horse in her string.

With a full stomach and a clearer head, Mayla paid her bill and wandered outside, weighing her options of what to do next.

Sainte-Chapelle was just a mile away. She could go there and submerge herself in its well of color, salving her soul. But a memory of last night—of Thiago, smiling with genuine joy, standing beside her, holding her while music fit for angels played—changed her mind. She opted, instead, to take the bus back to Polo Parisien.

Shortly after she was seated, her phone pinged with a text from her realtor.

Call me when you can. ASAP.

She checked her watch. It was still morning in America.

This could mean only one thing: her offer on the Kentucky property had finally been accepted. Her heart skipped a happy beat as she made the call.

"Ms. Alvarez… " The voice coming through the receiver sounded anything but happy. "I don't know what to say. We've lost the farm. I'm sorry."

Mayla felt as if she had taken a fall.

All the air left her lungs. A weight as heavy and unyielding as an anchor pressed on her, dragging her down, refusing to let her draw a breath.

Her head ached. Ashes coated her throat. She sat gaping, opening and closing her mouth like a fish out of water.

"It came out of the blue," her realtor said. "You are the only person to look at the property in months. No one but you ever came to inspect it or even inquire about it. They just bought it outright. Today. Paid full asking price."

Gone.

Her dream was gone. Blown away like a candle flame.

She couldn't even make a counteroffer. The asking price was seventy-five thousand dollars more than she could afford. But the place had sat vacant for so long and needed so much work that she had allowed herself to believe it was only worth what she offered on it. Clearly, the people who bought it knew better.

"So it's a done deal." Mayla stated the obvious, trying to buy herself some time to make sense of things.

"I'm afraid so. Paid in cash."

For reasons she couldn't explain, the man's soft Kentucky drawl made Mayla angry. "Not one word," she said between clenched teeth, "about God closing doors and opening windows, or so help me I will hunt you down and feed you broken glass."

"Well," he said. "Maybe this just wasn't meant to—"

"Not. One. Word."

"I understand your disappointment, Ms. Alvarez. But the right place is out there for you. We'll keep looking."

Yes, she would keep looking. She might spend the rest of her life looking. It had taken her nearly twenty months of searching until she found a property with everything she needed, in an ideal location, that was even within flirting distance of her price range.

"That's all I know right now," her realtor said. "I'll see what more I can find out. I'll let you know as soon as I know anything."

It didn't matter.

Curiously numb, Mayla watched the city pass by outside her window.

She had scrimped and saved for years, trying to get enough money for a downpayment to buy a place of her own. Most facilities in her price range were in such poor condition that they needed far more renovation than she could afford in several lifetimes. But this farm... This farm was different. As soon as she had set foot on the property, she had felt at home. Though it, too, needed rehabbing, its core components were solid. When she looked at it, she had been the first person in over a year to show an interest. She loved it. She wanted it. She had been willing to give everything she had for it.

But it wasn't enough.

⚜

Though Mourad held open the back door for him, Thiago headed for the front passenger seat of the Alpina.

Mourad took his place behind the wheel. "We are riding the shotgun, I see."

"Mourad?"

"Yes, sir?"

"That necklace."

"I have given the authorities my statement."

"I know, but—"

"I assure you, sir, I did not steal it."

"I know..."

"But?"

Thiago watched Mathieu's crew cart the various accoutrements of the shoot—scrims, folding chairs, racks of clothing—out of the museum and into their vehicles. The images they took today were merely illusions for the masses to *ooh* and *aah* over. Mathieu was a master at sleight of hand, orchestrating a clever fantasy from mundane reality. Yet the *real* reality was so much more intriguing.

"But—what happened?" he said.

"It would appear the thief was as unskilled as she is beautiful," Mourad brushed an imaginary speck of lint off his leg.

Thiago knew better. He held his tongue, waiting. The silence stretched, taut as an elastic band…Finally:

"I confess, sir, I did not follow your orders," Mourad said.

"Oh?"

"You told me to watch my wallet." Mourad shrugged, self-deprecating, a little embarrassed. "Instead, I chose to watch her. Very closely. As a result, my wallet, it is safe. The necklace also."

"There is no question that she took it—your video proved that. Yet she seemed genuinely surprised to discover the necklace was in her bag."

"What good would life be without genuine surprises?" Mourad coughed discreetly. "Perhaps the beautiful lady will have occasion to reflect on her actions. She may even decide she wishes to change her path. Embark on a different life. Perhaps move to a new city and make a new start."

Thiago held Mourad's gaze, searching for a tell, but finding none. "That's not easy to do."

"What is worthwhile is rarely easy. Surely the great Thiago Calvo knows this."

A pensive quiet filled the car, full of the myriad unspoken choices, both good and bad, that comprise a person's life.

Some time passed. Belatedly, Thiago realized they were still in the Orsay parking area. The engine wasn't even running, though Mourad sat with his hands on the wheel, patient and still as a park bench.

He looked askance at his driver. "Why aren't we moving?"

"You have yet to tell me where you wish to go." A statement of fact, rather than one of recrimination.

"The club."

They drove in silence until the Parisien's entrance gates loomed.

"Please convey my hellos to Mademoiselle Alvarez when you see her," Mourad said.

Thiago nodded. He removed the platinum precision Vevier Chrono-Métreur from his wrist, a "perk" from the photo shoot. "Not yet available in stores," he said, showing it to Mourad.

"Certainly not in the stores I am known to frequent," Mourad said, reverence in his voice.

Thiago placed the watch on the leather armrest between the two seats. "Consider it your bonus."

Mourad blinked, speechless with gratitude.

As Thiago unfastened his seatbelt, he never saw or sensed the driver move, but the watch was gone before he opened the door and left the vehicle.

Someone had been in the cottage in his absence. As he entered the door, the unmistakable aroma of fresh-baked brioche greeted him. A basket of bread and cheese sat atop his dining room table next to a bottle of a legendary white Châteauneuf-du-Pape. A note on exquisite linen paper was tucked into the basket:

A token of my appreciation. Many thanks to you and your Valentine.
—Vernon de la Foret

The gesture touched Thiago. He couldn't wait to share it with Mayla.

Mayla.

Worry hit him with unexpected force. He had been so shortsighted!

He had seen the hit she took. Perhaps she had been more seriously injured than he thought. Concussion or a serious sprain was not only possible, but probable. He checked his phone—

No. Mayla was fine. Rochelle had promised to contact him if she weren't.

But maybe something had gone further wrong with Cantata. Or one of the other horses. Any number of things could have claimed her attention. Any number of things could have been more important than meeting up with him.

He headed for the barn. If he knew her as well as he once thought, she was there, seeing to her horses. He would help if he could, then invite her to a quiet dinner, when they could talk without distraction over this excellent bottle of wine.

⚜

Wrath. Jealousy. Grief. Confusion. A fug of emotions, none of them good, enveloped Mayla as she cleaned feed buckets and mucked stalls. Rochelle had cleaned stalls in the morning, but Mayla needed something to do to focus her shaking hands.

For the past hour, she had tried to find a reasonable explanation for the news she had received. For the past hour, she had failed.

Her ears rang. Fury throbbed through her veins. Knowing that she had no good reason to feel this way did nothing to abate her anger. To the contrary, it stoked the furnace until it roared.

The last stall was Bogo's. As she positioned the muck bucket and began spot-cleaning, Bruno showed up outside the door.

"*Qué cagada!* I see you found a place where you belong." He cackled at his little joke.

In rapid-fire Argentinian Spanish, he spouted hatred and misogyny. "Polo is a rough game. A game of kings. Not of scheming, sucking *princesas.*" He cracked a mirthless grin with too few teeth. "It's too easy for you to get hurt."

She had heard it all before, though not as profanely, from Calvo Sr.

"*Comment?*" Mayla pretended not to understand his Bonaerense dialect. But Bruno wouldn't leave. He lurked outside the stall, spitting on the floor, spewing venom.

Eventually, she'd had enough. She loaded up her apple-picker with an enormous pile of fresh manure and threw it out the door—deliberately missing the muck bucket and hitting Bruno.

The barn went silent.

Mayla said nothing. Not "oops." Not "sorry."

She gripped her plastic pitchfork, half expecting to have to use it as a weapon. She waited for Bruno's howl of irritation. Instead, he smiled, cold and quiet as a shark, and walked away.

❦

As Thiago neared the doorway to the shed row where Mayla stabled her horses, Bruno stormed out, an unmistakable dark, wet, green spot staining his thigh. A little of the tension that had been building in the pit of Thiago's stomach eased. From the looks of things, Mayla was feeling fine.

He arrived as she trundled the muck bucket back from dumping it. Perhaps she would like to go for a ride with him. He opened his mouth to ask her—

Before he could say a word, Mayla saw him coming.

"YOU!"

She turned on him so fast, so palpably wounded, that he took an involuntary step backward. With her bright eyes and shoulders set in rigid defiance, she reminded him of a trapped wild mare, volatile and unpredictable.

He almost asked, "Is everything OK?" But obviously, it wasn't.

"When we first met, I thought you were The One," she said. The jagged shards of her words tore at her throat. "The One I could happily spend the rest of my life with."

"I thought the same," he confessed, at a complete loss.

He took a step toward her, hand outstretched as if he were approaching an injured creature. An unspeakable suspicion grated against his consciousness. "What happened? Did Bruno do something to hurt you?"

Bristling with disgust, Mayla grabbed her phone and shoved it in front of him so he could read the texted conversation.

Found out who the buyer is. Calvo Land Development, Internacional.

His heart dropped into his heels. *Oh no. This wasn't how she was supposed to find out.*

"I'm sorry," he said. "I wanted to be the one to tell you."

"Tell me what? That you somehow found the one place on the planet that I wanted, that I hoped to make my own and... " Mayla ground her teeth together. "How? How! How did my little attempt to purchase a farm even come on your radar?"

She suddenly went very still, all bluster gone, as she connected the dots. "Oh," she said, her voice flat and empty, joyless as a deflated balloon. "You talked to Rochelle. Used her to get to me. I see."

Mayla stuffed her phone back in her pocket. Without another word, she sidestepped him, picked up a brush, entered Cantata's stall and began grooming.

Thiago stood in the stall door. "I did speak with Rochelle," he said, watching her closely. "I didn't buy the farm for me. I bought it for you."

35

Past vs. Present

As Mayla brushed Cantata's smooth neck, she shook her head in disbelief. "If that's true, why didn't you discuss it with me first?"

Thiago's response was so quick, so cold, it threatened frostbite. "Because when I wish to give a gift, I am not in the habit of first telling the recipient."

Chocolate. Flowers. Wine. Those are gifts. They are small. Perishable. Portable. A farm is none of those things.

"I don't see you for ten years. We have one date and you buy me a farm. Who does that?"

Thiago moved inside the stall and stroked Cantata's flat forehead, rubbing the whorl of hair there. The mare closed her eyes halfway from happiness.

"You haven't seen me in years, true," he said. "But that's not for a lack of trying on my part." His voice was deep and rich as a well of honey.

"You betrayed me." Mayla gripped the brush as if it were an anchor helping her hold her ground. "Abandoned me when I needed you."

She had never spoken the words aloud; had never even let herself form the sentence in her head, always pushing the thought aside into the dark recesses of her mind before it could become fully formed. In the shadows, the feeling had festered, sending down roots, putting out shoots, growing stronger and more entrenched every time she muzzled it or pretended she had moved on without it.

Well, no more. An injured horse's stall was hardly the location she would have chosen for this conversation, but now that it had begun, she was game to finish it.

Did he buy the farm as a sort of atonement—to mitigate his guilt for leaving her when she most needed him? Or had she so bruised his pride that he felt compelled to rub her nose in the fact that such a purchase was mere pocket change to him? Either option was appalling.

"Abandoned? Never." He met her eyes and held them, refusing to look away. "I spent years—years!—trying to make amends."

Thiago moved toward her, elemental as a thunderstorm.

Mayla wanted to hold her ground, but she instinctively backed away.

In a few steps, she stood with her back pressed against Cantata's side. The homey, honest smells of pine shavings, timothy hay, and horse scented the air. She knew she could leave if she wanted to. But she didn't want to. The naked openness on his face transfixed her.

Cantata's barrel provided a solid wall of warmth on her back. Thiago reached for her, placing his hands on her arms as much to steady himself as to keep her before him.

"You don't understand," she said. "It took everything I had to try to realize my dream, and it still wasn't enough. But you...You just waltzed in and bought the place without even seeing it."

"That's not illegal, is it?"

"You can't throw money at a problem and make it go away!"

"I didn't. I was throwing myself at you."

To Mayla's utter horror, a lump of emotion formed in her throat. She never cried.

Never.

Now was not the time to start. Swallowing as best she could—though it felt as if a golf ball had lodged in her larynx—she pressed on, hoping that both the dam holding back her tears and the legs supporting her body continued to stand.

"You *had* me. Completely. We planned a life together, remember? But the first time I needed you, you weren't there."

"I could say the same for you," Thiago said, his eyes searching hers as if he were trying to memorize them. "We were foolish to think we would spend a lifetime together and never have a falling out. Life is messy. People make mistakes. *I* made a mistake. And then I wrote. I emailed. I called. You wouldn't respond. How can I say I'm sorry if you won't hear me speak?"

"You're sorry. You're *sorry*."

The muscles in Thiago's jaw clenched. Mayla knew her words and her tone stung him. She attempted to soften them. Her attempts met with utter failure.

"We did not have a 'falling out,'" she said. "Your father publicly humiliated me while you did nothing to stop him."

"I'm not making excuses for myself," Thiago told her. "But that was ten years ago. I was stupid! And young. Did you never do anything stupid when you were young?"

"Yes," she said, anger burning like acid in her veins. "I fell in love with the boss's son. Who left me alone when his daddy got mad."

"A lot can happen in ten years," Thiago said evenly.

"A lot did."

He drew nearer; so near she could see every individual thread in his expensive shirt. But it wasn't his shirt that mesmerized her.

His voice was little more than a whisper, intended for her ears alone.

No matter how much she reminded herself of his past faults, each word he spoke subtly altered the rhythm of her heart.

"I hate to admit this," he said, "but I was afraid to lose—"

"—your inheritance? Afraid of throwing your life away with someone who wasn't born to wealth? Not a blue blood. Someone who had to work and fight and scrap to make something of herself?" Hot tears threatened. She blinked them back; held them at bay. "Everything comes so easily to you. You never had to work for anything your whole life."

"Afraid to lose myself. I was so in love with you. I was afraid I would put you up on a pedestal and completely disappear."

His hands tightened briefly on her arms before letting her go.

"You never fought for us," he said. "I did for years, looking for a way to reach you."

"Well, there's no need to fight anymore," Mayla told him.

The words landed like an anvil, thudding into the space between them. Thiago's eyes darkened as border walls went up. Very reserved, he dropped his hands to his sides and backed off.

Without another word, he turned and left the stall.

Mayla found herself suddenly unmoored; adrift.

Cantata lifted her head to watch Thiago walk away. She whickered softly.

But he was gone.

⚜

I was afraid I would put you up on a pedestal and completely disappear.

Thiago's words to Mayla echoed in his mind.

She had no way of knowing that his fears had already been realized. It was too late for him. He had already lost himself to her. He had left the point of no return in his rearview mirror long ago.

She was an integral part of his life. A core part of who he was.

She so saturated his life that he had spent the last ten years trying to find a woman who would fill the gaps she left behind. But he had already found her.

It was Mayla.

It had always been Mayla. Only she could make him whole.

You never had to work for anything in your life. Though most people would have said such a thing with bitterness, Mayla stated it as a fact. She believed it to be true, but Thiago knew otherwise.

For years he had worked ceaselessly, using everything in his power to get his affairs in order so that, when the time came, he could show her how he felt about her.

The time had come.

But it was running out.

❦

"He bought you a farm." Rochelle stared at Mayla, stupefied.

"Yep." Mayla sipped her tea, wishing it were wine, but Rochelle had finished off the barely drinkable leftovers in the Mason jar and the rest of their flat was drier than a Prohibition era camp meeting—which, given her pounding headache, was probably best.

"Monsieur Calvo. Bought you. A farm."

"Not just any farm. *The* farm. Thing is, I never told him about it. Imagine my surprise."

The color drained so completely from Rochelle's face that her lips turned the color of sand. Mayla feared the girl might faint.

"OooOOooohhh… " The moan of dismay sighed through the room like wind through a canyon. "I might have…I mean, I think I—"

"I know."

"I never dreamed he would... " Rochelle covered her mouth with both hands, hyperventilating in horror.

"Believe me when I say that Thiago is a master of doing things you never dream he would do," Mayla said. "He excels at it."

She picked up the gag bit purse and handed it to her groom. "Here. It's the only bag I can find. Breathe in here."

A long moment of silence dragged itself between them.

"I am fired, yes?" Rochelle said weakly.

"Never. What would I do without you?"

Rochelle blew her nose and composed herself. "So the farm is now yours?"

"Of course not. I can't accept something like that."

"Why? He is rich. He can afford it. If you take the very beautiful man's very generous gift, then you can immediately do the renovations you want."

"No. No. And no." Mayla stood and headed toward the kitchen sink, trying not to favor her injured leg. Her mind conjured up an image of Thiago standing in front of her, dark eyes sparking with a hunger she shared as he moved to close the distance separating them.

Turning on the faucet, she splashed water on her face, drowning the illusion in reality and pushing it away. "I still want him—it, though. I'm going to offer to buy it from him."

"That will teach him."

Mayla looked up sharply, stung a bit by the reserve in Rochelle's tone. "What do you mean?"

"Trying to purchase a gift instead of accepting it from the giver practically guarantees you will never receive another."

"Fine with me."

But was it? *Was it?*

"I must say again that I am sorry. So very sorry," Rochelle said.

"You did what you thought was right," Mayla told her. "Never apologize for doing that."

With a final, heartfelt apology, Rochelle went to the barn for a last check on the horses.

Still wishing she had wine, Mayla finished her tea and went to bed.

She lay quietly, hoping in vain to drift off. The events of the day had left her exhausted. Her head pounded. Her shoulder ached. Her thigh throbbed; the scratch across it stung every time she moved her leg. But none of those were the reason why she couldn't sleep.

The only thing keeping her awake was Thiago.

A twinge of guilt stabbed her conscience as she replayed their conversation in the barn.

"You never fought for us."

He was right. The realization blindsided her.

Long ago, on the polo field in Argentina, his inaction had so offended her that she had never given him the opportunity—not to explain, for what he did was unexplainable—but to grow.

And he *had* grown. In some ways, he had grown more than she.

She had run away, rather than confront him. Why?

If she were honest with herself (and after the day she'd had, there was no point in anything other than complete self-honesty), ten years ago, she was afraid that if she stayed, it would be the first in a series of times when Thiago didn't stand up for her, didn't support her dreams. The thought that she might choose to stay with someone like that had terrified her. She didn't want to give up who she was in order to have him in her life.

But she had never allowed him the option of asking her forgiveness or of learning from their past. How much had they missed out on because she gave up without a fight?

Mayla was still awake, asking herself unanswerable questions when

Rochelle returned from the barn. After the girl locked up and went to bed, Mayla waited for her telltale light snoring to drift through the flat. It didn't come: proof that Rochelle was as awake as she.

The night grew blacker, with muted calls of nocturnal creatures outside her window.

Mayla made up her mind. In the morning, she would talk to Thiago. She would ask to buy the farm back from him, explaining that she appreciated the gesture, but he didn't have to atone for anything in their past, and she didn't want to feel that she owed him something.

"I'm sorry," she would say. "You were right. I ran. I should have stayed. I should have fought harder for us."

And then she would walk away.

Their time together had been too long ago, when they were both too young. They were older now. Wiser. Time to get on with their lives.

⚜

Thiago lay on his back, staring at the forest of shadows on the ceiling. What was it about being around Mayla that turned him into a bumbling teenager again?

He had hoped to have a rather lengthy, heartfelt conversation with her, touching on one or two other important matters, before telling her of his real estate purchase. But that hadn't happened. The only way his attempt to give her the farm she wanted could have gone worse would have been to show her the deed and then set it on fire.

Of course, she suspected him of trying to buy either her body or her forgiveness. Of course, she was furious with him. He wasn't particularly happy with himself.

His father's words from earlier in the afternoon echoed in the catacombs of his thoughts. "Forget her. You want a woman? Go get a woman! Step outside and whistle and you'll find ten women. You want her only because she's the one that got away."

Technically, he had not hung up on the old man; technically, he had said "good bye" before he had disconnected, though he suspected his father had not heard the word ground out like a peppercorn between clenched teeth. He believed with all his heart that his father was wrong on two counts:

He wanted Mayla for a list of reasons ten years in the making.

And she hadn't gotten away. Not yet.

36

Domestic Disturbance

THE MORNING DAWNED, overcast, with a moist wind hinting at rain.

Mayla awoke, then wished she hadn't. The muscles in her neck protested when they moved. Her back creaked but did not crack. A painful bruise covered the top of her head.

"It's almost like you got smacked with a mallet," Rochelle said.

Mayla grumbled and made a gesture that would have solidified Señor Calvo's "unladylike" opinion of her.

It irked her that even the most mundane action reminded her of Thiago. She couldn't afford the distraction. She didn't want to do anything with him—didn't want to see him, or talk to him, or have a single neuron form a thought about him—at least till after her final clinic session and after the last game.

The yoga mat lurked in a corner. At the sight of it, she sighed more heavily than she intended.

"What's wrong?" Rochelle said, freezing in the act of putting on her paddock boots. "How's your head? You feeling OK? OK to play?"

"I'll be fine." Mayla indicated the mat. "It's blasting me with guilt for ignoring it yesterday."

"I don't think that's how hatha works," said Rochelle.

"The word literally means 'force.' You think force is above using guilt as its henchman?"

Mayla unrolled the mat and positioned it in the middle of the floor.

"Stay there," she told it. "I'll get to you after I exercise. And feed. And finish up with my students. It's a date. Promise."

Rochelle cocked her head to the side, studying Mayla with her good eye. "I'd say I was worried about you... if only this sort of conversing with inanimate objects were atypical behavior."

"No reason to worry," Mayla said, heading out the door. "Everything is fine. You'll see."

Mayla's words were prophetic, especially with regard to Cantata. The mare ate well and moved easily, with no swelling or heat to indicate potential problems with her wound.

The morning passed in a busy blur of grooming, exercising, feeding, and cleaning stalls. Bittersweet sadness colored Mayla's mood as her students arrived for the final clinic session. She looked for Laudine, holding out hope that perhaps the woman had changed her mind.

But only six students on their horses gathered outside the shed row. Laudine was conspicuously absent.

"I hate saying 'goodbye,'" Mayla said. "I have so enjoyed working with you and getting to know you these past few days. I encourage you to continue developing your skills. Today, I want to show you some mounted drills you and your horse can practice to—"

She fell silent, noting Yvonne's phone affixed to a bracket mounted on her helmet.

"I'm sorry, but I don't allow video recording of my clinics. I believe I made that clear on day one."

"I know, Madame," Yvonne said, turning bright red with embarrassment. "I'm not recording. I brought Laudine."

She removed her phone and tapped it to switch the camera.

"Bonjour!" Laudine's wide, honest face filled the phone's screen. "Since I cannot come today, I begged Yvonne to let me ride with her, so to speak."

"I hope you aren't sick," Mayla said.

Proue stepped her horse back as if Yvonne's phone were contaminated. "Better to stay away then. Wouldn't want to infect the rest of us."

Laudine smiled out at them. "I am well enough. I won't be a bother, I promise."

"We're glad to have you join us, in any form," Mayla said.

While Yvonne seated her phone back in its bracket, Mayla mounted Widdershins.

"As I was saying, today we'll learn some drills you can practice any-where—both on and off the polo field. The more you do them, the more you will improve your balance, timing, and accuracy.

"Let's start with a dribbling exercise." Mayla tapped polo balls into place beside each student. "In my experience, amateurs generally make two mistakes: they hit too late and have the ball too close to their horse."

"So: wrong time, wrong place. Story of my life," said Doreen.

⚜

Thiago hung upside down, his knees hooked over a metal bar anchored into the wall of the Parisien's opulent workout area.

Calling the place a "gym" was to do a disservice to the painstaking attention to detail, the deliberate aesthetic, and the flawless use of space. Here, the *feng* certainly *shui*ed with all the *shui* money could buy. Large overhead fans circulated cool air. Discreet, recessed lighting provided glare-free illumination. Stone walls sparkled with flecks of multicolored quartz. The floor, comprised of some eldritch material that resembled wood, provided a slightly spongy non-slip surface. Pots of inventive topiary accented the alcoves.

Only two people occupied this palace of fitness: Thiago, suspended from the bar, and a balding man in expensive shoes who raced to nowhere on a treadmill while glued to the financial news displayed on the monitor a few feet from his face.

Thiago held a ten-kilogram medicine ball in his hands as he did a series of reverse sit-ups and core stretches. Twenty sit-ups. Then twenty twists, twenty arm revolutions, twenty wrist flexes, and twenty more twists, before returning to the sit-ups and starting the process over again.

This was a part of his regular routine. When at home, he sometimes used the gym equipment in the pool house. But often as not, he hung from a jacaranda tree near the driveway leading to the barns; it had a long, nearly horizontal branch three meters above the ground that was perfect for his reps. In the spring—late October and early November—vibrant purple flowers covered the tree, their fallen petals creating a carpet on the ground. When he hung upside down, he was suspended in a purple sea.

During his workout sessions, he always focused on improving his technique and building endurance. Since he didn't use complicated, expensive equipment, he had told himself his methods for staying in shape were available to anyone, just as the game was equally open to any player. All you had to do to succeed was want it badly enough.

But, of course, that was a lie—a cold, lifeless lie warmed on the compost heap of privilege.

Attempting to give Mayla his gift had forced him to acknowledge the extent of the gulf that divided them. They truly inhabited different worlds. In his, top-of-the-line exercise equipment in a well-appointed gym was available any time he wanted. It mattered not that he rarely chose to use it. Mayla's world offered no such choices. Likewise, his world included an army of influential people: lawyers, developers, producers, CEOs, and judges, all on a first-name basis; all happy to provide a favor to a friend. It afforded first-class travel, expensive cars at his disposal, and the family jet. It had a home base: a foundation, a security blanket of location and history and belonging to which he knew he could always return should disaster strike. He rarely called in favors, seldom indulged his wanderlust, and had never needed to take advantage of his safety net. But he could. He could. Anytime he wished. And that made all the difference. For Mayla could not. Her world operated under a different set of rules.

Then here he came, plowing through the reality of how she lived her life—a reality that involved years of careful saving, weighing the pros and cons of every purchase, making every expenditure a crucial decision. In a matter of hours, with a few phone calls, he had pushed everything she had worked for aside like mud in the streets after a storm.

He had never considered himself Superman. He identified far more readily with Bruce Wayne. But he was no superhero. Rather, Mayla must think him the most clueless, arrogant, patronizing fool.

Thiago did an extra set of reps, pushing himself until his abs burned in protest. When he finished, he dropped the ball, startling Treadmill Man, who stumbled and missed a stride, before returning his attention to the video screen.

Perhaps awareness of their differences was a form of progress. Perhaps he could come up with a way to clear customs and enter Mayla's world. Thiago hung motionless, hoping for the slight euphoria that often accompanied being upside down, but all he heard was the rhythmic swoosh of blood pulsing behind his eardrums.

❧

For the past forty-five minutes, as they practiced stick handling, hooking, and steering, Mayla had focused on the students who were physically present and largely forgot about Laudine monitoring the clinic from a vantage point on Yvonne's head.

"I am impressed at the progress you all have made," she said at the end of the last exercise, as students and horses caught their breath in the shade of a large acacia. "Four days ago, some of you had never hit a ball from the back of your horse. Now, look at you! Riding and shooting like pros."

She dismounted and loosened Widdershins's girth, indicating for her students to do the same. "Any questions?"

Yvonne removed her helmet and held her phone so Laudine could be part of the debriefing.

"That was so much fun!" Laudine said, grinning like a kid at a carnival.

"Could you see very well?" Mayla asked.

"Oh, yes. Though I probably should have taken something for motion sickness before watching some of the speed drills."

"Where do we go from here?" said Doreen.

"I'm glad you asked. You now officially know enough to be dangerous," Mayla said. "One option is to follow Proue's lead. I believe she has become one of le Parisien's newest sponsors."

Proue smiled, gracious, wealthy, and self-important, as the students broke out in spontaneous applause.

"Barring that, sign up for lessons and join a club. That will ensure you continue to challenge yourself to learn, to improve, and to—"

"LAU! YOU CALL THIS FUCKING SWILL COFFEE? GET OUT HERE, WOMAN!"

The bellow of outrage overpowered the phone's little speakers. Fritzing with distortion, curses crashed over them like an ocean wave near an oil spill, spewing toxic bile and foam. Pounding ensued. Heavy fists hammered on a wall.

The students stared at the phone in shocked astonishment.

Yvonne's hand flew to cover her mouth. "*Merde.*"

Mayla had a brief, vivid glimpse of Laudine's pallid face before the image blurred as she dropped her tablet. It came to rest on the floor of a bathroom, providing a skewed view of pretty lacy yellow and lavender curtains and an old-style toilet with an elevated water tank.

"You trying to poison me? Is this what you plot while I'm away? You are going to come out here. Right now. And I am going to watch while you drink every damn drop if it kills you."

"I'm sorry, ladies," Laudine said. "I've got to go."

"Don't you dare open that door!" Yvonne shouted.

"Who you talking to in there? I know it's not your boyfriend, 'cause you're too fat and ugly for anyone in their right mind to have you."

"Call the police," Mayla said.

"I've called them. Many times. They do nothing to help, and when they leave, it is worse." Laudine looked down on them from her vantage point. "But as I have recently been reminded: I am braver than I know."

Mayla's heart stopped when she heard the words of her email quoted. She grabbed her phone, unlocked it, and thrust it at Yvonne. "Call the police," she said as the cursing and pounding escalated. "I don't know Laudine's address. I don't want them to misunderstand my American accent. Call it in. Now!"

Laudine reached for the handle, ignoring their pleas for her to stop. As soon as she unlocked the door, it crashed open. A man in his fifties barreled into view, filling the doorway, spitting with rage.

On the periphery of the camera's field of vision, Laudine stood her ground. "Herb," she said, calm and firm, "I need you to listen to me and I need you to listen good. The police are on their way."

"You know they never listen to you. I'll make you so sorry you involved them."

They watched, helpless and impotent, as he clenched his hand into a meaty fist and raised it to strike.

Instead of following through, however, he froze. His mean, piggy eyes blinked in surprise. "What the hell is that?"

"This, Herb, is called a foot mallet."

Laudine brandished the missing mallet, swishing it through the air like a gladiator's mace.

The man's enormous nostrils dilated. He jutted out his jaw, condescending antagonism oozing from every pore. "What you going to do with it?"

"It was a gift for a friend. I have friends, Herb. Don't think I don't. But it's also a gift to myself."

Laudine advanced on him, coming further into frame. As she took a step forward, Herb nervously backed up.

"I learned a valuable lesson while you were away. I learned that you can become desensitized to accept anything. Even things you shouldn't because they can hurt you. All you have to do is keep picking away, doing the same thing over and over and *over*."

She took another step forward. "You are a goddamn chainsaw. You cut and you roar and you chop down everything you touch. And I've allowed you to desensitize me to *life*. Well, not anymore."

Herb kept his distance, backing away again.

"Let me be very clear, Herb. I'm not poisoning your damn coffee. I'm not cheating on you—though don't kid yourself that I couldn't. I'm not your punching bag. I'm not your Old Lady. I'm not your Ball and Chain. I'm not at your beck and call. I am your wife. And, Herb, I used to love you. I thought together, we could do anything. But I don't think that anymore. Because you are acting like an ass, Herb. And I can't be in love with an ass."

Herb's face contorted with murderous rage. He lunged for Laudine, but stopped short when she gripped the mallet and stood tall, biding her time, waiting for him to come in range.

"Smile, Herb. People are watching. Say hello." Laudine indicated the tablet on the floor.

Herb's face went slack with amazement; discovering he had witnesses appalled him.

"I suspect they are the ones who called the police," Laudine said. "They're not happy. And neither am I. I haven't been for a long time. It seems I don't make you happy either. So rather than be miserable together, let's see if we can find some happiness apart."

All bluster left the man. To Mayla's amazement, he began to cry. "I'm sorry. So sorry."

Laudine stood holding the mallet. To Mayla, even though the woman was middle-aged, a little paunchy, with tears running down her cheeks, she looked like an Amazon.

"No, Herb. You don't get to do that. You don't get to cry and grovel when people see how badly you have behaved. You need to leave. And you need to think about what you're doing. I'm staying here because this is my home.

"And you know what? This is your home too, when you learn to behave and treat me like a human being. But right now, you're behaving like a dog. And I know you don't like dogs, Herb. So until you can learn to like yourself, you need to leave."

Still blinking in surprise, Herb slunk away, accompanied by the sounds of sirens in the distance and the hearty applause of Mayla and her students.

37

Free Fall

MAYLA GROANED. She had known better than to lie down after her clinic, but yesterday's emotional rollercoaster, combined with last night's dreams and Laudine and Herb's morning drama, had so drained her that she had taken a short nap when she got back to the flat. In the past hour, her body had stiffened to the approximate consistency of a seasoned slab of oak.

Every muscle complained as she rolled over in bed.

Her yoga mat lurked on the floor, taunting her.

"Fine," she muttered. "A promise is a promise."

Gently moving through her routine of stretching and mindful breathing eventually made the stiffness fade. The pain abated. She could feel her heart beat, strong and rhythmic, pumping power through her body.

Mayla banished all negative things from her mind, refusing to focus on her aches and pains, on finances, on how inadequate she had felt among the beautiful people at the photo shoot, or on miserable, unhappy marriages. In the empty space vacated by all those draining thoughts, she placed positive images. Soon, a veritable mountain of memories arose, piled up like happy, golden eggs. Each one featured Thiago.

Mayla imagined diving into the center of the mountain, surrounding herself with everything it contained. There, she discovered a wonderful, glowing nugget of happiness. She reached out, grasped it, and pulled it to her. As soon as she touched it, soothing warmth spread through her body, into her limbs, her heart, her soul.

Mentally clutching the ember, scarcely thinking about the physical effort involved, she maneuvered her body through the steps to kapotasana. Shins on the floor... lift the sternum...release the head back... arch the body backward...reach the hands overhead.

When she attained King Pigeon pose, her back arched, chest raised, the palms of her hands holding her calves, with her face to the floor, it felt like the most easy, natural, and comfortable thing in the world.

Breathing easily, at peace and free of pain, she revisited her memories of Thiago trapped in the radiant nugget.

In her imagination, she opened her hand, releasing everything. The ember faded as she let him go.

⚜

Thiago couldn't get away.

For the past twenty minutes, he had tried several times without success to escape the knot of reporters clustered around him. He sat in a folding director's chair under the team's canopy tent, hoping every question he fielded was his last. He had tried directing the questions to Remigio, but the team captain kept lobbing them back his way. He had also tried saying, "I need to go get ready," but as he was already dressed to play and the horses were already saddled and groomed, the reporters refused to take him seriously.

"Is it true that Sergio Chavez is still in hospital?" asked one.

"Thiago is Chavez's replacement," Remigio said. "He'll tell you."

"Sergio is getting better every day," Thiago said. "The doctors had feared meningitis might develop, but they caught the strep and treated it in time. He will be back on the field very soon, you'll see. Until then, I am honored to continue in his place."

"Today is the last Monde du Polo game in France," a whippet-thin woman pushed a microphone at him. "Where will you be going next?"

Remigio stayed silent. He put his head back and placed his cap over his eyes, abdicating any responsibility to answer questions. The reporters closed ranks, encroaching on Thiago's personal space even as they turned their backs on the captain.

Thiago forced a smile. "It is a Goodwill League," he said. "So regardless of who wins, the schedule is already set. Team South America heads west. Switzerland, I believe. Then on to Germany."

"So it doesn't matter who wins?" The woman was skeptical.

"It always matters who wins," Remigio said from under his cap.

The reporters laughed.

"After the last match, in August, all scores are tallied. The team with the highest total score wins, with bonuses distributed both among the players and to the team's designated charity."

He expected the journalists to follow up and ask about the important work Team South America was doing to fight poverty, but they had other pressing concerns. "Is there someone special in your life? A Mrs. Calvo?"

For some reason, an image of Mayla gleaming with happiness as she rode a capricious colt filled his head. "Yes."

There was a collective sigh of disappointment. The assembled reporters pushed their recording devices a little closer for his answer.

"My mother," Thiago said.

He stood and backed away, putting his chair between him and the crowd. He inclined his head, hoping he appeared more gracious than he felt. "Thank you for your interest. I must leave now. Enjoy the game."

⚜

As Mayla and Rochelle were tacking up horses, Laudine approached, head held high, confident as the prow of a ship. Yvonne trailed in her wake. Each woman held a foot mallet.

"Laudine!" Mayla kissed the woman on both of her soft cheeks. "I am so glad to see you."

"*Merci.* It is good to be seen. I wanted to thank you for everything you have done for me these past few days, Mademoiselle Alvarez. You have literally changed my life."

Mayla grew quite serious. "You worried me. I was so frightened for you. If anything—anything—had happened to you because of something I said, I don't know how I would have lived with myself."

"Stop right there," Laudine said, as commanding as a queen. "My decisions are my own. As is my life. I live with the consequences of what I do and what I do not do."

"Still. I had no idea—"

Laudine nodded. "Good. For if you had known my situation, perhaps you would have treated me differently. I am grateful you did not."

Yvonne handed Mayla her foot mallet. "I am not proud to admit I pilfered this during our first clinic."

"I put her up to it," Laudine confessed. "She wanted to ask to borrow it, but I wanted to surprise you. I hope I caused no inconvenience."

"None at all," Mayla said. "I didn't even notice it was missing."

Laudine tilted her head a bit to the side.

Mayla wondered if she could hear the lie.

"I made this for you." Laudine handed Mayla a foot mallet with its shaft encased in a long cardboard tube. "I know you dislike surprises. I hope you will make an exception and like this one."

When Mayla removed the cardboard, she stared in astonishment. Beside her, she heard Rochelle's gasp of admiration. Laudine had elevated the lowly foot mallet to an exquisite art form. Interwoven knots carved into the wood gave the whole shaft a vaguely Celtic design. A series of horses capered throughout the knots, each pony painted to represent one of Mayla's mounts. Made of cherry wood, carved and painted with a master's hand, it was part totem pole, part magic wand.

Mayla swallowed with difficulty past a lump of emotion in her throat. "I am touched. I don't believe I've ever seen anything so beautiful."

Laudine glowed with pardonable pride as she and Yvonne prepared to leave. "I was afraid of getting hurt. But not anymore. 'Few fly,' you said. I may merely crawl in polo, but in life, I intend to soar."

⚜

Zoelie danced on light hooves. She felt the charge in the air and knew a game was near.

"Quiet, *princesa*," the Team South America groom murmured. He moved swiftly to one side, away from the flashing feet, then darted back to continue wrapping the legs as soon as the mare stilled.

"You're good with her. She likes you," Thiago said from the nearby stall where he was tacking up Milagro. Though he trusted anyone affiliated with Remigio's team to do a good job, out of lifelong habit he personally inspected every wrap, buckle, horseshoe, and strap before he rode.

"Thank you, Señor Calvo."

Thiago mentally kicked himself soundly in the ass. Four days he had been here. He had met the boy at the asado—had exchanged introductions and shaken his hand. The groom had helped feed, water, muck, tack, exercise, and turn out Sergio's horses. He had never been late. Had never complained. And damned if Thiago knew the kid's name.

"Do you play?"

A shrug. "It wasn't in the stars."

"Where are you from?"

"Buenos Aires."

"Me too! What part?"

The groom met Thiago's eyes, resigned and reserved. "Villa 1-11-14."

One of the country's largest shanty towns, so poor it didn't have a proper name. More mental ass-kicking ensued. They may share the same home city, but, like he and Mayla, they lived in vastly different worlds.

High time to open an embassy; begin to bridge the gap. To listen, rather than to rush in. To make a significant departure from How Things Had Always Been.

Thiago smiled. "Well, I'm glad you're here now. What's your name again?"

⚜

Every game was different.

Each time she played, Mayla discovered something new about polo that challenged her. Every chukker brought her something new to love. Each game had its own unique character.

As the third and final game of the Monde du Polo Parisien series unfolded, each team dug deep and played with ferocious skill. Neither gave an inch. Neither made a mistake. The hard-hitting war of yesterday was gone, as was the genial camaraderie of Friday afternoon. Both of them had been replaced by a ballet of sorts.

Team South America's superpower lay in its speed, while Team North America relied more on its superb agility. Both were quite evenly matched. All the players rode well, but every time Mayla shadowed Thiago, she felt as if she were chasing a centaur. He was one with his horse.

She threw herself into the game, a willing participant in the high-adrenaline, high-speed, high-stakes dance.

Play proceeded at a blistering pace, changing directions so often Mayla suspected the onlookers might get dizzy. The ball zoomed back and forth, crisscrossing the field as play after spectacular play was made.

With Team North America one goal ahead, she mounted Bogo for the sixth, and last, chukker. She had ridden him in the first chukker, but that was nearly an hour ago. He pranced beneath her, rested and ready to go.

As the ball headed down the field, she wheeled around, then encouraged her pony to stretch out. The chestnut responded like a racecar. With head straight in front of him and ears pricked forward, if he had sprouted wings, he couldn't have flown any straighter or truer.

She and Thiago converged on the ball. They were close enough to the South American goal that he would almost certainly score if he had the opportunity, but she had the better position. Mayla gripped her mallet and prepared to take control of the game.

Bogo flicked an ear backward.

Glancing over her shoulder, Mayla saw Bruno storming behind her, eating her dust. She wasn't worried. He had no chance of reaching the ball before she did.

With single-minded focus, she moved on. She raised her mallet to make her play—

Suddenly, the ground shifted.

The world turned upside down. It was as if the earth quaked. Or a cannonball blasted. Or a bomb exploded.

Time simultaneously sped up and slowed down. Everything happened so quickly, there was nothing she could do to stop it. But she noted odd details, as if freezing a film on a single frame.

Mayla felt her body leave the saddle and launch into the air. For a brief moment, she flew, upside down, her feet above her head, starkly outlined against a gunmetal sky.

She saw Thiago's eyes grow wide in fear...

Saw Bruno's horse come charging at her...

Saw Bogo's body above her, casting a wide, dark shadow...

Then everything went black.

⚜

Thiago watched Mayla ride. She moved with grace, poised in the stirrups, guiding her horse with pinpoint accuracy. He knew she had to be sore from yesterday's crash, but if she was, she didn't show it. How he loved playing against her; loved being on the field with her.

Today's match progressed with almost surgical precision. Both teams played with great technical prowess and with artistry. It was anyone's game.

In the sixth chukker, as he moved Ibby forward while vying with Mayla for the ball, he heard hoofbeats behind him.

Looking back, he saw Bruno coming up fast.

Too fast. What is he doing?

Out of position, Bruno chased after the ball as if Mayla weren't even on the field.

He veered neither left nor right, but aimed straight ahead.

His horse stretched out in a full gallop, surging twenty feet with every stride. Instead of sitting up, checking his rate, and slowing his pony down so he could safely maneuver around the others on the field, Bruno urged his mount even faster.

Then it happened.

The horse's front legs reached far in front of him just as Bogo's hind legs kicked out behind. The two horses' legs got tangled in each other, hooves slashing, shoes flashing.

Only then did Bruno pull his horse up. But it was too little, too late. He ended up on the animal's neck, hands clutching at the reins, scrabbling to stay on while his gelding struggled to stay on his feet.

Mayla and Bogo fared far worse.

Thiago stared, unable to do anything to stop the wreck as Bogo went down—hard—and Mayla went with him.

Thiago pulled Ibby to a halt and looked at the two bodies on the field.

Play stopped.

Time stood still.

38

Game Over

NO HORSE IS GRACEFUL on the ground. Bogo was no different. He lay on his side like a beached whale, a tangle of reins around his neck.

After a moment of shocked stillness, he rallied. Regrouped. With a sigh, the little horse rolled to his knees, then stood up, grunting, ungainly as a camel.

The crowd, which had been holding its breath, applauded.

Thiago noticed the gelding favored his left hind leg, but he didn't have time to assess what was wrong.

Without conscious thought, he leapt to the ground and ran toward Mayla. As he reached her, she rolled over and sat up. She shook her head a bit.

"Don't move!" he cautioned.

"I'm fine." Rage stretched her voice to the breaking point. "He ran over us on purpose!"

"The paramedics are on their way."

Mayla stood up, saw her horse, and staggered past him toward Bogo. She ran her hands over him, looking for damage. Her whole body sagged with relief when she realized that he was uninjured, save for losing a shoe.

As she mounted a new horse and prepared to take her penalty shot, Thiago's heart hammered with more concern than if he had been the one to take the fall. He couldn't take his eyes off her. Nor did he want to.

⚜

The rest of the game passed in a blur.

Mayla's left shoulder twinged every time she moved it. It would hurt like hell tomorrow. Right now, however, it fueled her fury at Bruno for running them down.

Of course, the game was dangerous. She knew that. And there would always be some who thought she had no business on the field. She had always known that, too. But at its heart, polo was a game of sportsmanship, played with genuine concern for the ponies whose heart made the sport possible. That someone would deliberately target her mount made her see red.

The score was tied until the final seconds, when Thiago scored the winning goal for Team South America. The crowd applauded, but after the drama from the wreck Bruno had caused, the end of the match was rather anti-climactic.

While the team farrier reset Bogo's shoe, the press descended on Mayla as she rubbed horse liniment on her shoulder.

"Aren't you afraid?" asked a woman wearing an enormous confection of a hat.

The question took Mayla by surprise. "Of what?"

"Why, of falling. Of getting hurt."

"I'll admit, hitting the ground isn't my favorite thing," Mayla said. "But riding is. And playing is."

"But it's so dangerous," the reporter pressed.

"You should talk to Carson: when he was a junior player, he had his nose broken by a pony's shoe studs."

Her audience gasped in horror.

Mayla smiled. "And if you want a real adventure tale, ask Coach Moe how he shattered his collarbone."

"I hear you once disguised yourself as a man to play," said a tall man in a rumpled shirt. Mayla suspected he would rather be at the racetrack.

"I wasn't the first woman to do so," Mayla said. "But things are getting better. Now people know we can hold our own."

"Until someone runs you over."

Mayla laughed because she knew she was supposed to. She moved her shoulder experimentally. It still hurt. "Until then."

❧

While many of the spectators, patrons, and new fans of polo sipped wine and converged on the field to celebrate Team South America's win, Thiago groomed horses and put them in their stalls to relax.

Relaxation for him was impossible. He couldn't get over how worried he had been when he saw Mayla fall. Not to mention how angry he was at the sheer vendetta Bruno had against her. That fall was no accident.

The sound of vacuous giggles and drunken laughter echoed through the barn.

"That's right!" Bruno's baritone boomed. "The game ain't for everyone. Gotta man up if you wanna play!"

Bruno rounded the corner, the star attraction in an inebriated knot of people.

Thiago stepped out of Ibby's stall. He stood in the center of the hall, crossed his arms, and waited.

Bruno stared at him, defensive and defiant. "*Qué?*"

"You're finished."

"Prove it." Bruno sneered. Snorting with derision, he started to walk on by.

Thiago moved and blocked his path. "Get your things and get out."

Bruno's response was so foul, it sobered some of his comrades and made them look at him askance.

"Don't believe me?" Thiago said. "Ask Remigio. Your stupid stunt endangered both a horse and a rider. Unacceptable."

"That woman shouldn't play if she can't take the risks."

As if they had minds of their own, Thiago's hands clenched into fists, begging to get involved in the conversation. He kept his voice quiet and level, though he now understood what fueled a tiger's growl. "You deliberately tripped a thousand pound animal in the middle of a game. You could have killed someone."

Anger hardened Bruno's face. He swung wildly, but his aim was so sloppy and his reasoning so compromised, Thiago easily dodged the blow.

Bruno did not get a second chance.

Thiago stepped forward, grabbed the man's wrist, and used the momentum of the punch to twist Bruno's arm behind his back.

"Careful," he said, pulling the arm high enough to make sure he had Bruno's undivided attention. "Wouldn't want anyone else to get hurt."

Bruno's hangers-on began to disperse, slowly at first, but with more enthusiasm when Remigio, a referee, and a club official arrived.

"He attacked me!" Bruno shouted. "Lemme go! Son of a—"

"I suggest you shut up," the South American captain said tersely.

Le Parisien's representative indicated the closed-circuit cameras at each end of the barn. "We will be happy to review the incident with you. After we have a little discussion about your conduct on the field."

Whatever words Bruno planned to say stuck in his throat.

As Thiago released his arm, Bruno jerked away, only to have the trinity gather around him and shepherd him out of the barn.

When he was alone again, Thiago reviewed the altercation. Something about it didn't sit right with him—something was off about Bruno's reaction—but try as he might, he couldn't figure out what it was.

⚜

Mayla groomed Bogo, rubbing his muscles with liniment while he drowsed.

"You're my boy," she said. "My tough boy."

Once again, she looked for areas of swelling or heat. Once again, she was relieved to find none. The little gelding appeared none the worse for his fall.

"What would I do without you?"

She rubbed the crest of his neck, tracing the muscles, gently massaging any tension from them.

"Feels good, doesn't it? Thanks to you, I understand why some players clone their ponies."

As she scritched along his withers, Bogo turned his head and nuzzled her, returning the favor.

"That reporter wondered if I was afraid. As if I'd be afraid on you! That would never happen." Mayla rubbed the soft nose. "But I am a little afraid of asking too much of you. Of losing you. I'm so glad you're OK."

She swung up on his back and lay down, looking up at the rafters, her head balanced atop Bogo's rump.

"When I ride you, I feel like I could fly. Sort of like when I'm with Thiago. He makes me feel that way, too. When I'm with him, the whole world is brighter, more interesting. I feel more alive. Is that silly?"

Bogo snorted.

Mayla patted his sides. "You think so? Maybe. But I can't help it. With him nearby, I feel like I could do anything. I...I *feel*. Recognized. Seen. Special. And he smells so good."

Bogo discovered some stray strands of hay, which he found infinitely more interesting than Mayla's one-sided conversation.

"All these years I thought maybe I was deluding myself that he was as great as I remembered. But if anything, I didn't give him enough credit. And I gave up too easily.

"I blamed him for what his father did. And I blamed him for being young. But what we lost isn't all his fault, like I'd convinced myself it was."

She sat up, stretched, and dismounted. Bogo minded his own business until she fished a peppermint out of her pocket, provoking pricked ears and jealous whinnies from several other horses in nearby stalls. Mayla rubbed his ears as he crunched happily.

"I hate surprises," she said. "Imagine my surprise when I realized that I'm as much to blame as he is."

⚜

Thiago quietly slipped into Cantata's stall.

"Hey there, girl," he whispered.

He moved toward her haunches and examined the cut Bruno had inflicted yesterday. Straight and clean, it was obviously done by something sharp. Deliberately.

He tried to remember as much as he could about Mayla's rideoff with Bruno, envisioning the field, the ball, and the moment of impact. The incident appeared utterly typical. Straightforward. The sort of play that happens a score of times in every match.

Mentally adding the riders, their polo mallets, and the horses' tack didn't help. Nothing unusual there either. Neither Mayla nor Bruno wore spurs or carried a whip. Both of their mallets were in their hands—nowhere near the cuts on either horse or human.

And yet...And yet...

Something about his conversation with Bruno still bothered him.

Every word the man had uttered was etched in his memory. Every nuance. Every change in tone and expression. As he reviewed it again, the hint of a suspicion occurred to him.

He left the stall and turned toward his team's barn when he heard the gentle murmur of Mayla's voice.

Changing course, he headed in her direction, intending to tell her his hunch and involve her in his quest. But as he neared Bogo's stall, he made out the words:

"When I ride you, I feel like I could fly. Sort of like when I'm with Thiago."

He stopped short, out of breath, as if someone had sucker-punched him.

Something crunched under his foot. Bogo snorted at the noise.

Thiago froze. Standing motionless, his heart racing, afraid to make a sound, afraid to break whatever spell was causing Mayla to bare her soul, he couldn't believe what he was hearing.

"I didn't give him enough credit. And I gave up too easily."

Belatedly, he realized that he shouldn't be listening, but he couldn't make himself stop. Every word Mayla said was one he had longed to hear. He wanted to do the honorable thing, to give her the privacy she thought she had, to quit eavesdropping, but something stopped him.

It pained him to admit he was afraid. It wasn't something he was proud of, but it was true. He feared that if Mayla saw him walk around the corner, she would stop talking. And then he would never be able to hear the words that fed his hopes, revitalizing them.

One of Carson's horses, a little bright-eyed mare, noticed him. She came as close to him as she could, pressing her muzzle against the vertical iron bars on her stall door. She nickered a friendly greeting.

Every horse in the vicinity swung its head in his direction. Every ear turned toward him. Carson's mare blasted him with a sharp, high-pitched whinny. A few other horses echoed her.

He stayed where he was, straining to hear more. But Mayla had fallen silent. The only sounds were those of horses eating and moving around in their stalls.

Time to make himself known; maybe say a few words of his own.

Thiago coughed. He cleared his throat, making enough noise to alert Mayla that she was not alone. He turned the corner and walked to Bogo's stall. The gelding came to the door and blew on him with minty breath.

But Mayla was gone.

39

End Game

BACK IN HER FLAT, Mayla showered off the dirt from the match, then coated her shoulder with more liniment that seeped into her muscles, heating them and numbing them to the pain. Bruises from her fall were already purpling on her left hip and cheek. Her neck would be sore again in the morning, giving her shoulder some company in its misery.

She really should start packing, she thought, as she dried off and dressed. If she didn't, she'd be stuck with the whole job tomorrow.

But a cursory look at her luggage, with its neatly rolled clothes she hadn't yet used during her stay here, changed her mind. Living out of a suitcase had been her M.O. for years. She was a pro at it.

The room grew brighter, as if from a power surge. The sun had finally broken through the cloud cover.

Time for a little soul lift. One last time.

She peeked into Rochelle's tiny, closet-sized room, intending to tell the girl she was headed out. But Rochelle was snoring, out cold in the throes of a power nap, so Mayla said nothing. Instead, she wrote out a quick note: "Taking a mental health break. Back soon."

Soon afterward, she walked briskly along the wooded pathways of the *bois*. Might as well stay active. If she didn't, the bruise on her hip would set, like a blood stain, and refuse to leave. As it was, she would likely be stiff tomorrow anyway.

In pieces and fragments, the accident came back to her: standing like a jockey in her stirrups, crouched over Bogo's withers as he ran. Preparing to take her shot. Bruno chasing her down. The moment of impact—cracking and clutching and grabbing and jerking. Flying through a gray sky, unmoored from her horse, untethered by gravity. Then slamming to the ground because gravity sucked.

Such a fall, caused by such a vindictive worm, didn't result in her being afraid to ride or play. It just left her numb.

Nothing would happen to Bruno. He might get a fine or an official censure—a half-hearted slap on the wrist that was essentially meaningless—but even if the Monde du Polo kicked him out and banned him for life, most national leagues didn't communicate with each other in such matters. He would be playing for another team, endangering other players and horses, by this time next week.

That was reality. The nature of things.

At the northeast corner of the woods, Mayla struck out due west across some of the city's least pedestrian-friendly terrain. She dodged the nightmare of traffic crossing Avenue de Neuilly, darted through the grassy eye of calm of the *Place de la Porte Maillot* roundabout, then hurried across a tangential boulevard to make it to the safety of the metro station, where she headed underground.

The stark reality hit her as she descended into the harsh fluorescent lighting and rather lurid wall art: Team North America had lost the series. This seriously dropped their standing in the Goodwill League stats. A week ago, she had been so certain they would come out on top. She had even given some serious thought as to how she would invest the bonus money...on the farm that wasn't hers.

A mournful saxophone played nearby, echoing through the

concrete tunnels. Mayla stood on the platform, waiting for her train. She rubbed her sore shoulder and smelled the menthol of horse liniment. A sign declared that she was in the Neuilly Porte Maillot station. But the sign was wrong. She was in Limbo.

Thiago pulled the chain to turn on the overhead light as he and a skeptical league official entered Team South America's tack room. The sweet, spicy scent of horse sweat, hay, and quality leather greeted them. Mallets, blankets, helmets, and other equipment hung from pegs. Rows of racks held dark, well-oiled saddles and bridles. Affixed to each saddle rack, a small placard bore the name of the rider who owned it and the horse the saddle fit.

"What exactly is the problem?" The official scanned the room. "All looks in order."

The racks labeled "B. Carrizo" were at the far end of the southernmost wall. While the official remained in the doorway, Thiago checked every one of Bruno's bridles and reins, looking for stray buckles or odd bits. He found none.

After investigating the bridles, he turned his attention to the saddles.

Ten minutes later, Thiago knocked on the door of Mayla's flat. He had to force himself not to bounce up and down like an impatient kid.

Rochelle opened the door. "Monsieur Calvo."

"Is Mayla here?"

Rochelle shook her head, icy and reserved.

He smiled, though he suspected she knew he did it to mask his disappointment. "I have something to show her."

He held out a stirrup iron for her inspection. Perplexed, she took it and examined it.

She immediately recognized the problem, as he had in the tack room. Most of the stirrup was made of smooth steel. But one side, just above the tread, had a wicked-looking burr. About a centimeter long, a tiny piece of metal was soldered so it stuck out sharply on the outside of the iron. It wouldn't endanger the rider's foot or the side of the horse that wore the saddle, but it would pose a significant threat to any horse or rider unfortunate enough to come into contact with it.

"Careful," Thiago cautioned when Rochelle touched the burr. "It's sharp as a blade."

"This is what cut Cantata!"

"And Mayla."

Rochelle studied the weapon again, but made no move to invite him in. "And Bruno has more like this?"

Thiago shook his head. "Not any more. I may have knocked on one or two other doors before I came to see Mayla. Where is she?"

"As if I would tell you."

Rochelle's ire stung like a scorpion.

"You used me," she said. "'A small favor,' you asked for. 'Is Mayla happy? That's all you care about,' you said. 'What makes her happy?'" She stamped her foot with frustration. "I told you about the farm because I thought you wanted to be a part of her life. What do you do? You immediately fanny off and buy it so you can hold it over her head."

"I wanted to give her a gift. Something she really wanted. Something to show her how I felt about her."

Rochelle peered at him with her good eye, as implacable as a prison warden.

"You wanted to showboat. If you think Mayla is the type who needs some big, expansive gesture to get her attention, you don't know her very well. Just like I don't know you very well. I thought you were a man of honor. I thought I could trust you."

"You can," he said. "Where is she? Please?"

Rochelle handed the stirrup iron back. Shaking her head, she started to shut the door, closing him out.

"She could have died today," Thiago said.

The door stayed open, but Rochelle remained unfazed. "You would have her to play it safe?"

"No. That's not at all what I—"

But Rochelle wasn't listening. "I always wanted to ride," she said. "But Mama never let me. 'You'll break your leg. Oh! Then you couldn't dance!' *Quel dommage!* What a tragedy.

"From the day I took my first step, she invested all her time and energy into making me the dancer she always wanted to be. Dance was her passion, so it became my life."

She leaned against the door jamb, astutely blocking his way. "Have you ever been to a dance competition, Monsieur Calvo?"

"I can't say that I have."

"It encases you in sequins, perches you on heels, leeches whole days away from your life, and refuses to give them back.

"Every chance I got, I would sneak off to go ride. I got a job exercising racehorses, but Mama found out and made me quit."

"She worried you might get hurt?"

"*Oui.* If that happened, I could not win. And I must win. Winning was the goal. Nothing else mattered. Mama made my costumes, chose my partners, choreographed my routines. My last competition, she affixed sparklers to our clothes, insisting the spectacle would help us win. But there was...an incident."

"And—?"

"And now I wear this." Rochelle indicated her eye patch.

Thiago wasn't generally squeamish, but he winced involuntarily.

"As soon as I got out of the hospital, I left home and have not been back. I began my apprenticeship that summer. If I am going to get injured, it will be doing something I love. I no longer play it safe," Rochelle said. "Neither does Mayla."

"Thanks to Mayla, I quit playing it safe years ago," Thiago told her. "But I don't think she knows that. I need to tell her."

Rochelle wiped a tear from her good eye. "Tell her what?"

Thiago didn't need to search for the words. He answered without hesitation, before Rochelle had finished speaking.

⚜

Tourists packed into Sainte-Chapelle, but Mayla barely noticed the mass of people. She stood in the center of the vast room, lost in the jewel-like colors splashing across the top floor.

Someone moved to stand behind her; she knew without turning around who it was. Her heart jumped like a startled rabbit, dispersing her tenuous calm.

"You played well today," he said. "I love playing with you."

Though his voice sent ripples of happiness shivering through her, she couldn't leave the obvious double entendre uncontested.

"I don't want a playboy," she said, keeping her voice low, hoping it wouldn't shake and betray her.

"May I remind you that I am not a boy anymore," Thiago said, his mouth so near her ear that only she could hear his words. "I am a man."

"Men don't play. They stay."

He moved closer, his body a tower of strength behind her. "I have had ten long years to see what my life is like without you in it. I don't want to experience that for one more day."

Leaning against him, she smelled a wild palette of grass and sweat, horses and dirt. He hadn't yet showered from the game. She wished she could bottle the scent and keep it with her forever.

Keeping a scent or a memory was one thing, but they each had commitments. They led separate lives. Exhibition games were scheduled all over Europe as part of the Monde du Polo Tour. How could they make things work?

"Team North America goes south next week to Cadiz. Then Barcelona," Mayla said.

"We're scheduled for Zurich. Then Berlin."

"After that, Athens."

"Geneva."

"Then we're in Milano."

"Imagine that," Thiago said. "So are we. It's a date."

Mayla nodded. "So is this."

"Mourad—"

"Your note-writing, flower-giving driver?"

"The same—is in the car outside, with a truly remarkable bottle of wine that promises a memorable evening."

"It already is."

Thiago wrapped his arms around her, enfolding her. "Since my last attempt to give you something was met with some resistance—something I expect to argue over at great length in the near future," he said, "I wanted to tell you that I am thinking of giving you a rather large diamond ring. Shall I discuss it with you first?"

She snuggled into him, pulling him closer, surrounding herself with him. "Yes," she murmured. "Please do."

"Fair warning: I expect this discussion to occupy most of the next few days. And nights. Until then, please accept this ring of steel as a token of my undying affection." Pulling one arm away from her, he retrieved his phone from his pocket and showed her a photo.

Mayla saw the picture of the evil-looking burr on the stirrup and immediately recognized what it meant. She turned to face Thiago, her eyes full of unspoken questions.

He nodded. "Bruno is out. He deliberately endangered both horses and riders. The World Polo League has expelled him and, since he had been warned about his poor sportsmanship before, he has been stricken from the books."

"Permanently?"

Thiago nodded. "Also, league officials have sent video footage of his recent fouls and photos of his customized stirrups to every other professional polo organization. No one will take him on after today."

"Fighting my battles for me, now?"

"No." As brilliant colors shined on his body, Thiago looked into her eyes, past the happiness that sparkled on the surface, into her very core. "Just standing up for the woman I love. Like I always—always—will."

He kissed her—a kiss so strong, so wild and full of promise, that his hands tightened, holding her more tightly, drawing her even closer to him until their two bodies begged to be one.

Mayla closed her eyes, shutting out the colors that danced and dazzled. Their surroundings were unimportant. No matter where she was, as long as she was with Thiago, she was home.

Acknowledgments

I'M SWIMMING IN AN ENORMOUS OCEAN of gratitude to everyone who helped make *Paris Polo Match* a reality. When I started writing it, I had an agent who specialized in genre books: horror, romance, spec-fic... Much of what I normally write is further off the beaten path and doesn't fit into a neat little genre box. So I set out to write something that would make my agent's job easier—a fun, frothy beach read with a little intrigue, a little romance, and a lot of horses. The agent and I parted ways, but by then I was rather invested in making sure that Thiago and Mayla had a chance of getting their story told.

Thank you first to the United States Polo Association (USPA). Some years ago, I worked on a manual for their trainer certification program. At the time, I knew nothing of polo. Kris Bowman, the USPA Executive Director, and Jessica Downey, USPA's Polo Performance and Education Manager at the time, did a stellar job of introducing me to the game. I am forever in their debt, and am also indebted to each of the top-tier players and instructors who love the sport and who explained it to me with the patience of Job. Anything I got right about the game is because of them. Any mistakes are solely my fault.

Thank you to my fabulous language consultants: Lili for her delightful help with my woefully inadequate French (special thanks for the fascinating primer on French swears!) and Ana Margarita Horta for her charming assistance with Argentinian Spanish. Languages are not my specialty. Truth be told, the language element nearly kept me from publishing the book because I was genuinely afraid I'd unwittingly insult an entire demographic. I owe every correct foreign word to Lili and Ana. Any word that is incorrect (you'll notice a theme here) is, again, my fault.

Thanks to my wonderful publishing pros, especially Rae Ganci Hammers for her phenomenal design, Marie Kuipers for her mad eagle-eyed proofreading skillz, and Christian Dufner for helping me launch with ease.

Thank you, Rheo, for putting up with me during the lengthy manuscript preparation process. You are the brightest light in my orbit, my dear. If every mom had a kid like you, the world would be a better place.

And finally, thanks to you, Dear Reader, for taking the time to read every. single. word. in this book! I hope it brought a smile to your face and put a little song in your heart. I would be eternally in your debt if you told a friend or two how much you liked it and left an online review. However, even if you keep things to yourself, I am grateful to you for spending some time with my story. You make my soul sing.

Ami